I, Red Skelton

Here I am doing the donut routine (circa 1938) which first helped me become a comic face above the crowd.

I, Red Skelton
Exit Laughing

or,
A Man,
His Movies,
and
Sometimes
His Monkeys

a novelized memoir
by **Wes D. Gehring**

BearManor Fiction
2011

I, Red Skelton: Exit Laughing... or, A Man, His Movies,
and Sometimes His Monkeys

© 2011 Wes D. Gehring

For information, address:

BearManor Fiction
P. O. Box 71426
Albany, GA 31708

bearmanorfiction.com

Cover design by John Teehan

Typesetting and layout by John Teehan

Published in the USA by BearManor Fiction

ISBN—1-59393-365-7
978-978-1-59393-365-4

To Cassie and our daughters:
Sarah & Emily
and
Chelsie & Cierra

Table of Contents

THE GUY THEY CALL THE CLOWN

Einstein and Edison
Were certainly wonderful men,
But when their names are mentioned,
It's never with a grin.

But there's a man
Who's greater in his craft,
For, when anyone says "a clown"
It's always with a grin.

To say that he's a genius
Would be putting it quite plain,
Let me tell you what he really
Does in a musical refrain:

The guy they call the clown
Chases away gloom and Mr. Fright,
And tells you, "Up and go! The
World's a stage and you're the show."

The guy they call the clown
Puts blue in the sky
And a twinkle in the eye
That's why I'm proud to say—

I'm the guy they call the clown.

– Red Skelton

Foreword
by Conrad Lane

"I recently took an economy flight. There wasn't any film but they flew low over drive-in movies."

– Red Skelton

WES GEHRING RANKS among the most accurate of biographers, but his new book represents a departure for him. It might be categorized as a pseu-do-memoir or "non-fiction fiction." This text, entitled *I, Red Skelton*, is the product of Wes Gehring's imagination, but it is a very informed imagination. He has written two previous biographies of the great comedian, both me-ticulously researched. Gehring is not content to sit in his ivory-tower office, doing research on line. Rather, he has gone to the scene of Skelton's forma-tive years in Vincennes, Indiana and has interviewed many who knew Red's background. Gehring also journeyed to California and New York for much information, and sought out persons such as Red's granddaughter, Sabrina Alonso, a documentary film-maker based in San Francisco, and the come-dian's daughter, Valentina Alonso, an artist living in Oregon.

What emerges is a work that is entertaining, informative, and incisive. We learn much about Red Skelton in this highly-readable book. Among the more revealing items is the story of Red's parentage – a well-documented story that would be unbelievable if dramatized on film, but which does not strain credulity if one is familiar with Gehring's previous work. We learn much about the women in Red's life, notably the indomitable Edna Stillwell, the first wife, whose guidance and drive were most responsible for Red's early success. There is also an intriguing portrait of the beautiful but troubled Georgia, his second wife, who was probably the true love of his life.

For film enthusiasts, there is much material on Buster Keaton, the comic great who contributed so much to Red's comedy successes, such as *A South-*

ern Yankee (1947). There is an especially suspenseful section wherein Red teams with Keaton to try to solve one of Hollywood's most famous unsolved murders: the 1935 death of Thelma Todd.

So many Hollywood biographies fall into the category of hagiography or hatchet job. *Goodness Had Nothing To Do With It* is one example. Mae West's book, though very entertaining, is just so much self-serving puffery and can hardly be termed objective. An example of the other category is Gary Crosby's *Going My Own Way*, a full-frontal attack on his dead, defenseless father.

I, Red Skelton is neither of these. It is a fair-minded, objective observation of a legendary entertainer. It contributes greatly to our better understanding of this remarkable clown: his inner demons and his visible comic genius.

– CONRAD LANE

Conrad Lane is a Ball State University emeritus professor who remains active as a film essayist and a nationally recognized Elderhostel movie history instructor. He also formerly hosted the PBS film program *Now Showing* on WIPB-TV in Muncie, Indiana.

Author's Preface:
In Red's Shoes

"I have a sixth sense, not the other five. If I wasn't making money, they'd put me away."

– Red Skelton

I MET, INTERVIEWED, and sometimes hung out with Red Skelton during his performing visits to the college where I teach – Ball State University. I also gave the keynote address at the BSU ceremony in which Skelton received an honorary doctorate. Since then I've written 30 film books, generally about comic personalities, including two biographies of Skelton: *Seeing Red: The Skelton in Hollywood's Closet* (2001) and *Red Skelton: The Mask Behind the Mask* (2008). An early excerpt of this book appeared in *USA TODAY Magazine* as: "What Would Red Have Said?" (July 2007). Thus, anything in this text which might be construed as controversial has been anchored in actual events documented in the research for my second Skelton book, which was a *Foreword Magazine national biography finalist at Book Expo* (New York City, 2009).

The Skelton research has taken me to archives across the country, including an amazing treasure trove of private papers at Vincennes College (now in the holdings of Indiana Historical Society, Indianapolis), and Western Illinois University (Macomb, Illinois). Other pivotal research stops included the Performing Arts Library, New York Public Library at Lincoln Center; the Margaret Herrick Library, Academy of Motion Picture Arts and Sciences, Beverly Hills, California; the Cinema-Television Library at the University of Southern California, Los Angeles; and the Vincennes Public Library (Vincennes, Indiana). See the book closing bibliography.

Writing this text also had me combing references by and about many of Skelton's contemporaries. The memoirs of several comic personalities, including Charlie Chaplin, Buster Keaton, and Oscar Levant, also provided brief bits of dialogue. Additional background material was provided by now defunct period newspapers and journals. Two earlier comic novels I wrote, *The Charlie Chaplin Murder Mystery*, and *The James Dean Murder Mystery*, were also a model, of sorts, for the book in hand.

The novelized memoir which follows draws upon all these materials, as well as interviews with various Skelton family members. This includes the comedian's only surviving child, Valentina Alonso, who did the foreword for my second biography of Red, and Skelton's only grandchild, Sabrina Alonso. My youngest daughter, writer Emily Gehring Long, also provided a poem for this book. In the text her free verse is credited to Holly Caine.

I was drawn to this "novel" form of a mock memoir by my inability to let go of the provocative private papers his third wife and widow, Lothian Skelton, gave to Vincennes College. As the first scholar given access to this memorable material, I've merely maximized its potential. One might call it the creative fruits of an academic haunting. That is, while I tapped into the same bombshell subjects in my second biography of Skelton, the "nonfiction fiction" format of this "memoir" allows for greater freedom in exploring some of Skelton's inventive tendencies about his biography. ("Nonfiction Fiction" is a phrase coined for the breakthrough writing of Truman Capote and Norman Mailer in the 1960s. But other pivotal models for me would range from Peter Viertel's *White Hunter Black Heart*, 1953, a novel about the making of *The African* Queen, 1951, and Jerry Stahl's novelized memoir about comedian Fatty Arbuckle, *I, Fatty, 2004*). Like many of us, Red saw himself as a simple person, yet he was anything but that. To paraphrase an old biographical axiom, "One can never be sure of the absolute truth on a given subject, so the writer's goal is to find the best truth possible." For me, this book comes closest to that "best truth possible" about Red Skelton.

This novel is anchored in the mountain of research I did for my two Skelton biographies. Numerous people helped make these books possible, starting with Valentina and Sabrina Alonso. Marvin L. Skelton, Red's nephew, did several insightful interview sessions with me. The comedian's widow, Lothian Toland Skelton, answered a number of questions for my first biography of her husband.

Dr. Phillip M. Summers, President Emeritus and Project Coordinator of Vincennes University, generously opened the Red Skelton Collection to me (now held by the IHS), even though the holdings were not then fully catalogued and available to the general public. Two of his assistants, Billie Jean Primus and Jackie Bloebaum, were especially helpful. Indeed, Billie Jean's knowledge of the materials was invaluable. Robert "Gus" Stevens, of Vincennes College's Lewis Historical Library, provided invaluable advice and shared his own research on Skelton.

An interview and correspondence with Brenda Grant, the daughter of Carl Hopper (the apparent model for Skelton's Clem Kadiddlehopper) was a major plus. Correspondence with Janice Thompson Dudley, the sister of Red's first childhood sweetheart, provided an interesting window on his childhood. Earl Williams, a Skelton friend and former general manager of Ball State University's Emens Auditorium, provided background material on Red.

University of Southern California archivist Ned Comstock always goes out of his way to be helpful on my books. Western Illinois University Special Collections archivist Marla Vizdal also went the extra mile to assist me in my Skelton research.

Friends Joe and Maria Pacino provided both valuable research assistance and a place to crash when I was in the Los Angeles area. David Rulf shared some fascinating eleventh hour insights, via his physician's assistant grandfather Jack Wolfe, on Red Skelton's psychiatric Army hospitalization during World War II. Film historian Conrad Lane was always available for manuscript advice. As usual, Janet Warrner logged time as my copy editor. The computer preparation of the manuscript was done by Jean Thurman and Kris Scott.

As always the love and support of family and friends have encouraged me to soar, like a fantasy figure in a Marc Chagall painting.

– WES D. GEHRING

Born in a Brothel

In looking back at my long mixed-up life, the observation I most relate to was made by my dear friend Oscar Levant: "There's a thin line between genius and insanity... and I have erased that line!"

I WAS BORN FOUR DAYS LATE—I was in no hurry to join the most dysfunctional of families. My alcoholic father, Joe Skelton, had already died of drink months before my July 18, 1913 birth. In later years I would puff him up as some world famous clown—but that was just me blowin' smoke. Indeed, I laid it on so thick as a young man—wishful thinking about my dad—that his alleged fame wouldn't go away, like that old line, "He might be dead but he won't lie down."

Anyway, Joe Skelton was a "clown" all right, but not in the traditional sense. Oh, he might have done some amateur clowning for one of the "Odd Fellow"-type organizations to which he belonged. But his day job was neighborhood grocer in Vincennes, Indiana, the small-town site of my birth. However, my father was an expert in unhappiness and an all-around hell raiser, character traits he came by naturally.

But now comes the strangest part of my story. My dad's mother, Ella Cochran, ran a brothel in Washington, Indiana, another small burg near Vincennes. Ella's favorite "girl" was a prostitute named Lillian. Dad felt the same way, even though he was married to the woman the world knows as my mother, Ida Mae Skelton. Despite all the drinking, Joe was quite the "swordsman," and he managed to simultaneously knock up both Lillian and Ida Mae. He would screw anything with a pulse. As the kind of crass man who always saw himself as the tallest hog at the trough, this double pregnancy was one of his crowning achievements. He was braggin' all over both towns about it. I think that if Gandhi had ever spent any prolonged period with my father, even the little Indian guru of peace would have brained him with a large blunt object.

Surprisingly, Ida Mae didn't want Joe murdered, and he was born to be murdered. As if to prove this point, Joe and Ella had both been frequently hauled into court on assault and battery charges. They were quite the mother-son duo. The catalyst for their final joint court appearance was the result of Ella trying to kill my dad—because he got her biggest moneymaker pregnant. The sizeable earth mother Ella went after him with a knife, and this was one runaway train of a madam—just the shadow of her backside must have weighed 200 pounds.

My dad survived this show of "tough love," only to die of booze a few months later. Sadly, Lillian passed on during my birth (my weigh-in was over 14 pounds), while Ida Mae's baby was stillborn one week later. Ella orchestrated my being raised by Ida Mae. When my adopted mother later told me the truth about my birth, I affectionately nicknamed her "Murr," after the murky nature of my origins. She did her best, but as an overworked charwoman, "Murr" frequently left me unsupervised at home, where I was terrorized by my three older half-brothers, Death, Plague, Pestilence... I mean, Ishmal, Chris and Paul.

When they weren't dragging me behind their homemade motorcycle or throwing me in the local rock quarry lake, the boys beat it into me that I wasn't part of the family. But just looking into the mirror underscored my outsider status. I was the only Skelton kid with red hair and freckles, just like my prostitute birth mother. I was sort of a cinderfella, sleeping in a tiny attic room on a tick bed. During the winter, I would wake up with snow on my quilt blanket, and in the summer the heat was so unbearable I would sleep on the roof.

If you were to put a dull butter knife to my throat (I hate to think you'd pull a gun on me), I really believe that my later comedy success was less about talent and more about my intense drive for wanting someone to love me. When you're starved for affection, it becomes as simple and straight forward as the alphabet—with just as many possibilities... somebody in that laughing audience has to love me! If ever a sad story needed a plot twist, mine did. Until that twist occurred, I cried myself asleep many a night in that sorry little attic room. But not wanting to generate any more abuse from my half-brothers, I kept my crying as quiet as possible, making about as much noise as a mouse peeing on cotton.

My whole provocative past had me stunned for much of my childhood, like a lost ball in high weeds. I had no self-esteem, one of those cases where the juice ain't worth the squeeze. That's why I made up those circus clown stories about my dad. Given my past, I was driven to create a new life story. Then, when I decided to become a clown myself, having a circus father just made it a more poignant family picture. But like my comedy hero, Charlie Chaplin, used to say, "The more you stir an old turd, the more it stinks." That is, I've spun so many tales about both my father and the past that I'm almost reluctant to start this memoir. But with age comes a certain freedom. As some singer once said, "I used to care, but things have changed."

My best childhood days were spent under the babysitting care of either grandmother, Ella Cochran or Ida Mae's mother, Granny Fields. I don't believe I ever referred to Ella as "grandmother." It was always "Ella." I wasn't prompted to call her that. She just had a certain bearing about her, despite the notorious madam background, that made me give her a lot of respect. Of course, she had a scary cough that sounded like an old Hoover Vacuum that sucked up a penny, but I loved to listen to her stories.

She had been married four or five times—it varied from telling to telling—with spouse number three, William Cochran, being the most violent. During a drunken fight he even shot one of Ella's sons, Chris Earhart, my dad's half-brother. William was convicted of attempted murder and sent to Michigan City prison for ten years. That effectively ended their marriage, though Ella was always worried that he would return, like a bad penny. But strangely enough, she kept out his picture for a time. I don't know if she was playing it safe, so if he popped in on her, Ella would look like the dutiful lover. I preferred to think she was like one of those military commanders from the past, who kept the enemy's picture on the wall to better study him.

Either way, the first time I saw this picture, I nearly soiled myself. He had brillo pad eyebrows and crinkly eyes so deeply set they could have been peeking directly from the recesses of his brain. And his cartoon-like ears seemed to want to jump away from his head. William might have doubled for the image of the proverbial axe murderer cornered in the hayloft, or an ad about the dangers of inbreeding. Ella herself confessed, "He was so ugly he could have turned a funeral procession up an alley." Still, she would laugh and say, "Aren't we one big family?" It was only later that I got to thinkin', "All those people in Greek tragedies are one family, too."

I once asked Ella why she had stayed with Cochran so long, if he was that scary. She told me in the most matter-of-fact manner, like someone would say "Please pass the butter," that "Cochran was hung like a horse, and could go all night long." Yeah, it was sort of a punched-in-the-gut effect, coming from a grandmother. But she was a madam long before the grandmother business. Plus, like Mae West, or most women, "She liked a man what took his time." Needless to say, you always knew exactly what the score was with Ella.

To back up the bus a second, Ella's first husband was an attorney named Elmer Skelton. He lived in a small town called Princeton, not far from Vincennes. Ella was a teenaged maid Elmer could not keep his hands off, despite being a respected town elder with a wife and family. Ella became pregnant, and their subsequent marriage was a major scandal, which probably led to Elmer's death shortly after the birth of my father, Joseph. Ella's second union was a common law arrangement with Joseph Earhart, which is probably where my dad got his first name. In fact, during my father's adult life he even flip-flopped on his full name, sometimes calling himself Joseph Skelton, other times going by the moniker Joseph Earhart. You gotta love this whole *Chinatown* background….

I later tidy things up a bit, since I was also listed as an Earhart on my birth certificate. In the mid-1950s I had my name legally changed to Skelton. Also, I went back to Vincennes and cased out the approximate location of my father's grave. Between a cheap original marker and a later flood, the exact spot was long lost. Well, I had a large gravestone put up, with "Joseph E. Skelton" on it. No more of this Earhart business. Yet, the funny thing is, the more I try to fix the facts, other odd bits of family history creep back in, like smoke under the door. But you'll see, as this strange story unwinds.

Ironically, just as I never knew my father, he also never knew his dad. Regardless, Ella soon replaced Earhart with the infamous William Cochran. But once he was shipped off to Indiana's version of the Big House, her liaisons were of a briefer duration, though one or two might have qualified as a common law marriage. All I know is that Ella was fun to be around and very kind. Her home was the only childhood place in which I felt like I belonged, even if one of my chores involved being a towel boy in a brothel.

If chaotic childhood represents a time when one is metaphorically caught in a midair freeze-frame, Ella's whorehouse represented a safe zone for me. Granted, like her sex talk, she never sugar-coated anything. For example, once after a funeral for one of her "girls" (a victim of a botched abortion), I asked her if the woman was in a better place. Ella responded quietly, "I don't think so, not unless dirt is better than air." She always extolled me to enjoy the here and now, adding, "Shrouds don't have pockets." Ella had seen so much of life's darker side that she used to laughingly suggest a walking heart-to-heart with her would necessitate the constant refrain, "I'm going to need a longer street!" She was also fond of the axiom, "If hard knocks don't build character, they do build characters!"

You know, Richard Pryor was raised by a brothel-running grandmother, too. Her name was Marie Carter but everyone called her Mamma. Like my Ella, Marie was also a big battleship of a madam with a talent for insights colored with comedy. Richard and I used to trade brothel grandmother stories whenever we ran into each other. Here are two of Richards's favorites about Marie. When she first came to Peoria, Illinois, Mamma said, "We was so poor even poor folks didn't speak to us." Later, when Richard told her he wanted to be a comedian, she asked, "You all know how black humor started? It began on slave ships. Cat was rowing and a dude says, 'What you laughin' about.' He said, 'Yesterday I was a king.'"

Regardless, despite all the hogwash I later spun about my father the clown, I think my decision to be a comic entertainer was born of my amusing grandmother, the madam. After all, a small town whorehouse was a major source of entertainment back then, and Ella had that great earthy sense of humor. For instance, the last joke she told me—this was during World War II, just before she died—was quite profane for the time: "What were Custer's last words?" "We be fucked!" (My later infamous "blue" rehearsals at CBS, "Red's Dirty Hour," were sort of a Rabelaisian homage to dear old Ella.)

Compared to Ella, my Granny Fields was pretty low key. Moreover, in direct contrast to the lively trade of running a brothel, the Fields family had long been involved in operating a funeral parlor. I always wanted to write a book about my grandmothers and their two trades—I even had a great working title: *My Grandmothers, They Got You Cumming or Going.*

Granny was a great storyteller, too. But whereas Ella had spun tales about the most dysfunctional of families, A. C. Fields had been related to the great 19th century minstrel man Al Fields. The Fields family also had a number of wood carvers and portrait painters. So maybe the inspiration for my later obsession with painting clowns was first planted by Granny Fields. The only downside to Granny was her miserly ways with food. She always claimed the cupboards were bare... which they were. But in exploring her tiny house by the railroad tracks, I found she hoarded canned goods under her bed and in a box in her creepy fruit cellar. Granny seemed most partial to canned peaches and two kinds of soup—mock turtle and oxtail. Sometimes my half-brother Paul, my only sibling to sometimes treat me fairly, and I would steal canned peaches and have an impromptu picnic in a nearby field. Of course, we often spilled a great deal of the contents, because we never had a proper can opener. We did the best we could with a dull pocket knife. (My childhood was largely meatless, other than an occasional stolen chicken. I don't ever remember having a steak until I was long gone from Vincennes. I still enjoy telling people, "I love animals... I just like to eat them!")

To Granny Fields' credit, she never called Paul and me out on taking her peaches, and I'm sure she must have eventually known. Don't misers always keep a running tabulation on their goods? Years later, after the Cuban Missile Crisis, I pulled my own Granny variation on hoarding canned goods. I became convinced an atomic Apocalypse was upon us, and I started stockpiling all manner of canned goods. But getting back to Granny, I don't know what her excuse was—probably a lifetime of tough times.

I never blamed her for lying, especially after Paul and I turned it into a game. Indeed, that eventually sort of became my philosophy: "Life is a game best played just for the fun of it." After Paul and I developed the nerves of a blind burglar, we applied our practical thievery to another, more important, task. Vincennes was crisscrossed with railroad lines, and during the winter we stole coal from passing trains. We would board at a railroad water stop on the outskirts of Vincennes, and when the opportunity presented itself, fill our sacks from the coal car. When the train passed near our home, which was always some shack on the tracks, we tossed our coal sack off and just jumped.

Once, however, Paul almost died during what had seemingly become an easy routine. Just before our jumping off spot, he fell between the coal and baggage cars—our normal hiding place, just a foot from the tracks. What saved him was a metal bar he desperately held onto, as well as my grabbing his leather belt. Luckily, we both managed to hold on until a sharp railroad grade just outside of town, where the train slowed way down. We managed to extricate ourselves from a tight spot and hike back to Vincennes, retrieving our sack of coal on the way.

In later years I came to find out that an army of Midwestern poor boys found various ways to get winter coal from passing trains. My dear friend Joe E. Brown, who lifted funny to the level of fable—best known now for his dirty old man in *Some Like It Hot* (he falls for Jack Lemmon in drag)— probably found the easiest coal scam. Remember, his signature trait was that huge mouth, winning him such comic nicknames as "cavernous-mouthed," "funny face," "monster-mouthed," and "Grand Canyon."

Joe himself once told me, "Red, the only thing I could ever do was make people laugh… And I can take only second billing for that talent. Nature met me more than halfway when it threw a handful of features together and called it a face." Thus, young Joe hit upon the idea of using his "crater-mouthed" mug to make faces at the passing train firemen to get free coal thrown at him. This was also the first time the youngster realized his "cavernous" cavity could be an advantage. (When he told me this funny face story, I asked him, "What do you think the East German judge would have given you?")

Besides Paul and my misadventures on the rails, trains were a pivotal part of living in early 20th Century Vincennes. Years before the Depression made hopping a freight train a safety valve exit for oversized poor families, it was a regular pattern in my hometown. In fact, each of my siblings drifted away in that manner. For that era, a train whistle represented almost a romantic "song" of adventure. But it was also a source of humor, since we always lived right on the wrong side of the tracks. "Murr" used to tell us boys, "Some people buy auto parts and others live near railroad crossings."

For a time, I even created an after school job on one of the local trains— selling homemade sandwiches. I was a bit of a huckster. The meat and the lettuce would literally be hanging out of the edges of the sandwich—with very little in the center. Occasionally, this got me in hot water with the conductor. But I had a lot of moxie and fast feet, so I got by. That reminds me, when I later did a picture called *Three Little Words* (with Fred Astaire), I played a songwriter (Harry Ruby) who spent more time trying to be a baseball player. That was a laugh, since I was so unathletic I couldn't throw a cat out a window. Regardless, during the production I hung out with Hall of Fame pitcher Lefty Gomez. When I asked him the secret of his success, Lefty said, "Clean living… and a fast outfield." I love that line. If truth be told, I even used it as one of my own on a couple of occasions. But yes, fast feet frequently got me out of tight situations as a youngster.

Coming from a dysfunctional family also allows you to be better prepared for screwed-up situations. That is, you're already a veteran of seeing the shit hit the fan. Consequently, you've mastered a little two-step out-of-the-way (again with the fast feet), and that ye old shit can then hit someone else. Naturally, sometimes you still get caught in the crossfire, and you're like a vampire on a day pass. I can hear the Greek chorus chanting now, "You must eat so you can suffer."

Anyway, the only downside to my sandwich racket on the train was staying out late and then falling asleep in school the next day. But education was never one of my strong suits. It didn't help that I was in a "special class," which the recess crowd translated into being a "dumb kid." While none of my half brothers was exactly a scholar, I was by far the dunce of the world. I only received a GED years later when my first wife and manager, Edna Stillwell, got on my case. For a time, we actually had a tutor traveling with us in vaudeville. I got so much ribbing about it that we eventually put him into the act. Stealing a bit from the Marx Brothers' old *Fun in Hi Skule* vaudeville routine, Edna and I ironically cast the tutor as a poor student!

The education paradox for me, related to that *Fun in Hi Skule* sketch, was that I had dropped out well *before* high school. But the county school board was especially pleased, since I had worn out several truant officers. This is because, except when the circus was in town, they never knew where to find me. Still, I can't say my Vincennes school days were completely without merit. A patriotic principal in junior high first planted the seeds of what later became my most successful spoken routine—a personalized "Pledge of Allegiance." Otherwise, my philosophy of education was cribbed from Mark Twain: "I never let school interfere with my education."

Of course, my class clown tendencies had never been limited to school. I was always "on." Though my early material was pretty thin, like picking up a dachshund and pretending to eat it because it was a "wiener dog," I was one lively fellow. It distracted from all the hurt in my life. To borrow a line from my later good friend Frank Sinatra, if I had thought about my life, "I would have felt like the crappiest piece of crap in crap town."

Here's a quick story about Frank—who I first got friendly with back in his Tommy Dorsey vocalist days. By the time Frank had become "Chairman of the Board," rare was the person who could make jokes at his expense. But since we went all the way back to the movie *Ship Ahoy* in 1942, with Frank in singing support to my star turn, he was all right with my kidding him. For example, when he got his footprints immortalized in cement at Grauman's Chinese Theatre, I quipped, "Bing Crosby's footprints walked out in protest."

Now flash forward to the 1950s, when I played in Las Vegas at the same time as Frank and the Rat Pack. I hung out with them quite a bit and even had a cameo in *Ocean's Eleven*. One day Frank told me, "Dean [Martin] just pulled one of your tricks [got smart with me]." It seems that Frank and Dean ended their joint Sands Hotel engagement each night with some comic patter. But even though Dean was almost playing straight man to Sinatra, Martin was always getting the bigger laughs. Frustrated, Frank had them switch lines—yet Dean still generated the most laughs. Mystified, Sinatra later confessed to Martin, "I don't get it."

Dean replied, "You're just not funny, Frank."

Besides my early ongoing tendencies to be funny, I always had moneymaking schemes to help a poor family. For instance, by racking balls at Kramer's Pool Hall (two cents a rack), I was able to pick up discarded playing cards. This led to my first practical application of my art skills. By a combination sleight of hand and colored pencil doctoring, I turned the cards into "new" novelty decks for sale in neighboring towns. I worked the gullible citizens right on their main streets. As the old huckster comedy character Simon Suggs used to say, "It is good to be shifty in new country."

Sometimes my jobs were fairly traditional, like crating boxes in a Sears store, ushering at Vincennes' Moon Theatre, and washing dishes at various greasy spoons around town. I even pulled a Charlie Chaplin and entertained on street corners, singing and dancing for pennies. At seven years of age, I also started selling newspapers before and after school. At three cents a paper, I made a penny for each street corner sale.

Even here I would try to be a performer, yelling things like, "The same old thing, only happening to different people!" On occasion, I might also concoct an exciting story that was *not* in the paper. In general, my business principles left something to be desired. In later years, my customers told me I was "fresh, impudent and even insulting, and that they often bought my ware to avoid embarrassment."

My most famous yarn connected to boyhood newspaper sales involves how I met vaudeville legend Ed Wynn. Now, whether it was really Wynn, I don't know. You have to realize that the Rosetta Stone to understanding me is my tendency to varnish or gild the facts, all in the spirit of telling a better story. I take to creative fibbing like a fat boy to cake! As my favorite Indiana humorist, Kin Hubbard, once said, through his Abe Martin character, "It's purty hard t' be interestin' without embellishin' th' truth a little."

If you can still trust me, here is what really happened. I was selling newspapers in front of Vincennes' Pantheon Theatre, a major vaudeville Mecca which sat 1500 people. A stranger asked me, "What do you do for excitement in this town?"

I told him, "Well, sir, we've got a big show coming into the theatre tonight. You could go to that." When he asked me if I was going to attend, I told him I had newspapers to sell. Darn if he didn't buy all my papers and give me two bits for a ticket and a treat. But that wasn't the biggest shock. I'll never forget how surprised I was that night to see that the guy who had bought all my papers was the star of the show!

So why did I later credit Wynn with being that thoughtful vaudevillian, even though I don't for the life of me remember who he was? As a youngster, I'd always admired his "Perfect Fool" character, a country rube with a high-pitched voice that later influenced my own comedy character of Clem Kadiddlehopper, another cluck from the country, more crackers than crackerbarrel. Though my greatest funny figure was the tramp Freddie the Freeloader, a cross between Chaplin's Charlie and Emmett Kelly's Weary Willie, Clem was with me the longest and best represented my Indiana roots.

Thus, I felt that I owed Wynn big time for that influence. Plus, when I had him on my television show in the early 1950s, he was going through a tough time in his career. And sometimes people just need to be rescued. The next thing I know, I'm spinning this yarn about Wynn befriending me as a child—right there on national television. Poor Ed, if you look at a kinescope of the program, he has this "What the heck?" expression on his kisser. But to his credit, he played along. I just did it out of love, to give his career a little sympathetic boost. And I think it helped. It wasn't too long before he was even getting some serious acting jobs, like playin' in a drama on the old television anthology *Playhouse 90*. Indeed, he would eventually get an Oscar nomination for his supporting role in *The Diary of Anne Frank*. But that was a little deep dish for me; I liked him better as Jerry Lewis' fairy godfather in *Cinderfella*.

Regardless, my little fib about Wynn soon developed a life of its own. The tale's feel-good nature has now made it one of those legendary entertainment stories, about the mantle of comedy being passed from one generation to another. But that part of it is actually true. That is, whoever this generous vaudevillian was, he opened up a mesmerizing new world to me. I had never before seen a professional stage show, and I was definitely hooked. So what's the harm in giving a little credit to someone like Wynn? In truth, I don't know if I'm soft-hearted or soft-headed. But the day I stop spinning yarns, you could probably proclaim, "Look up, Jesus is a comin'," because time as we know it will have come to a close. (Since penning these lines, I've received a letter from a Vincennes fan, Doug Carroll, suggesting the thoughtful vaudevillian might have been comic Raymond Hitchcock—who played my hometown at approximately the same time credited to Wynn's alleged visit. And to be honest… I think Doug is right.)

Sadly, while I did a good deed related to Wynn, I have never before now acknowledged an additional inspiration for the aforementioned Clem Kadiddlehopper character. One of my childhood friends was a boy named Carl Hopper. His family were north Vincennes neighbors of the Skelton clan. Carl, two years younger than I was, suffered from a severe hearing loss which caused many to consider him not quite "all there." This misconception resulted in cruel putdowns when Carl misunderstood what people said and replied with under-his-breath asides and patented "Huh?" Even Carl's parents felt that there was no need for him to receive an education, consequently, he acquired a lifetime habit of butchering the English language. Carl's high-pitched voice was also a result of his hearing loss. Despite these problems, he remained a remarkable upbeat farm boy who was especially taken with hats and laughing at his own jokes.

Since everyone picked on me, too, including my own half-brothers, Carl and I formed an "us against the world" pact. I also included him in any of my comic pranks. At some point I nicknamed him "Kadiddle," possibly playing upon the slang definition of "diddle," which meant idling away one's time. Later combined with his name, Carl-diddle, it soon became Kadiddle. Since my joking often softened the attitude of mean-spirited boys, I created an affectionately comic imitation of my friend. Carl never found this offensive. In fact, years later, when I met his daughter while I was performing at the Indiana State Fair, she shared that Carl had taken great pride in my modeling Clem Kadiddlehopper, in part, after him.

Carl was the only one of my characters where there was such a direct connection with a real person. I did, however, sometimes credit my father with being the inspiration for Freddy the Freeloader. But that was back when I was still claiming that Dad was a world famous clown. If Freddie really had any model, it was Chaplin's Tramp.

Freddie was created during my otherwise difficult second season (1952-53) on television. After my Emmy Award-winning first year, I fell victim to the small screen's glass furnace phenomenon—where years of accumulated brilliant material is burned up. Or, as I joked at the time: "TV is a remarkable medium. You have to work ten years on stage, in hit shows, to make people sick and tired of you. This you can accomplish in only a few weeks on television."

Anyway, Chaplin has always been my hero, even after the Joseph McCarthy Communist witch-hunting crowd got him booted out of the country in 1952. My interest in jumping ship from movies to this then-upstart called television was fueled by the parallels I saw with Chaplin being a movie pioneer. If you do something first in a new medium, you're writing on a blank page. You set the bar/standards, and define the rules. I wanted to do that in television, like Chaplin did for the movies.

Naturally, with all that focus on Chaplin at the time—my period interviews keyed upon him so much you would have thought I was his press agent—I started thinking about spinning off a character like his Charlie the Tramp. From this catalyst, Freddie the Freeloader was born. At first, I even kept him silent, like Charlie. But eventually I had Freddie, this comedy diplomat from the dump of life, talking, and when I mixed pratfalls with pathos… and the occasional custard pie, I had my universal character.

Though I was fond of my other funny figures, they were often one-note characters. For example, boxer Cauliflower McPugg had a brain to match his name, and had seen more canvas than a pup tent salesman. Sheriff Deadeye was anything but a deadeye, while his constantly slipping holster gave him a sissy-pants walk. San Fernando Red was a con man wheeler dealer with a bigger pitch than Dizzy Dean. (My old writer, Johnny Carson, later patterned his Art Fern, the tea time matinee movie host, on San Fernando.) Even my "Mean Widdle Kid" Junior, of "I dood it!" fame, was basically just Dennis the Menace on diet pills. Of course, my comedy team of Gertrude and Heathcliff was fairly unique—television's only stand-up comedy seagulls. But my playing of these two birdbrains was done sparingly, usually during my television program's opening monologue. There were other characters, but these are the ones I remember most fondly.

Of these secondary characters, I think San Fernando was my favorite. Though he was not based on any one figure from my childhood, San Fernando conjures up memories of my early Vincennes years, back when the sunlight seemed so bright it danced. Being from southern Indiana, I knew plenty of fast-talking hucksters, which is essentially what San Fernando represented. The definitive example from my youth was "Doc" Lewis, who had a Patent Medicine Show which came through Vincennes every summer.

As a wannabe performer, I would petition him each season to be a "gopher" in his operation, helping sell his magic elixir and/or taking part in the comedy sketches "Doc" put on in order to raise a crowd. I was after him from about the age of ten on, and by the time I was a teenager, he let me become part of his Patent Medicine Show. It even helped out at home, since I was gone for the summer, with "Murr" getting a modest financial allotment from "Doc."

My audition, after telling "Doc" I could sing and play the ukulele, had not gone well. But my freckle-faced, carrot-top enthusiasm must have won me some sympathy, because "Doc" merely drawled, in W. C. Fields overtones, "My boy, you've misinformed me. Try selling the medicine." So, I began getting the product to him on a makeshift stage, as he sang out, "Hurry, hurry out with some more [bottled medicine]. Don't be the innocent means of depriving these wonderful people of an opportunity to purchase glowing health for such a minute sum." (I should add that this alleged cure-all, called "Hot Springs System Tonic," was composed of water, sugar, and Epsom Salts—which we mixed in a big wooden barrel outside of each town we targeted.)

My young enthusiasm to keep "Doc" supplied with bottles soon resulted in the most providential accident. In my delivery boy rush to the stage, I tripped over an uneven patch in the wooden planking and took a spectacular unplanned pratfall into the crowd. When it was clear that I was okay, and only two bottles of the tonic had paid the ultimate price, the audience showed its appreciation with sustained applause.

This was an epiphany for me, and in later years taking a major pratfall was the opening to my vaudeville act—usually falling into the orchestra pit, with an already torn snare drum as my target touchdown spot. The wear and tear of slapstick has taken a toll on me—I now have braces on both legs—but physical comedy is still my favorite way of provoking laughter, what someone once called, "a humorous backdrop."

"Doc" Lewis, ever the showman, immediately decided to incorporate my comic fall from the stage into each new show. But being a practical businessman, we managed to make sure no more bottles of his precious product were broken. My tripping was to occur just as I handed the elixir off to Lewis. We even milked the routine further by having him stumble about the stage almost dropping the bottles, while I launched myself into pratfall land. Eventually, my repertoire did expand to include singing and playing the ukulele, as well as the occasional minstrel sketch.

Another chore I did for "Doc" even briefly assisted my first innocent romance. The medicine show sold candy as well as elixir. Borrowing from the "Cracker Jacks" sales pitch, Lewis' treats also had "A Prize in Every Box," an added selling point for impoverished customers. Now, here's where I out conned the con man. I was in charge of stuffing the candy boxes. My first sweetheart, Vincennes' Velma Thompson, had been so pleased when she got a fake silver spoon in one of these boxes that I vowed to get her a set of six.

I felt bad putting one over on Lewis, but it was my first romance. So, I managed to salt away half a dozen spoons and presented them to her just before the medicine show left Vincennes for the next stop on our summer tour, which also included forays into Illinois, Kentucky, and Ohio. Unfortunately, my love-motivated sneakiness went for naught—Velma's parents eventually put the kibosh to our romance. The only explanation I ever got was that my background was too impoverished; I didn't have a future. But I always assumed it had something to do with my grandmother Ella having a whorehouse in a neighboring town. I mean, that can't really help a fella's standings. Plus, there was a whole court docket full of additional Skelton family infractions I haven't yet shared.

Besides periodically being arrested and/or fined for having a "house of ill repute," Ella was frequently jailed for the illegal manufacturing of moonshine, the illegal sale of said product, and the catch-all charge—"public nuisance." Moreover, once Ella got out of the whorehouse business, she kept petitioning the court to drop all past charges about her being a madam—so her colorful background in the sex trade just never went away. For Ella, the past wasn't dead; it wasn't even past. Add to this my half-brothers, who worked hard at being apprentice juvenile delinquents, and poor "Murr"'s attempts to keep our dysfunctional family together, and it probably looked like "I didn't have a future." But a local Vincennes entertainer would help me to change that sorry prediction.

The "Professor,"
the Prostitute, and Ella

> "The ability to walk on water made it difficult for Jesus to learn how to swim."
> —Clarence "Professor" Stout, my first mentor

MY GOOD FRIEND, FRENCH MIME MARCEL MARCEAU, also had an excellent command of language. During yet another Arab-Israeli conflict in the 1960s, he told me, "War over religion is like killing someone over who has better imaginary friends." But in truth, I told you that story in order to tell you this one. Marceau often enjoyed repeating an old French axiom, "Tell me whom you haunt [whom you befriend] and I'll tell you who you are." It's an adage I have pondered often through the years. I think I gravitate towards friendships that can result in mentorship—personal growth. Though my life as a traditional student was a disaster, I am attracted to people who can stimulate me to the point of trying to find the right direction. You might call these folks "cultural swizzlesticks." For instance, my first wife, Edna Stillwell, made me a better comedian by writing several of my early classic sketches, such as the donut-dunking routine and the "Guzzler's Gin" sketch. Later, when I wanted to attempt more serious creative projects, I hooked up with journalist turned biographer Gene Fowler. His best book, *Minutes of the Last Meeting*, was a group profile of four brilliant but self-destructive drunks, comedian W. C. Fields, actor John Barrymore, painter John Decker, and poet Sadakichi Hartman. Fowler taught me everything about writing, including the courage to write this memoir.

Gene had this wonderful story about how writers were perceived in different countries. I think he lifted the tale from someone else, but it went like this: "In America only the successful writer is important, in France all writers are important, in England no writer is important, in Australia you have to explain what a writer is." Gene was the greatest raconteur I ever knew, and that covered a lot of gifted Hollywood storytellers. Though he also scripted a number of films, writing biographies was his great passion. Yet, he tended to embellish his "facts" quite a bit, like his biography of Mack Sennett—*Father Goose*. Delightfully entertaining, but as the title suggests, the book is often in fantasyland. Since my tendencies already embraced the creative fib category, Gene's influence further pushed me into that camp.

My first mentor friend type, other than brothel grandmother Ella, was Clarence Stout. He was the proverbial big fish in the small pond. That was Vincennes—the town known in vaudeville as the perfect place to be when the Biblical Apocalypse occurs—because everything takes five years to get there!

Clarence, whom I usually referred to as the "Professor," looked that academic part—small built, owlish eyes, and a general bookish demeanor. Stout's one vanity weakness was dying his hair—it was always as black as ten feet under. All in all, the Professor wore several professional hats. His main day job was as a pit band musician at Vincennes' Pantheon Theatre, at Fifth and Main Street. But he also toured the Midwest, or at least Indiana, Ohio, and Illinois, as the leader of "Stout's Minstrel Follies." Nationally, he was known for the songs he sold to various music publication houses. Indeed, his "O Death Where Is Thy Sting?" had been featured on Broadway in the celebrated *Ziegfeld Follies of 1919*.

The pioneering black entertainer Bert Williams had chosen and performed this song. A friendship developed between the two men, with Williams nicknaming Stout "Hoosier Boy." Unfortunately, Williams' unexpected 1922 death from pneumonia ended their plans for later collaborations. Naturally, Stout took the entertainer's death hard; and it was difficult for him to mask pain. In contrast, tough-skinned Ella might have said something like, "Everyone gets dead, it was his turn," or one of her favorite darkly comic lines, "I'm not afraid of dying. I just don't want to be there when it happens." But with relationship to my future in comedy, I should add that the Williams-Stout pairing on "O Death" was rooted in humor, just as were the Professor's opening comments on Jesus the swimmer. That is, the song title comes from a satirical member of a congregation quizzing his pastor. After hearing in the sermon that hell is full of vampish women, whiskey, gin, and dice, he comically asks, "O Death Where I Thy Sting?"

Another major black entertainer, with whom Stout maintained a close friendship was W. C. Handy, often called "the father of the Blues." The Professor and his wife Inez, a great mimic, would often visit Handy at his home in Chicago whenever my local hero would have a new batch of songs to peddle. As Stout's friendships with Handy and Bert Williams suggest, the Professor was color-blind. While he never got up on a soap box about his then liberal views, he did have a story I dearly loved about a racist getting his come-uppance. Fittingly, it involved one of those trips to Chicago to see Handy. When a Michigan Avenue bartender served the two men drinks, he said to the Professor, "That will be fifty cents for you, and five dollars for him [pointing to Handy]." Handy, by this time a very successful entertainer/composer, lackadaisically took a twenty dollar bill [then a week's wages for most] from his pocket and blasély placed it on the bar. "Keep the change," he said to the amazed bartender.

Stout loved telling that story, a tradition I've taken up recently. Years before Jessie Jackson, the Professor used to talk about all the races as a "rainbow"—sort of heaven's promise in Technicolor. Because of the Professor, I could never understand racism. I always tried to make friends with everybody. For so long blacks were not treated as human beings… and in some parts of the country it's still that way now, which is sad. To me a racist was a Neanderthal type, so dumb he was only attracted to shiny objects that make noise when they rattle.

If truth be told, my poor status ("We didn't have a pot to pee in," as "Murr" was fond of saying) also gave me more in common with disadvantaged blacks in and around Vincennes. In fact, the local black barber, Dudley Miller, usually gave my half-brothers and me free haircuts, "because your widowed mother was having a hard time." I never corrected him about "Murr" not being my real mother. I didn't want to get into the whole brothel thing; besides, I was taught to "Never look a gift horse in the mouth." However, I think he knew the real story, anyway. Regardless, with another local black, Stout's minstrel friend Gabe Jackson, teaching me how to play the ukulele, I was soon just as color-blind as the Professor.

Of course, beyond such a valuable life lesson, the Professor was my college of one. He taught me so much about show business. He instructed me in comic timing, how to parody a personality (my first socko bit was a spoof of Al Jolson), and the nuances of pantomime. But some of his suggestions initially went right over my head. I was like the target of that old Hoosier axiom, "He ain't even got the sense God gave a goose." For example, the Professor used to tell me to be more sensitive in my observations of people—like a woman. But I thought, at first, he just wanted me to invent a comic woman character. So I came up with an early version of what later became one of my most acclaimed sketches—a woman getting ready in the morning. This involved everything from putting on pretend make-up to attempting to get into an imaginary girdle. Only later did I realize he just wanted me to be as observant as the fairer sex in my finding comedy material in the world around me.

Besides Stout's mentoring, he also represented a surrogate father-figure. When he first spotted me as a kid dancing and clowning to coax pennies from passersby near the Pantheon Theatre, I think he saw a miniature kindred spirit. The Professor and Inez were always incredibly kind to me, and their daughter Frankie taught me all the latest dance steps. (After dancing professionally, Frankie later opened her own studio in Vincennes. Like her dad, she had a great sense of humor. The sign one first saw upon entering her studio proclaimed, "A dancer is one who makes motions for a living.") Inez should have had a comedy studio—her mimicking skills were that good. Inez was tall and thin, with the most expressive face, a female Stan Laurel. But I most remember her divine, old-fashioned chocolate fudge. It was so rich that after two bites you were flirting with gout.

Still, I felt a bit like a sociologist around the Stouts, though I wouldn't have actually known that word as a child. That is, the Professor, Inez, and Frankie were the first "normal" family I'd ever seen up close. But after so much non-traditional parenting from Ella, and simply having a dead dad and an adopted mother always working, it took me a while to believe the sincerity of the Stouts. Compared to my dysfunctional family, the Stouts were only a difference of degree… 180.

My initial confusion about trying to comprehend normalcy is not unlike that old comic question about why they call it "raw sewage," as opposed to what—"cooked sewage"? What is normal? When your family tree is pretty much "naughty" pine, the Professor's traditional family might just as well be a species from Mars. Plus, Stout was more focused than a snake charmer—much more. My experience with people up until that point in time might have been described using a popular definition of a producer when I first landed in Hollywood: "A man who doesn't know what he wants and wouldn't like it if he got it." Stout always said the key to focus or discipline is finding one's passion. Thus, if someone had asked me to compose an epitaph for the Professor's tombstone, I'd have written, "Whatever gets you up the hill."

The ultimate secret to the Professor's drive, however, was anchored in the most basic of obsessions, something I heard him say 1,000 times: "I became an entertainer because the stage gave me such joy." This was something I could sink my teeth into, too. Moreover, he wasn't some stranger I was reading about in a discarded movie magazine. Clarence Stout was someone who had made it from my own hometown, and I knew him! Best of all, as Ella liked to say, "The Professor kept himself common"—no change in hat size here. I felt blessed that he was going to show me the entertainment "ropes."

The Professor helped make 1929, when I was sixteen, my break-out year. Besides appearing in the Old Cathedral parish circus, put on by Vincennes' Father Henry Doll and the YMCA circus (orchestrated by Y director Ray Beless), Stout starred me in his minstrel revue. Though I greatly enjoyed the circus exposure, which ranged from playing clowns to doubling as a Spanish Señorita chased by a bull (two of my siblings—how fitting—in a costume), these were modest amateur affairs that made a point of including *everyone*. I'm reminded of that old joke about how peaceful it is living in a small town. You don't do much. You're afraid to... you're sure to get caught!

In contrast to my "circus" work, "Stout's Minstrel Follies" made every attempt to be a professional operation. The Professor used fellow musicians from the Pantheon Theatre band, as well as entertainers he could hire from the vaudeville circuit that passed through Vincennes. If Stout took a chance on a newcomer like me, he spent forever training us in the basics. Vincennes represented our shakedown cruise. After several local performances, we took the "Follies" on the road for several summer months, with periodic swings back through Vincennes to briefly catch up on life at home.

Given my dysfunctional family, these periodic homecomings didn't mean much to me, though Ella made one very memorable. While she was officially out of the brothel business by 1929, Ella still maintained close ties with most of her former prostitutes—which she had nicknamed the "Busy Body Brigade." Ella had missed my "Follies" debut, and for this return engagement she and six Brigade members were anchoring the front row. Decked out in the most colorful and feather-dominated finery this side of an explosion in a chicken coop, they were quite the eyeful.

Now, while they were the most responsive of audience members, especially when I was on (my "Rainbow 'Round My Shoulder" number was their favorite), don't think for a minute that Ella had gone all grandmotherly in support of young Red. Here's what really made the night unique for me—I was a sixteen-year-old virgin on the verge of becoming a man. Since my involvement with the "Follies" seemed to preclude my leaving Vincennes permanently sometime soon, Ella decided it was time to break my proverbial cherry. Normally, having one's grandmother orchestrate that first game of hide the salami might sound weird. Actually, go ahead and drop the "might sound weird." It definitely rings up as strange. But when you factor in that brothel background, who would question Ella's innate wisdom in these matters? (I've always been fascinated by various types of folks but like most young males, the only key kind of person at that time was spelled: G-I-R-L-S.)

Like most clownish-looking teenage virgins, I was all in favor of this proposed sexual rite of passage. I was a youth inching towards—make that, running towards—his expiration date. But being the easily embarrassed type, I had not yet mustered the courage to take part in what might be called the "casing the goods" process. Well, former madam Ella solved that problem with one brilliant step—if you can't bring Mohammad to the mountain, you bring the mountain to Mohammed. Ella's front row Busy Body Brigade represented my very own sexual line-up card. Happy birthday to me.

Consequently, you can imagine how nervous I felt that night—my opening to the Jolson impression (with an assist from Inez) came out so high it sounded like I'd been sucking helium all day. I was a boy locked in the candy store—free to sink his teeth into any bonbon he so desired. While the general audience at the Pantheon that evening thought the show was coming from the stage, the real performances were taking place in the front row.

There were six varieties of come hither looks, much pursing of lips, discreet caressing of breasts, and one delightfully unexpected parting of the legs, which made me swallow my gum. I was dumbfounded, or maybe just dumb. But I was smart enough to hold my prop derby just below my belt buckle. Through all this Ella, the queen bee, sat beaming. Presumably, all these tricks, no pun intended, had come directly from the long time brothel madam. Regardless, I was on stage three times that night: as Jolson, in a scene from *Uncle Tom's Cabin*, and as part of the "Follies" centerpiece minstrel show. But each time I changed my mind about which girl I would bed. My initial choice could have doubled for silent cinema's poster child of girlish innocence— little Mary Pickford, all blonde curls and cupid lips.

There was no doubt, after my Jolson bit, that "Mary" was the one. But during the *Uncle Tom* segment, that suddenly changed. My eyes rediscovered a girl, to continue the movie star analogy, who resembled the iconic Louise Brooks, with the short black helmet hair and the fuck me red lips. Brooks is best known today for her two German films with director G. W. Pabst—*Pandora's Box* and *Diary of a Lost Girl*. While both came out my stage debut year, they were much too steamy (spelled seamy in Vincennes) for my hometown. But I had already fallen for her provocative looks in an otherwise innocent silent film called *It's the Old Army Game*, a W. C. Fields comedy where she clerks in his store. (I have always been a huge Fields fan, and *Game* was the basis for the comedian's greatest sound picture, *It's a Gift*.)

Okay, I was definitely set to bed my "Lulu in Hollywood" look-alike. I would have bet the house, or since I was just finishing *Uncle Tom*, I would have bet the plantation, that she was the one. But then it was time for the minstrel portion of the "Follies," and when I returned to the stage a third time I lost my heart to yet another of Ella's "Busy Body Brigade"—a beautiful little black girl called Artina, like the Langston Hughes poem "To Artina." She was better than any silent star I had ever seen. Her skin tone was a light mahogany, what blacks of that time used to call "high yellow." She had big bedroom eyes, lovely high cheekbones, and a sliver of a smile that could quickly turn to laughter. Her flapper-style garb revealed shapely long legs. In short, I ached to be inside her. Though I would soon learn that she was completely without the harshness of Hughes' Artina, the poet's closing lines also perfectly described my selection's hold on me: "I will take your heart for mine, I will take your soul, I will be God when it comes to you." Yes, Artina was a prostitute, but in my eyes Snow White would have come off as a tramp in comparison.

Normally, I savor my every moment on the stage—still do. But that night

I was sooooooooo anxious for the "Follies" to be over. Yet, as if to expressly torment me, the hometown crowd was very kind, and there were several encores. Indeed, the Professor even singled me out for special praise, with the *Vincennes Commercial*'s later review crediting me with "some high powered [Jolson] impersonating." But that night, of all nights, reviews were the last thing on my mind. Still, I was more than a little curious as to how this would all play out.

Finally, the "Follies" were over, and I dashed to our makeshift group dressing room, with containers of cheap cold cream to help remove the burnt cork from our skin. Ironically, here I was taking off blackface, in order to have sex with a chocolate fantasy. Several of my fellow thespians were going out, and they tried to convince me to join them. One particular friend, a round wannabe comedian nicknamed Fatty, was adamant that I come along. I was as afraid as a turkey in November that he would mess up my special night. In Hollywood, overtime used to be referred to as "golden time." But for me, that long ago Artina night in Vincennes promised to be a truly "golden time."

Ella came to my backstage rescue. Weaving through the cast and crew like a halfback on a long, broken field run, my most non-traditional of grandmothers was soon announcing to everyone in earshot, "Family emergency, I need to get young Red home immediately!" With that, we were soon out a stage door into an alley adjacent to the theatre. All six girls stood waiting on my decision. While much of my later life has felt like there was a Warner Brothers cartoon character about to drop an anvil on my head, at this precise moment I felt incredibly blessed. Though some might have called Ella's little scheme pure nonsense, I saw it as a higher kind of sense. I had never wanted anything as much as I wanted Artina.

I huddled with Ella and told her my choice. She then broke up the brothel group, except for Artina, and the three of us went back to the boarding house Ella owned and operated—purchased with her whorehouse profits. She had collected some rather provocative people there, what you might expect if the later darkly comic novelist Nathanael West had run a boarding house. But we'll save that for another chapter. We went to my grandmother's second story room and she started to make coffee. Suddenly, I had this fear that Ella planned to watch or give me pointers while I did my business. Trying to calm this sense of panic, I glanced about Ella's book-strewn room, with my eyes finally coming to rest upon a love seat pillow. Embroidered on this cushion was the axiom: "To write simply is as difficult as to be good." As I smiled at the appropriateness of this sentiment for my brothel grandmother, I heard the most delightfully musical of laughs. Turning to Artina, I realized we had both happened upon this saying simultaneously.

This modest moment of bonding brought Artina to my side, and she gently took my hand, letting our fingers interlock. As she squeezed my hand,

Artina nodded towards Ella, and my grandmother said, "I need to go downstairs and look in on Widow Cummings; she's feelin' poorly. I could be quite a while. You two be good now." Pouring herself a large cup of coffee and slipping a bright red shawl over her shoulders, she shuffled out the door humming the Ethel Waters song, "I Want to Be Somebody's Baby Doll So I Can Get My Loving All the Time."

Ella's bed, a large bird's eye maple four-poster, was behind a beaded curtain to the left of the room. Parting this dangly wall, Artina led me to the bed and slowly undid the buttons on my blue workshirt. Making quick work of a task my thick fingers always struggled with, she had soon pulled off my shirt and undid my pants. Then, playfully pushing me back on the bed, she took off my shoes and socks and trousers.

Embarrassed by being down to my underwear, I climbed under the quilt coverlet and sheet. But my eyes never left the lovely Artina. What followed was a slow matter-of-fact disrobing by Artina, with her big brown eyes just as locked onto mine. I had been around brothels enough to know that this was part of the show, but it didn't mean I enjoyed it any less. When she was down to some yellow lace panties, Artina suddenly bolted into bed beside me, like she, too, was embarrassed.

The explanation she whispered in my ear, however, was, "I'm cold; warm me up." For the longest time we simply held each other. Before Ella left, she had lit a kerosene lamp on the marble nightstand, which bathed the room in a soft sepia-tone, making Artina, to borrow another line from Langston Hughes, "golden like the sunshine." She also had the slightest cleft to her chin. When I kissed it, Artina said, "Mama told me it meant I was 'touched by God.'"

In time we slipped off our undergarments, and though I was tall and gangly and Artina was long-leggedly petite, we fit together wonderfully. She said she wasn't supposed to kiss "Johns," but it would be okay if I kissed her. She seemed even younger than my sixteen years, but when I softly brought my lips to hers, Artina's tongue was immediately in my mouth. For me, the novice, it was like that old joke about Paris: "The best thing about the French capital are its girls. They're so gifted they invented a new way of kissing." Not surprisingly, I was soon exploding inside Artina, and I literally shook with each thrusting ejaculation.

Surprised with the quickness of the act, I lay there not exactly knowing what to do next. Artina excused herself, and taking a towel from the nightstand, she briefly disappeared through the beaded curtain into the outer room. But she soon slipped back into bed and asked, "Would you just hold me?" Nodding my head "yes" too many times, like the village idiot or my later character Clem Kadiddlehopper, she curled up in my arms. As I kissed her bare shoulder I noticed a small pock mark on her arm, as if an impression had been made with a penny. I repeatedly told her, "I love you," to which she just smiled and put a finger to my lips, as if to shush a talkative child.

As we continued to hold each other I could feel her small, round, perfect breasts against my chest, and I was soon hard again. As Artina felt this she asked, "Would you like to come inside me?" I tried to whisper, "Very much," but it came out almost indecipherably, like a French punch line, "Viva moo." When I started to fumble with again entering her, Artina said, "Can I be on top?" At this point I would have said "yes" to anything short of the Lincoln assassination. So she was soon riding me like a pony, and this time Artina moaned softly with each downward thrust of her body. God bless women who make pleasurable sounds. Men need all the feedback they can get. We might not be bright, but we're imminently teachable. Still, Artina hardly had a corner on the noise department. I moaned myself as I cupped my hands over her breasts and almost lifted my buttocks off the bed so that my member would be all the more upright for her riding pleasure. It took longer for me to come this time, and though she might have been just acting, I think we had a simultaneous orgasm.

The second time Artina slipped out of bed she didn't come back. Sadly, I never saw her again, though I thought I saw her later that summer in the balcony of Vincennes' Moon Theatre. As with many American communities of that time, the cheap seats in the film theatre balconies were known as "Nigger Heaven," the only place blacks were allowed to sit. But what is now often forgotten is that many poor whites sat there, too, since these seats were less expensive than those on the main floor.

In point of fact, Ella bringing her former prostitutes to the front row of the Pantheon Theatre should not have happened on several counts. First, these were, after all, whores, and the Pantheon was the top (respectable) theatre in town. Second, there was a black in the group, Artina, and people of color were not allowed on the first floor. Third, Ella had recently spent a couple nights in the local pokey—another of her assault and battery charges—for roughing up a dry-good salesman for implying she needed what would now be called an "extra large" corset. Why he did this, short of a death wish, I have no idea. But Ella beating up on fools was sort of the narrative of her life.

At some level I think she believed that whoever scuffs most wins. Though she was always kind to me—never more so than with Artina—Ella could condemn the world with her eyes—and fists—quicker than anyone else I ever knew. Ella would just go crazy. I wouldn't put it past her pushing you into an abyss… and then jumping in after you, so she could further beat on you on the way down. While someone else might apologetically say, "Forget what I said; I'm just having a nightmare," Ella pretty much was the nightmare. So until that hyperbolic event occurs, "When monkeys fly," you did not want to tangle with Ella.

Of course, beyond the fact that no one in Vincennes wanted to contest whatever Ella and company planned to do—like a night in the theatre with her whores to see her grandson—Ella also had the dirt on anyone and everyone of prominence in town. This included the mayor, the sheriff, and the country KKK Grand Wizard. All of them and many more bigwigs had long frequented her Washington, Indiana brothel, as well as an earlier one in Vincennes.

Ella not only had a memory like an elephant, she had saved every personal note, IOU, letter, and any other paper trail item that would incriminate these pillars of the community. Obviously, she had also made it well-known that "things would come out" if she were not treated with a certain degree of deference and respect. As she was fond of saying, "Politicians, ugly buildings, and whores all get respectable if they last long enough."

Consequently, because of Ella, Artina sat in the front row and changed my life. Though I never saw her after that one amazing evening (it was someone else in the balcony), not one day has gone by since then that I haven't thought of her. If truth be told, despite three wives and countless lovers, Artina still remains the vision in my head when I bed someone. Inside my now damn old body I'm still young with feelings for her. I know, she was a prostitute gift from my grandma! But that in no way lessened the ache which remained for her. Regardless, I later figured there was a certain symmetry in lovin' a prostitute... since my mother was a prostitute.

So there you have the three pivotal people in my young life—the Professor, Ella, and the sweet Artina, who treated me like a courtin' fellow instead of just another "John." When I tried to track her down after the summer "Follies" tour, she seemed to have vanished, gone back to "her people" in Kentucky. I was never able to find out more than that.

When I solicited Ella's help, she kissed my forehead, rubbed my unruly red mop of hair, and said, not without gentle affection for both Artina and me, "Let it go child; she's a whore." So I let it go, but that aforementioned ache remained. Interestingly enough, I later learned that Ella had gifted my father with a prostitute for his first time, too. But like everything else about my dad, who was abrasive by nature, it had turned into an ugly situation. Joseph had felt humiliated by coming before he was even inside the woman and had ended up beating the poor girl. "He was a bad one," said Ella. "Even though Joe was one of my own, I'm not sorry he was taken early. God help him. And God help me for saying that. But you're a good boy, Red, like your mother Lillian, not at all like Joe."

Ella's general take on things was that if you lived long enough, you'd see lots of bad things come down. She was fond of saying "cynicism" was just another way of spelling "realism." But occasionally, like with Artina, there were blessings, too. This made perfect sense to me, because at sixteen I'd already seen more than my share of harsh times, starting with those murderous half-brothers, half-crazies. Many a night I'd lain awake wondering if suffering was just suffering, or was there any way to funnel it into something good? With Artina I maybe had an answer—suffering made you really savor those fleeting moments of joy, a phenomenon always in short supply among the poor. So while falling in love with a prostitute might seem funny/sad, it gave me something to hold onto at a time when day-to-day life was trying its best to overwhelm me. Romantic hope might be a frail ally, but it was the only ally I had.

The day after being with Artina, the "Follies" and I were back on the road in a beat-up bus so old it ran on peat moss, and headin' for the next one-horse town on our jerkwater circuit. After the romantic "riches" of being with Artina, I was back to being another hand-to-mouth, gypsy-like entertainer, with shoe soles so thin I could step on a coin and tell whether it was heads or tails.

On the Road: From Donuts to the Clap

On an extended vacation with my family in the 1950s, my children's favorite stop was Washington, D. C.'s "Air and Space Museum," but I kept thinking, "Shouldn't this place be empty?"

I LOVE TRAVELING, a trait born of all my early years of touring as an entertainer, from Clarence "Professor" Stout's "Follies," to crisscrossing the eastern United States during Vaudeville's last hurrah in the 1930s. My warmest nomadic memories, however, were from 1929, my first summer with the "Follies." As we went from one Midwestern small town to another, I still remember the Professor's winning way with each local audience. He always used the same opening line, other than substituting in whatever burg we were in. For example, "It's really good to be here in *Marion*. I'm not from around here. But I came as soon as I heard about it." Moreover, since there was invariably some sort of road work and/or building going on, it gave the Professor some additional standard lines, like: "You'll have a great town here… as soon as you get it finished." Or, "It's a small world… but I wouldn't want to paint it."

For added publicity purposes, we always tried to arrive the day before our opening. Stout was fond of saying, "If you can't be on time, be early." Early meant we could make our presence known around town, from hanging out at the local barbershop to visiting the various greasy spoon cafes. We put up posters and talked the "Follies" up so much we sounded like that old Groucho Marx line, "You must have been vaccinated with a phonograph needle."

The Professor would even volunteer to man the theatre ticket booth, with some of us performing out front. For instance, years before my television show's "Silent Spot," I was doing pantomime. My best routine was the aforementioned bit about a woman getting ready in the morning, from putting on make-up to wrestling with a girdle. But even then I had a semblance of a later classic sketch—where I pantomime an old man watching a Fourth of July parade. You have to remember that when I was a boy, the nation's birthday rivaled Christmas as the country's number one holiday.

I can still remember Vincennes' Civil War Veterans watching the July Fourth parade. Between those memories and my close relationship with my grandmothers, I've had a great affinity for older people. I especially like their constant mix of humor-tinged advice. Ella, my grandmother who ran the brothel, was fond of the following equation for a long life: "Sit down every chance you get." I also remember her gentile admonition when anyone got smart alecky with her—"Don't go clever on me."

Ella was the only one I really missed on the road. But generally, touring was the most crackerjack of times. Things might not have been quite that great, but that's how I remember it, memory being what passes for personalized reality in life. Like director Kurosawa's *Rashomon*, a movie I discovered on one of several later trips to Japan, which has a story that explores four characters' varying takes on the same incident, the Professor's slant on the 1929 "Follies" tour would probably have been different. But as an artist once observed (I think it was Picasso, or maybe it was my barber), "Art is a lie that tells the truth." Or, screw the details. While looking back is not without its dangers (remember what happened to Lot's wife), it's pretty much required when doing one's memoirs.

Regardless, I mention this Professor-encouraged show business outreach because this set the pattern for all my future touring, right into my senior years. Mingling with the folks always helps sell tickets. When I played college campuses after the S. O. B.s at CBS cancelled my TV show, I would stay in the local student center hotel. Hanging out with college kids was always news. (I even won a "Campus Entertainer of the Year" award—so much for CBS' claim that my television audience numbers skewered too old!)

Now, don't get me wrong. While being accessible to the folks is good business, I'm very much a people person. Like Lincoln, that Cinderella in prairie boots and one of my favorite heroes, I believe in the common man's inherent wisdom—fooling the people is as hard as trying to sneak a sunrise past a rooster. Of course, with a brothel-running grandmother, I am also conscious of all negatives caused by the small-town blue-nose types. Someone once said, "There are two classes of people: the righteous and the unrighteous. But the classifying is done by the righteous."

Beyond celebrating the people, observing them has been my greatest source of finding material. This is a common research tool for comedians. Oliver Hardy once told me, "I spent hours in the parlor of my mother's boarding house studying people. My character's embarrassed fiddling with his tie bit came directly from one particular milquetoast boarder. And that exasperated expression I got whenever Laurel did something stupid—stolen from another lodger, Mr. LaFong, who looked that way whenever he didn't get seconds of my mother's fabulous beef and noodles!"

As a sidebar on Hardy, he was one of the first comedians I cornered upon my initial brief stay in Hollywood for *Having Wonderful Time*. I approached him as a fan, even had him sign an autograph book—one of my many hobbies. Anyway, I always felt Hardy was the underrated one in the team of Laurel & Hardy. Stan was great, too, but Oliver's long-suffering frustration over dealing with child-like Laurel made them. I also loved the team's description of their characters—"two minds without a single thought." No matter how you cut it, they were an inspired comedy pair.

Getting back to my own comic exaggeration of the world around me, I owe a great deal to my first wife, Edna Stillwell. I was tanking in a Montreal nightclub called the Lido, back in late 1935. I had made the mistake of trying to be a Hoosier Maurice Chevalier. But Indiana's French Lick isn't quite Paris. Well, Edna said, "I could write better stuff than what you've been cobbling together from those joke books."

I got all sarcastic and said, "Okay Mrs. Hemingway, why don't you. This is certainly the time for you to reveal any hidden talents."

Surprisingly, she went on to write some of my signature material, starting with a career-making donut-dunking sketch. This pivotal routine was born the next morning. We were sitting in a diner, too broke for anything but coffee. It was then that she noticed a man at the counter dunking a donut. Edna had a eureka moment, as she observed, "There's our first sketch." Darned if she wasn't right. What evolved was a routine where I demonstrated several types of dunkers, from the flamboyant personality who overstates his every gesture, to the timid soul who attempts to dunk on the side. But my favorite was the poor sucker who miscalculates his pastry submersion time… dissolving the donut!

Years before gross-out Gallagher, I embellished the bit by also throwing "sinkers" into the audience and occasionally talking with my mouth full— "broadcasting" donut chunks in every direction. The *Milwaukee Journal* critic praisingly called this merry mess of a routine "the donut-dunking massacre." Since the bit involved sitting at a table with a plate of sinkers and coffee, I could even write my "ad-libs" on the paper tablecloth!

There was, however, a comic downside to this bit, which I played for *years* in vaudeville. Each show necessitated eating *nine* donuts… and I did *five* shows a day! After a while, I'd eaten so many sinkers I started to swell whenever it rained. But the numbers further fueled the publicity. By 1938 a *New York Daily Mirror* critic covering my ability to slaughter donuts in wholesale lots entitled her article, "Red Ate 12,000 Sinkers and Each Made 'em Roar." By the time RKO Studio called me to Hollywood that year to put the sketch on film, in *Having Wonderful Time*, I'd put on a ton. Would you believe I used to weigh fourteen pounds?

They practically killed me in the studio gym, but if you ever catch the picture on TV, you'll see that they Stan Laureled me right down. I hate exercising. My only workout routine today is getting the mail. I also enjoy telling people, "I get plenty of exercise carrying the coffins of my friends who exercise." I later got rather sneaky on the subject of weight while I was at MGM. Whenever they claimed I'd put on weight, I'd buy oversized tailored suits and parade my apparent sizeable losses past whatever bigwig wandered into my domain. They always bought it.

But getting back to my pastry problems, sometimes the difficulties had nothing to do with added poundage. Often it was difficult just maintaining the sinker supply. I needed five to six dozen donuts a day; four dozen were for the shows, with the extra covering the random hungry fellow vaudevillians who would eat the "props." But one time, shortly before our first show of the day in Milwaukee—this was 1938 or '39—Edna and I got to the theatre to find nothing but empty donut boxes.

At first we thought it was a prank, or overly ravenous performers. But it soon became apparent that our Boston bulldog, Jiggs, had eaten 60-plus donuts. While the various stage acts on the bill fanned out in the neighborhood in search of "props" for my act, Edna and I took care of a very sick pooch. This was the same dog I used to lower out of a third-story boarding house window, where pets were not allowed, for his late night constitution. One night this caused a passing drunk to stumble back to a nearby bar and shout, "There's flying bulldogs out there!"

When I eventually preserved my donut sketch on film for RKO, I joined a long line of Depression era comedians who built comedy routines around food. Granted, every age does it, from Charlie Chaplin stealing hot dog bites from a child in *The Kid*, to John Belushi (with that body of an out-of-work plumber), instigating a food fight in *Animal House*. Still, during the accent-on-hungry days of the '30s, movies were literally peppered with eating sequences.

The champion Depression eater was Joe E. Brown, with that Grand Canyon-sized mouth. In one of his definitive films, the baseball classic *Elmer the Great*, he managed to tackle the largest movie breakfast on record: stacks of pancakes, ham, apple pie, gingerbread, donuts and jam, and assorted fruit (especially a comic's favorite—the banana), while drinking coffee and a large glass of milk. Also, like me talking away in my donut sketch, Joe's nonstop patter had him "broadcasting" breakfast items, too.

Of course, some '30s comics took a more surreal path to the foodbag. For example, in *Sons of the Desert*, loopy Stan Laurel is frequently munching away on wax fruit, while Oliver Hardy eats his hat in *Way Out West*. But the comedy king of oddball eating is Harpo. In one of the Marx Brothers' early Depression films he eats a telephone and later downs an inkwell like an alcoholic chaser. Groucho's theory on his mad mute of a brother was that he personified reincarnation—Harpo had been a goat in a previous life.

I know I'm taking the long way around the barn describing my early touring days. But I have one more Edna-related story that will shed some light on my nomadic nature. In the late 1940s I was trying to get out of my MGM contract. Though this was the studio that billed itself as having "More Stars than the Heavens," it was no place for a comedian. If a camel is a horse designed by a committee, MGM is the studio that hired that committee. What with being humor-impaired, they proved to be a comedy graveyard for many of my favorite funny men, including Buster Keaton, the Marx Brothers, and Laurel & Hardy. But enough with the negatives. As "Professor" Stout used to observe, "If you can't say something nice… make an anonymous phone call."

Ultimately, I had a press conference where I announced that I would buy out my MGM contract for $700,000. Well, this was big news—made all the papers, including some of those late editions they used to print. That was a lot of money—still is. As I now like to say, especially since I have a much younger third wife, "A millionaire is a man with enough lettuce to choose his own tomatoes."

Regardless, I got my $700,000 buyout statement all wrong back in 1947. It turned out that would be my projected earnings… if I *stayed* with MGM for the length of my contract. Poor Edna, who also then doubled as my business manager, had to call another press conference for damage control. For me, the safest thing would be to keep my mouth shut. Have you noticed a lot of quiet types get credit for being conservative when they are only stupid? Still, her press conference was the catalyst for probably the most insightful thing anyone ever said about me: "If you want a good story, talk to Red. If you want the truth, talk to me."

I'm what old-timers, like my mentor the Professor, would call a storyteller "six times over"—each time I would embellish the facts into a better tale. Eventually, it would bear little resemblance to what really happened. Plus, when you add in the times I simply didn't understand something—like my $700,000 MGM buyout statement—you can see how I would not be the most creditable witness.

So how does this relate to my entertainment wanderings as a youngster? I fibbed *a lot* when relating my story to reporters, especially when I was starting to hit it big in the late 1930s and early 1940s. Just as I had falsely claimed my father was some world class clown, I made it sound like I had permanently left home as a ten-year-old, starting with "Doc" Lewis' medicine show. But my "Doc" days were limited to summer vacations and didn't start until I was a teenager.

"Professor" Stout's "Follies" were where I really got my feet wet as a performer, and as a fibber. In fact, lying almost became like breathing to me. Since the "Follies" involved a minstrel segment, scene re-enactments from *Uncle Tom's Cabin*, and vaudeville-like segments (where I would do my Al Jolson impersonation), I would later tell reporters I toured in separate companies for each of these areas. And when I did move on to something else, like briefly hooking up with a regional circus as a clown, I tended to exaggerate both my duties and the length of my stay.

I did, however, enjoy being with the circus—though I spent more time doing "grunt" work (feeding the animals, putting up tents, selling tickets, and so on) than actually performing as a clown. But by then I had started almost believing my stories about my father being a circus clown. Like Mark Twain's visit to the Middle East, where he felt a sudden sense of bereavement over being near the final resting point of his beloved long lost relative Adam, I could get downright tearful over my fictitious circus connection with a father I never knew.

Even though I wasn't with the Hagenbeck and Wallace Circus long, all did not go smoothly in big top land. During my first circus parade, I found myself with little to do on my bandwagon perch. Unfortunately, the procession route took us by a series of luggage shops, still a special temptation for me, what with my gypsy tendencies. Thus, I constantly found myself glancing back at the store window displays of the to-die-for trunks. But soon I would feel like dying myself. No one had warned me that "to look over your shoulder during a circus parade is regarded in big top circles as more foolhardy than attempting the 'triple' with a drunken catcher and no net below."

Among the very superstitious circus folks, this looking back infraction meant heavy fines. Who knew there were circus police? Anyway, my total bill would have had me working gratis long enough to test my meager math skills. With this reversal, I had a sudden weeping melt-down. But I soon found that circus folks were even more sentimental than superstitious. By the following day, not only was my fine forgiven, I found that my dog-eared suitcase had been replaced with a new monogrammed wardrobe trunk. The circus company had taken up a collection for an overwhelmed young man.

I also had a brief entertainment stint on a Mississippi River stern-wheeler showboat called the *Cotton Blossom*, which was owned and operated by one Horatio Hittner. Captain Hittner had these headlamp-sized eyeballs and a ramrod posture that meant he sat straighter than a school teacher at a poker table. I did a little bit of everything, from comic stories to playing my ukulele and singing. Since I mingled with passengers as I performed, this was excellent training for a job I would soon have during the Depression—an emcee for those endless walkathons.

Though I later credited myself with several seasons on the *Cotton Blossom*, I barely lasted through one. Oh, it wasn't for a lack of enthusiastic performing. I still literally threw myself into my work, with a major pratfall being a signature opening and closing to my act. I was, as Ella used to say, "A hard dog to keep on the porch." My pink slip was the result of an aborted romance with Captain Hittner's daughter, Mary Ann. Her cabin was not far from mine, and she was always asking me in to "just talk." She was Mae West shapely, though rather plain to look at. But Mary Ann had that one trait to which so many men are attracted—she was easy.

Unlike Ella's gentle prostitute Artina, who had stolen my heart, Mary Ann's rough sexual activity resulted more in the bruising of other organs. Though always demure in public, the perfect Southern belle under multiple petty coats, behind closed (bedroom) doors she was the proverbial hellcat— tag team wrestling would have been more restful. But Papa Hittner only knew little miss pure as the driven snow (before she drifted). I am reminded of my friend Oscar Levant's line about Doris Day, "I knew her before she was a virgin."

Though my heart still belonged to Artina the whore, she was way off in Indiana, and Mary Ann was only two doors down—making it Saturday night every night. Or so I thought. On a July 4th evening Mary Ann was so anxious for our "festivities" to begin that she came to my room before I had even changed out of my performing costume—the garb of a 19th century riverboat gambler. As she helped me slip out of my trousers, Mary Ann began stroking my "package." Then, dropping to her knees she went down on my "little fireman." And that gal could have sucked the chrome off a trailer hitch.

Given the unusual blackness of the night, just as I climaxed the riverboat hit a sandbar. The sudden stop rocked the cabin, causing pictures to fly of the walls, and bric-a-brac about the room to fall to the floor. Talk about rockin' the molecules! Simultaneous with all this, a patriotic late nighter set off some fireworks along the shore. So amid "rocket's red glare" and "bombs [seemingly] bursting in air [or at least in my cabin]," I had a riverboat stopping orgasm for the ages. It's the only time after fellatio that I've ever been so moved as to treat my partner like an affectionate puppy—I actually patted Mary Ann on the head and said, "That's a *good* girl!"

Now, when one has these rare magic moments, there is a tendency to delay ending them. Such was the case here. Mary Ann continued to remain plugged-in, so to speak. Indeed, she reached around me, with each of her hands squeezing one of my buttocks—pushing my member even deeper. Mary Ann was successfully navigating what another age would label Linda Lovelace's *Deep Throat* territory. (That reminds me of a joke. Do you know how Lovelace's grandmother died? She went down on the *Titanic*.)

While I would normally be the last one to speak out against prolonged fellatio, my tenure aboard the *Cotton Blossom* would probably have been longer had we stopped immediately after the "rocket's red glare." Though running aground added to my sexual—the earth moved—titillation, I forgot about the concerns of a father, as in Captain Hittner. He came tearing down to Mary Ann's cabin. Finding it empty, he was in even more of a panic. But the ship's sudden stop had evidently thrown open my door, and when the Captain stuck his head in to ask about his daughter… well, let's just say he had his answer.

Like one of my pantomimes, no words were necessary. Of course, plugged-in Mary Ann was speechless anyway. Me, who's normally like one of those pioneering talkin' dolls—Chatty Cathy—had nothing. And the poor Captain had immediately gone into an Old Testament imitation—turning into a pillar of salt. When speech did eventually return, all he could muster was something that sounded like, "You're firrr…." At first I thought he was putting some sort of wrath of God curse on me, turning me into a biblical pelt—you know, fur. It was only later, after he closed the door and walked away, that I realized I was fired.

Years later, when I had a modicum of fame and I first shared a sanitized version of the story with the press, I made the Captain out to be the most revengeful of fathers. I actually claimed he pitched me into the Mississippi, with nothing but my almost new circus trunk to act as a life preserver. In truth, it was all much more civilized. Like me, the Captain was not into confrontations. One of the other performers knocked on my door at eight the next morning and informed me that once we were off the sandbar, I would be dropped at the first available landing—which turned out to be some burg near Mark Twain's birthplace, Hannibal, Missouri. I was relieved. All night I had been checking the locks on my portholes and door like I was Anne Frank. At the bare minimum, I had expected the Captain would make me walk the plank or something.

As I surveyed the sunset later that day from nowhereville, Missouri, I was content. I had survived a tight spot with no visible wounds, and nature never seemed so perfect. Well, maybe the sunset could have used a bit more red, but it wasn't bad. Unfortunately, I counted my chickens too early. It turned out, Mary Ann had given me a little parting gift—a touch of the clap, what we used to call the "French disease." Not knowing what hit me, other than it burned to pee, I walked to Hannibal in search of a doctor. Desperate for relief, I gave him my $12 nest egg. Back then they were still treating the condition with mercury, but I will spare you the details.

As I think back on what someone in the military might now call the "collateral damage of sex," I am reminded of a poem I wish I'd read *before* bedding Mary Ann. This inspired bit of verse had come from a university student named Holly Caine, forty or fifty years after my *Cotton-Blossom* experience. I was playing some Midwestern campus, and she interviewed me for the university paper. During our talk Holly said she really wanted to be a poet, and wondered if I'd look at some of her work. Given my own poetry writing, I agreed. And when I checked out of the hotel the following morning, there was a folder for me. What follows is my favorite Caine poem, "Condom," from a collection later published as *Words*:

> Here I sit between the pregnancy tests and lube
> On your Wal-Mart shelf
> Promising pleasure in colors, textures, and tastes
> To be grabbed by a shy teenager or a drunk frat brother
> Placed in wallets, purses, even night stands
> Will tonight be the night
>
> Will I be used today
> Called up to the big show
> Enjoy the best
> Be used
> So used
> Ripped open
> Slid on and done
> Filled and done
> Only to end up in the trash
> Taken out with yesterday's trash

Ella would have loved this poem, too.

As I recovered from my embarrassing French disease predicament, I made some silly vows, like giving up women. (This would last roughly six weeks.) But I still honor one career decision I made back then. When I first toured with "Professor" Stout's "Follies" I was going to be the greatest comedian that ever lived. However, when I thought I was dying of the clap, I resorted to one of those pacts with God we're always makin' when things aren't going well. You know the drill. In my case, I promised to give up assorted sins (especially loose women) and be more humble if I could only pee without pain.

Luckily, I had lived a fairly sinful life, so I could offer up many sacrifices to God. Years later I remember reading a Mark Twain story, where he had advised a friend on the finer points of how to give up various vices when one hammers out a "help me" pact with the Lord. But the humorist was horrified to discover that his acquaintance had never cultivated any weaknesses, and thus, was without bargaining chips in her heavenly negotiations. As a boy born into a brothel, I would never have given Twain anything to worry about.

Though most of my clap promises to the Almighty eventually turned to "claptrap" (such as avoiding easy women), the humble commitment stuck. I was reminded of this a few years back when Muhammad Ali was spouting his "I'm the greatest!" claims. Now, don't get me wrong, I greatly admire Ali. In my day, boxing rivaled baseball as America's number one sport. And I think Ali could have taken my favorite fighter—Jack Dempsey, something I never thought I'd hear myself say.

Still, Ali's "I'm the greatest" is something a young naïve person says, when you think you're bulletproof. Granted, such confidence can, to recycle "Professor" Stout, help "get you up the hill." But as you become older and/or stumble through various life lessons, your aspirations soften. You simply want to be a "gamer," someone who loves his profession and gives 110%. So much of life is just showing up.

Let me sandwich in one brief story about Ali. We did a joint charity appearance late in his boxing career—he had just regained the heavyweight title for the third time, the only fighter to ever do that. We were at a gym on La Cienega Boulevard in Los Angeles, preparing to do a three-round comic sparring match. But the laughs were coming before we even got in the ring, starting with his chiseled physique versus my gone-to-seed build, which was beginning to resemble the name of one of my early comedy characters: "Willie Lump Lump."

As we met at the center of the ring, I further milked the setting's comic potential. For instance, when the ref (played by black comic Slappie White) said no hitting below the belt, I pulled my pink pansy-covered trunks up to my armpits. Then as Slappie directed us to grasp gloved hands at the break, I dropped to my knees in pretend pain over Ali's vise-like grip, all the while staying in character as my loopy punch-drunk boxer "Cauliflower McPugg."

Ali generated equally big yucks by simply playing it straight—acting like this was yet another fight. But as he started to shadow box in his corner before the opening bell, he did something that started to make me nervous. Looking directly at me he repeatedly mouthed the words, "I'm going to kill you!" With each of these silent explanations the crowd went wild, chanting "Ali, Ali, Ali!" But for Nervous Nel me, I immediately started studying his face, looking for some telltale flicker of a smile, or a wink of an eye. I got nothing… other than excess stomach acid.

All the while there's that thunderous "Ali, Ali, Ali!" from the crowd. But I'm thinking, shouldn't my Cauliflower McPugg be the underdog here? Eventually, I put it all, or most of it, out of my mind. I told myself, "He's just a great showman." So now it's the first round and we're dancing around in the ring. Actually, he's the one gracefully "dancing"—doing his "float like a butterfly" movement, while I'm lumbering around like the overweight donut-dunking clown that I am.

Soon Ali starts bringing his laser-like punches to within a paper-thin fraction of my noodle—you know, my second favorite organ. I couldn't believe the speed and control he had with those gloves. So, I start worrying again: "Sure, Ali has great reflexes but what if he has some sort of George Frasier flashback, and he lands just one of these haymakers? My *Cauliflower* McPugg would end up really being a vegetable. I'd start talkin' like Edgar Bergen's dummy Mortimer Snerd, or Frank Fontaine's drunk, Crazy Guggenheim." (I'm reminded of a boxing bit from one of my many joke books: "Why is marriage like a prize fight? Because the preliminaries are generally better than the main event.") Regardless, the second round I was feelin' more confident—Ali hadn't killed me yet, and I was even mimicking his back-pedaling movement. Of course, with me it was so stiff; there should have been a ringing sound, like those neighborhood ice cream trucks.

Just as I was fantasizing about turning professional, maybe recycling Bob Hope's old boxing alias, "Packy East," Ali starts silently mouthing to the crowd and me, "Out in three! Out in three!" Naturally, the pro-Ali crowd immediately joined in, too. These audience members were probably direct descendants of those pioneering Roman Coliseum sports fans, who were always betting on the lions, even though they could have gotten great odds on the Christians.

To calm down, I reminded myself that Ali was famous for predicting the round in which he would end a fight. Then, as the second round ended and we headed for our separate corners, he whispered to me, "Next round, swing big for my chin." This time he winked. What was he up to? I was about as confident as the class dunce at a spelling bee. But if Ali wanted me to swing for the fences, I would try to oblige him.

As we maneuvered about the ring at the start of the third round, there was less "dancing" on his part. He was "off the bicycle," as they say in boxing circles. Plus, Ali's chin seemed out, and with his arms at his sides, he was asking for it. I started swinging my right arm in a full 360-degree movement, like the cartoon character of your choice, accelerating for the haymaker of the century. We hadn't worked out exactly how I would "pull my punch," but between all my comedy sketches, and his years in the ring, that didn't seem to be a big problem. Surprisingly, this was in direct contrast to a *Lucy-Desi Comedy Hour* I did in the late 1950s. Lucy and I performed a Freddie the Freeloader duet—both of us dressed as my tramp character—and she had a conniption whenever I ad-libbed anything. Lucy was definitely *not* into improvising. Ironically, while she was a great comedienne, she had bought into MGM's philosophy that the script is sacred—definitely a minority opinion among the funny bone bunch.

Anyway, with Ali and the haymaker, I knew I couldn't hurt him, even if I didn't perfectly pull our bout-ending punch. Still, in the back of my mind, there was a modest concern that I might upset him. Then, in a split second, he could accomplish Ralph Kramden's ongoing threat to Alice, "Boom, zoom, to the moon!" And I was too young to be that kind of astronaut… you know, simply propelled by a knuckle-sandwich.

Thankfully, my fake knockout punch came off without a hitch. Ali allowed it to graze him slightly on the chin, and he dropped like a stone. He continued to embellish the upset, by repeatedly kicking up his legs, as lively as a frog on a hot plate. Slappie White then made a great show of declaring me the champion, while two sexy pretend nurses made a provocative show of helping Ali up and into his robe. At this point, he did some inspired improvising of his own. Borrowing a page from James Brown, Ali aped the singer's closing routine, where feigning exhaustion, he is helped into a robe and slowly escorted from the stage… only to comically repeat the process. The crowd really ate all this up. Here I had beaten the champ, so to speak, and he still won the fans, and at my own game of ad-libbing, too!

This off-the-cuff comedy with Ali reminded me of my early free-wheeling entertainment days, when Edna and I were making it up as we went along. Those misadventures will be the focus of the next chapter.

Edna — The First Mrs. Skelton

I'm no stranger to pain, I've been married three times."
                                            – Slappie White

As the Good Witch of *Oz* suggests, "It's always best to start at the beginning." Well, like Slappie White, I've been married three times, too, and though I've known my fair share of pain, I can't blame it on any of these women. I will eventually get to the other two wives, but for now I'd like to focus on my first spouse, Edna Stillwell, who created so much of my early material. As the saying goes, "Success has many parents." But Edna was the one most responsible for putting me on top. She made me rich and famous—you know, the well-upholstered air.

Of my three partners, Edna was also probably my best friend. Even after our 1945 divorce, she remained my manager and chief writer into the 1950s. To borrow a romantic comedy line frequently used by scriptwriters pitching a story, Edna and I "met cute." I was a seventeen-year-old burlesque comic, while she was a fifteen-year-old head usherette at Kansas City's Pantages Theatre, a vaudeville house. I was playing at the Gaiety, just a block down the street from Edna's theatre. But with vaudeville being a step up on the entertainment chain, I spent every free moment at the Pantages—ever available if an act failed to appear. One night the balcony stooge for one of the Pantages acts did not show and a desperate stage manager pressed me into vaudeville service. It was left up to flashlight-leading usherette Edna, in the sexiest little short skirt, to both lead me to the box and flesh out what was expected of me.

The bored and sometimes "drunken" heckler and/or disruptive audience member is a special treat for the student of comedy, since this bit of stage shtick is as old as the theatre itself. Filmed examples stretch from Charlie Chaplin's (please cue the hallelujah chorus for my hero) *A Night in the*

Show, to those old men muppets who sabotage *The Muppet Show* from their balcony perch.

That night in Kansas City I drew my actions, in part, from the afore-mentioned Chaplin short subject. I knew the movie from my ushering days in Vincennes. *A Night in the Show* had Chaplin playing two disruptive parts: a drunk in the auditorium (Mr. Pest), and a blue collar type in the balcony (Mr. Rowdy), with the latter figure frequently in danger of tumbling to the main floor.

Okay, so I do the drunken heckler bit and get a great response from the audience. But the gorgeous usherette Edna is not impressed. Normally, this would bother me. Yet, she was so sexy I let it pass. Being a leg man, Edna had the greatest pair of gams I've ever seen, before or since. And this was back in the good old days, when air and water were clean, and sex was dirty. Think-ing back on it now, the teenage Edna was not unlike the leggy Cyd Charisee (though blonde) in the noirish fantasy from the `50s film *Singin' in the Rain*. It was the sort of image that makes a guy's teeth sweat, followed by choking on his Jujubes. To borrow an old burlesque line, "She could have caused car-diac arrest in a yak."

Ignoring her indifference, I gave her some of my best lines, like, "The applause were thunderous, I was afraid I'd have to check myself for ruptures." Or, "I recently shared a tiny office with a lady contortionist, six inches smaller and it would have been adultery." These bits "killed" in burlesque but I got nothing from Edna. She was like a tree with eyes, and a heart the size of Hit-ler's. Entertainment artists are paid to metaphorically dance on the edge of the cliff but with an audience of Ednas, I would have felt like literally diving over a cliff.

Still, I kept trying. Besides being easy on the eyes, her brassy nature sort of reminded me of my brothel grandma, Ella—always ready with a smart re-mark. For instance, if you told Edna, "It takes all kinds," she'd come back with, "Is that what it takes; I always wondered? Or, if you complimented her outfit, Edna might shoot back, "Yeah, I bought it at an exclusive shop—'Everything must go!'" She was also cuttingly comic about other acts, calling one "No more substantial than cigarette smoke." On another occasion she railed, "Just having an act doesn't always mean anything—my dog can hump a table leg but that doesn't give you puppies."

Of course, she could be totally self-deprecating, too. Before Edna dropped out of high school to help support her single parent mother, she had played six-girl basketball, a popular Midwestern sports format into the 1960s. Unfortunately, Edna's team never won a single game, and she used to say, "We were so bad, we couldn't beat ourselves in a scrimmage." Yet, a lot of that smart aleck nature was a protective outer shell. Once she got to know and trust you, her tone was considerably softer. But again, like Ella, I was also amused by the ease with which Edna could segue an everyday question into something bawdy. For example, if you asked, "Could you do me a favor?" She might reply, "Does it involve a donkey?"

Given Edna's defense mechanism sarcasm, not to mention seeing a lot of quality comics as an usherette, she was neither a fan of my vaudeville baptism under fire, nor my subsequent subbing opportunities at her Pantages Theatre. My basic routine, after graduating from audience heckler, was heavy with slapstick—opening with a spectacular fall into the orchestra pit and coming up with a bass drum wrapped around my neck.

After taking the fall, I would yell at the orchestra from the pit, "Wise guys! Movin' the stage on you when you're not looking." Struggling to get out of the pit, I would add, "Why don't you fill that in, that hole." Then I would go into some of my pantomime sketches. Not only was Edna not impressed, she tried to get her stage manager to fire me! But this more forgiving man, not without his own comic talents, had the perfect comeback: "I don't have to fire him. He'll probably kill himself falling into the orchestra pit!"

Edna's initial reservations with me, however, were much broader than I ever imagined. After we were married she confessed, "I didn't like your act, nor the way you dressed, nor the way you talked." Not surprisingly, when I first attempted to date her, I received a freezing brush-off. That was tough, because behind my cocksure façade, was a not-so-sure character. I could talk the talk but people like Edna would trip me up on the walk. Allowing myself one obvious cliché, I was the breezy burlesque comic, who was the saddest of clowns in private.

Being on a burlesque circuit that also included St. Louis, Indianapolis, South Bend, Chicago, Toronto, and Buffalo, Edna and I then parted company for several months. We would next meet at the El Torreon Ballroom in Kansas City. While some things had not changed, such as the city and Edna's icy demeanor towards me, both of us were now in different jobs. Edna was the El Torreon cashier and I was the emcee for a Walkathon at the Ballroom. Walkathons were a new quasi-sadistic entertainment born of the Great Depression, which had been precipitated by the Wall Street Crash of the previous year (1929). The Walkathon (also known as the Danceathon and the dance marathon) involved dozens of couples in a competition to be the last duo standing. With no time limit, the event could go on for weeks as the couples staggered around a dance floor fighting the exhaustion which would eventually wean their numbers down to a winning pair.

Competitors were allowed one ten-minute break per hour for food and bathroom needs. Colloquial comedy of the time nicknamed the Walkathon the "fallen-arch marathon." But behind-the-scenes we called it the "walking dead," and compared it to other drawn-out "entertainments" from the period, like the 6-day bike races. Years later another Hoosier-born artist, director

Sydney Pollack, immortalized the Walkathon/Danceathon phenomenon in the movie *They Shoot Horses, Don't They?*

As good as Sydney's film was, there wasn't much humor, and that's something my Walkathon shows always had. Granted, the Depression was tough times, and even though these marathon competitions could be grim, my mission was to lighten things up. We're all put on earth for a purpose, and mine is to make people laugh. For me, a humorist is a person who, even when he feels bad, he can manage to feel good about it. In contrast, some people are so humor impaired, you could soak them in a joke for a month of Sundays and it would still never get through their skin. And without a sense of humor, you're like a car without shocks—jolted by every "bump" in the road.

For all my comic drive, being a Walkathon emcee was quite the challenge, starting with those *ten-hour shifts*! My non-stop patter included a running commentary punctuated with jokes, comic songs, impromptu impressions, my signature pratfalls, kidding encounters with contestants, and whatever other distractions I could conjure up. Once, I even "borrowed" a mounted policeman's horse and road it around the Walkathon dance floor—just to keep a tough audience involved. I figure you can't escape from life; but you can escape into it."

Being a Walkathon emcee also helped my standings with Edna. Burlesque didn't have the best reputation. Plus, she also felt my self-proclaimed billing, "youngest comic in burlesque," was egotistical. Ironically, the knock against burlesque was unfair. While I was in this field we only specialized in spoofing pop culture films and plays. For example, we did two different parodies of the sexy silent Latin star Rudolph Valentino. One was a take-off on *The Sheik* called *The Shriek of Araby*. The second routine spoofed Valentino's *Blood and Sand*, and we titled it *Mud and Sand*. In both bits I played Rudolph *Vaselino*. The dialogue never got any racier than a Vaselino the doctor bit I did in both parodies. Here is a typically innocuous line. After a less-than-voluptuous woman gets a breast exam, I say, "I'll charge you my *flat* fee!" (Cue the snare drum.)

Anyway, it was only after I left burlesque that it started to get raunchy. That is, with tough times and the added difficulty of finding paying customers, burlesque had moved from sometimes peppering its parody format with sexual innuendo, to outright strip-tease acts. Or, as Red Buttons used to describe it, "Burlesque came from the old Latin expression, 'Bring on the broads.'" Regardless, the spoofing format had gone from a specific take-off, to a "broad" take-off.

Even if I'd been interested in returning to burlesque, local blue laws in Midwestern cities often closed these theatres, making the once dependable burlesque circuit an iffy proposition for comedians like me. Moreover, in the days before air conditioning, burlesque and smaller market stage productions often shut down during the summer. But Walkathons initially proved to have year-round popularity.

Some of the accounts Edna and I later gave of our first joint Walkathon had her as one of the contestants. But you know me and my "creative" take on the past—where the history runs deep and the folklore deeper. (If I was one of your tall tales, I'd definitely be the tallest.) Thus, having Edna be one of the struggling participants just sounded more romantic. But had she been part of this exhausted group, Edna would have been too tired to appreciate my humor. And that's what eventually won her over.

The victory, however, was not easy. For a month I tried to thaw her out. Then one night from the stage I tossed out a joke at which she laughed: "Jobs don't come easy. For months at a time, I forgot what kind of work I was out of." Soon I got Edna with another bit: "Last night two kids were caught sneaking into the Walkathon… we fixed them… we made them see the whole show."

Paradoxically, once the romance was on I had to cope with the fact Edna lived on the distant outskirts of Kansas City. Why, that streetcar went from the downtown area to what seemed like the California state line. Edna would later relate my joking marriage proposal tied to those long streetcar trips: "After about three months Red said one night, 'Why don't we get married and save me all this travel?'"

Despite all the faults Edna initially found in yours truly, we had a lot in common. First, neither of us had known our father. While my dad had died before I was born, Edna's pop had abandoned the family while she was still a baby. Second, both of us had worked from a young age to help support a struggling household. In fact, like me, Edna even had an undertaker in the family. Her mortician uncle was always after her to come into the business. We used to joke that he was "The 'boxer' who always wins," and "The fellow in the end who always lets you down."

Third, though Edna never thought of herself as a performer, even after later stooging for me in our act, both of us were drawn to show business, the profession that made you part gypsy and part suitcase. And with joint aspirations for vaudeville, that smorgasbord of the theatre, we were hopeful to catch-on someday. As noted earlier, Edna eventually found her entertainment gift to be writing comedy. Fourth, each of us was driven to succeed, with Edna channeling her talents into making me a star. (My brothel grandmother used to joke, "Ambition is a poor excuse for not having sense enough to be lazy.") Fifth, as in most teenage marriages, there was also a certain growing-up together factor, too. We essentially raised each other, as we entered that institution (marriage) once described as "A quiz show you lose if you give the right answer."

While Edna was younger by nearly two years, hers was the dominant personality. Plus, her mission to remake me was not limited to show business. Later in the 1930s George Bernard Shaw's celebrated play *Pygmalion* was inspiringly adapted to the screen. Edna's transformation of me that same decade did not quite approach Shaw's makeover of a Cockney guttersnipe into a lady (the later basis for *My Fair Lady*), but it was close—a photo finish. Besides the aforementioned high school equivalency exam I eventually passed, I even took some college extension classes on comedy. Getting a historical perspective on my profession gave me a great slant on there being no new jokes. For instance, here's a bit Edna and I later wrote, "A comedian is a guy with a good memory… who hopes no one else has."

My favorite example of this old joke syndrome from my college extension classes was drawn from Mark Twain's novel *A Connecticut Yankee in King Arthur's Court*. The title character in this time-tripping book finds himself stuck in the past and forced to listen to the court humorist. Here's the Yankee's take on the situation, "It seemed particularly sad to sit here, thirteen hundred years before I was born and listen again to poor, flat worm-eaten jokes that had given me the dry gripes when I was a boy thirteen hundred years afterwards. It about convinced me that there isn't any such thing as a new joke possible." (Twain loomed large in my marriage to Edna. She even footnoted the writer in one of her standard greetings, "What about you Huckleberry?")

Though my relationship to Edna was often that of a student to a teacher, a better analogy was parent and child. She later said of our marriage, "I discovered that he needed a guardian angel… or at least a guardian." Not surprisingly, all three of my wives would give me endearing nicknames which suggested a caretaker scenario, such as "my man-child," "kidult," and "boyman." I'm almost embarrassed to confess that my pet name for Edna was "Mommie." Along related lines, I've always loved the fog—it shuts out the rest of the world. Well, Edna was sort of my special fog machine. She managed to shut out most of the adult world. I just didn't have to deal with it.

Fittingly, another of Edna's parental terms for me was "Junior." If that sounds familiar, Edna later used me as the model for my popular radio character "Junior"—the brattin' kid whose tag line was always, "If I dood it I get a lickin'… I dood it!" Moreover, that expression had "legs"—show business' term for staying power. The year after it was introduced on early 1940s broadcast, newspapers across the country borrowed the phrase to describe Colonel James Doolittle's surprise World War II bombing raid on Tokyo—"Doolittle Dood It!" I even did a movie called *I Dood It*, and Junior remained my most popular radio character throughout the 1940s.

Regardless, I have always needed a great deal of support—a situation which applies to numerous entertainers. Neglected and/or underloved as kids, we need the ongoing affection which comes through applause. For years whenever I was on stage, Edna had to stand in a prominent position in the wings where I could see her. Once during a radio broadcast, when my success should have made me more confident, I glanced at the usual place and she was gone. I almost had a panic meltdown. After the show, I told her, "Don't ever do that to me again." To better understand the unique comfort zone represented by Edna—at the time of this incident, we were divorced, and she was my manager and writer/producer.

These developments, however, are getting ahead of the story. In 1931 we were like many young Depression couples—struggling to get by. As my favorite Hoosier humorist, Kin Hubbard, had written shortly before this, "Two can live as cheaply as one… just not as long." Physically, Edna and I were also reminiscent of the then phenomenally popular newspaper comic strip duo *Mutt and Jeff*, where skinny Mutt towered above his short pal. Similarly, at six-foot-three I towered over the pretty petite Edna. Adding to the dissimilarity was my carrot-topped head, versus her blonde bob, though she colored it brunette in later years. This comic contrast was pertinent to the act, since I used Edna as a theatre stooge later in the 1930s. While not having to pay an assistant was the chief reason for Edna doubling as my sometimes sidekick, an amusing physical difference is always a plus in a comedy act. (My favorite example of this would be the conflicting shapes of Laurel & Hardy.)

Of course, I should hasten to add that I was not completely goofy-looking. During our Walkathon days, and even initially in vaudeville, management had me pretending to be single. They thought it was better for business. Consequently, poor Edna often had to pretend she was my sister. Yet she *never* complained. Edna was that focused upon making me a headliner. Still, she might have funneled some resentment into her first Walkathon bit of stooging—a heckling audience member, not unlike my aforementioned drunken balcony heckler. As soon as I came on Edna would start to yell things like, "Take him off!" and "Kill the bum!" She was always a hit with the crowd, and Edna later told a local paper, "I like to holler, and it feeds my brother lines, too."

But this chronicles a time when we were an established hit. At the beginning of our marriage I was still just a former burlesque comic trying to make it in the world of Walkathons. Indeed, my mother-in-law had originally objected to her daughter marrying a burlesque comedian. It didn't help that I kiddingly told her I was going to reform and become a dope-peddler. But I eventually brought her around with a bunch of corny jokes about her brother the undertaker. For example, "No matter how busy he is, he can never bury himself in his work." (Don't blame me; I was just starting out. Besides, the jokes worked on Edna's mom.)

As I followed the Walkathon phenomenon from city to city, I eventually became confident enough as an emcee to eventually ask for a percentage of the gate instead of a straight salary. But consistent with my childlike tendencies, I would naively accept promoters' box office numbers, even if they were watered down. These were guys whose every word was a lie, including "and" and "the." And their first pictures were probably mug shots. They were "businessmen" who would have written history with a pencil, or produced attendance figures as bogus as claiming my Indiana was the only state without an active volcano. Back then I thought I had common sense, but I wasn't even close. They shouldn't even call it common sense; it should be called "rare sense."

This is when Edna first came into her own as our money manager—negotiating Walkathon package contracts that also made her the cashier (as she had been back at Kansas City's El Torreon Ballroom), so she could check on the box office numbers. Eventually, she would work our weekly Walkathon income up from $75 to $500—quite a raise for someone who had to borrow his $3 marriage license fee from his bride!

As good as these numbers were for the Depression, Walkathons were not always steady work. Plus, one never knew when they would end. There was inevitably down time between engagements. Moreover, our forever on-the-road expenses ate up most of the money—covering food, lodging, and transportation to the next Walkathon city. Early in our marriage, when we were just hoping for that $75 a week, I often had to get creative to survive. I fell back on the huckster skills I'd employed as a child back in my Hoosier hometown, like doctoring old playing cards and selling them as new novelty decks. Thus, when we found ourselves stranded in St. Louis, I created a fog-preventer for car windshields. All this amounted to were slivers of soap wrapped in recycled tinfoil taken from discarded cigarette packages. But it was not so much the product as the moxie to sell anything on a street corner—especially drawing upon the shakedown skills of "Doc" Lewis, the medicine man salesman/grifter for whom I worked as a kid. Edna stooged for me as the eager ice-breaking first fog-preventer "customer" *and* lookout for any patrolling street cops.

Ironically, despite these huckster skills, which I later used to create my wheeler-dealer confidence man character San Fernando Red, I was still that man-child who could not handle himself. I was also a sucker for competing scam artists and any sob story involving a handout. In addition, after a lifetime of impoverishment, any extra money would, to borrow a popular Depression era phrase, "burn a hole in my pocket." Befitting a husband she called "Junior," Edna put me on a modest allowance and handled all money matters. Even years after our divorce, when she was still managing me, all my checks had to be co-signed by Edna. This was both a safeguard to protect me from bad investments, and simply an exercise in basic bookkeeping—I was bad at keeping records of my purchases. *If* I wrote anything on the check stub, it was usually something goofy, like "None of your business."

What proved even more exasperating to my first wife was that for much of our long association I refused to be concerned about money. Or, as Edna liked to phrase it, "He's allergic to financial worries." I think this was a product of my never having had anything—yet always somehow getting by. My real life personality seemed fueled by the central characteristic which attracts us to most comedians—the resiliency factor. Yet, the financial freedom with which Edna gifted me, by playing purse strings parent, was a strain on our relationship.

Another mini-melodrama for us involved my proclivity for pets—an outgrowth of both my overgrown youngster nature and the unconditional love animals tend to give caretakers, something to which I definitely related. Our menagerie often included multiple dogs, once a duck, and a polar bear cub we briefly used in the act. To say Edna was in charge of pet "damage control" was to state the literal truth. For instance, when the aptly named polar bear cub, "Snowball," got loose in a hotel dining area, a Keystone Cop-like scenario ensued. But I most remember Snowball chasing the waiters. They were pretty fast afoot but so was the cub. They'd cut and twist among the tables like a halfback running a broken field but they couldn't shake Snowball… There was considerable furniture and glassware smashed in the melee and no doubt a few nerves were shattered but I think the hotel people overreacted.

Besides playing diplomat over these pet problems, poor Edna also had to be a fast-talking arbitrator for those occasions when I allowed my Walkathon comedy to take on destructive surreal silliness. For example, during a Minneapolis competition I invited a contestant to sing a song on stage. As he launched into his rendition of "Singin' in the Rain," I had a light bulb moment—simulate a raining backdrop, and see if this sudden "storm front" would derail the wannabe warbler.

I began my fun attack by squirting the contestant with a seltzer bottle, just as Harpo had tried to quiet a blaring radio in my favorite Marx Brothers picture, *Duck Soup*. When that did not phase the singer, I doused him with a couple buckets of water—still nothing. But egged on by an appreciative crowd, I moved to my comedy coup de grace—spraying him off the stage with a fire hose. This was such a hit with the audience that I decided to turn the hose on the crowd. Though this topper greatly pleased the dry portion of the audience, the soaked-to-the-bone section was less than pleased. I literally had to go into hiding. And the Walkathon manager was all in favor of killing me over the piffling matter of the organ under the stage… which was not waterproof.

However, the initial anger and follow-up intermediary skills necessitated by Edna after my funny fiasco with the Minneapolis Walkathon organ was nothing compared to the ire and draining diplomacy exhibited by my wife when I chopped off the legs of a rare and very expensive piano at a Walkathon in Atlantic City. I could blame such chaotically zany comedy on the then contemporary influence of the always absurd Marx Brothers, the team once punningly described as, "All gall, divided into three parts." But in all honesty, when I slipped into a creative comedy zone back then, everything and everybody was at comedy risk. For me life is a comic classroom, and I'm the designated prankster—a poet of the funny bone. While Edna would always loyally give a tip of her hat to my zany inventiveness, she also had to constantly bail me out of trouble for being so iconoclastic. Moreover, after several such incidents, she got tired of circling the metaphorical wagons in my defense.

Like the "thrill comedy" actions of silent film star Harold Lloyd, forever synonymous with the *Safety Last* sequence where he hangs from the hand of a skyscraper clock, I was also happy to put myself in harm's way for comedy's sake. When you're young you feel bulletproof. Consequently, at one Walkathon I rode a midget bicycle along the railing of a balcony overlooking the auditorium stage. After taking an unplanned fall and nearly going over said railing, I decided to begin the next night's Walkathon festivities by hanging from a beam over the stage. This proved such a thrill comedy hit that the following evening, I planted a dummy dressed like me on the beam, called to the crowd again, then pushed the dummy off into space. People fainted all over the establishment and once more it was only Edna who saved me from being torn limb from limb by the Walkathon powers that were.

Naturally, all these *Edna to the rescue* stories merely reinforce the parent-child dichotomy mentioned earlier. I wish I could say I eventually grew-up but my next two wives also had to mother me, too. It's funny, jokes about marriage usually target the woman. For instance, "Everything in life is fairly simple except one's wife." Or, "Nobody works as hard for his money as the man who marries it." I even wrote one along these lines which is frequently anthologized, "All men make mistakes but married men find out about them sooner." Still, in all three of my marriages, I was the challenge, not my wives.

The genius of Edna was that she used my childlike ways in the act by basing "Junior" on me. She even had a set line about how it came to pass: "I had to watch Red the way Junior's mother had to watch Junior, or he's bound to get into mischief. Red has the same approach to life: 'If I dood it, I get a whippin'... I dood it!'" Like Edna's creation of my aforementioned donut-dunking sketch, it was comedy born of simple observation. But instead of an eating act being drawn from a stranger at a coffee shop, Edna simply had to sketch Junior from, to paraphrase period humorist James Thurber, "her life and hard times with me."

Of course, this art mirroring life phenomenon is only one side of the equation. American comedy has long been fueled by the arrested development of the male. The first movie clown I remember seeing at what we called the "flickers" was John Bunny—a child-man not unlike the later W. C. Fields. Both of these comedians were forever trying to escape controlling wives for a night out with the boys… or maybe the girls, too. (Bunny's signature line from his stage career was the following toast: "Here's to our wives and sweethearts… may they never meet.")

Though this arrested male development situation, what I like to call the "Peter Pan Syndrome," is very prevalent, I think I could have qualified as the poster child. My overly dependent relationship on Edna was the catalyst, in part, for my later erasing her from my life. While I'm not proud of having done this, blotting people out of my consciousness was how I once coped with change. They say knowledge is power, but for me knowledge (at least about self) is often pain.

Regardless, given Edna's controlling nature, or maybe because of it, we often quarreled as a young couple. At one point she even left me on the road and returned to Kansas City. But that was precipitated by me giving a pretty waitress some free passes to the Walkathon—a very naïve thing to do when one's wife is the cashier! But I was lost without Edna and I showered her with long-distance communications. And even though my boy-man tendencies were a major part of our problem, they helped me win her back, too. For example, here's Edna's *Photoplay* take on the subject several years after the fact: "Ultimately, I was a sucker for his little boy approach to anger. He never stays mad longer than two consecutive minutes and can't understand other people who keep on being mad when he isn't."

Soon after her return, Edna began writing those career-making comedy sketches—starting with the aforementioned donut routine. And to borrow a line Jackie Gleason's writers used to apply to their work, Edna was great at "Feeding the Monster"—getting me material. But I'd like to quote something she wrote to my old Vincennes mentor, "Professor" Stout. The source is a letter I recently found in one of my joke filing cabinets. (You know the definition of a filing cabinet? A place to lose things alphabetically.) Anyway, after several affectionately detailed pages Edna observed, "Gee—this isn't a letter it's a visit." Even after all these years, I was moved by the genuine "aw shucks" charm to her correspondence. It makes one think, "how appropriate she should be writing comedy material for such an 'aw shucks' Hoosier humorist." The Professor always said, in a voice so deep that it seemed to start at his toes, "Edna's a good egg; she's really a good egg."

Let me share, however, one more Edna story. We were staying in a rather scary New York boarding house around 65th and Broadway, years before the building of Lincoln Center revitalized the area. This was in the early 1930s, when we were trying to establish ourselves in the Walkathon craze. Nearby was a porn theatre, though they couldn't call it that at the time. I think the term "European" was in the title, a period euphemism for all things erotic. Well, the marquee always said: "Open at 7 A. M." And I'll always remember, one night Edna looked up at that starting time and said, "Now, I'm not opposed to porn—but it's a whole new perspective when you have to set an alarm!"

All in all, this brings my saga of Red and Edna up to the verge of what the Depression era often called a "Cinderella Man success," which is the subject of the following chapter.

Me——A Bob Hope Model?

"Comedy is like food and music—it's a universal."
– Edna Stillwell Skelton

I ROOT FOR THE CHICAGO CUBS during the rough spots… I think they're called seasons. I identify with them because I have been an underdog my whole life, too. But things really came together for Edna and me in 1937. There are maybe four or five times in your life when you can do no wrong; this was one of them. And the secret was the donut sketch Edna had written. Suddenly I was getting major bookings, including Loew's State Theatre in New York City—*the* vaudeville house on Broadway's Great White Way.

Edna and I were so focused on fine tuning the act that there was no time for anything else. For example, I remember some fellow vaudevillians wanting us to play a board game one night on the train, between engagements. Well, it could have made me spit nails. See, I have enough stress without fake problems that come in a box… I don't want to have my good times come down to rolling a six.

Regardless, you would have thought my beloved brothel grandmother was writing these rare 1937 reviews. My favorite notice was *Variety*'s take on my Loew's engagement: "[Skelton] is a young comic whose chances appear exceptionally strong. He has an easy, affable manner of working, quickly ingratiates himself and is pretty well equipped with material… He's not going to have any trouble at all getting along in this or any other town, either on stage dates of this character, in picture houses or on nitery [nightclub] floors."

On this same Loew's bill we had a sexy mystic named Minnie, who was always attributing our success to those "signs" in the stars—which always struck me as so much crap. That is, those star pictures are always supposed to be Greek warriors or bulls and such. But if you want to be honest about all those random stars/heavenly dots, you'd have some sign called "the measles."

51

No, the career year Edna and I had in 1937 was all about us making our own luck… plus that donut routine.

Our 1937 critical kudos also resulted in an invitation to appear on the popular coast-to-coast radio program, *Rudy Vallee Varieties*. This was my first exposure to a national audience. Vallee had started his career as a popular singer, the first to be labeled a "crooner." Between his music and the periodic movie part, he had also been able to land this highly influential radio program, which soon became famous for showcasing new talent.

Vallee might have had a soft spot for Hoosier performers, since one of his favorite guests was Indiana-born veteran comedian Joe Cook—frequently billed as either a "one-man vaudeville," or simply the "nut comic." Though forgotten today, his persona was often of a zany, fast-talking huckster along Groucho Marx lines. Fittingly, Cook was on Vallee's program the night Edna and I first appeared. And when I kiddingly called his Evansville hometown a "suburb of my Vincennes," we soon had an affectionate radio feud on our hands.

Oh, it was not in a league with the celebrated radio feud between Jack Benny and Fred Allen that began in 1936, or even the later comic battle royal between W. C. Fields and Edgar Bergen's dummy Charlie McCarthy. But Cook and I doing a Hoosier-based one-upmanship was popular with Vallee's radio audience, and we were invited back for more comic dueling. This was generous of Vallee, since I had initially upset him with one of my too revealing, off-the-cuff lines. He was already ticked that I wasn't following the script and when he tossed his pages out of exasperation, I quipped, "Rudy's ad-libs are scattered all over the floor."

My high profile 1937 also led to a lucrative twelve-week movie commitment in Hollywood, where I was comic support to Ginger Rogers, Douglas Fairbanks, Jr., and Lucille Ball, in the romantic comedy *Having Wonderful Time*. (Lucy and I hit it off from the beginning, two redheads—well she wasn't a redhead yet—who lived to be funny. But while I was always "on" in public, Lucy tended to save it for those camera moments.) While my first feature, not released until 1938, wasn't quite the hit I had hoped for (more about that later), it was obvious that movies would need to be part of my future. By this time vaudeville was largely reduced to stage shows in support of large city film palace screenings. And who knew how long that would last?

Moreover, Hollywood just seemed to be throwing money at you. As an honest, hardworking Midwesterner from a born-to-be-unimportant background, I didn't feel deserving of all that easy cash. For instance, I was recently looking at one of my two dozen oversized scrapbooks and revisited my 1937 thoughts on that first Hollywood job: "Why, I didn't really earn one penny of that [$2,000 a week] salary out there [in California]. I do more work than that just for an audition or a free rehearsal."

Of course, Edna and I did enjoy exploring "La-La Land," and my autograph book was a constant companion. Yes, even though I was in a movie I remained star-struck. Plus, it didn't hurt that the famous folks I was meeting, like Fairbanks and Rogers, were so nice. Ginger even gave me tips on another of my hobbies—photography. This outgoing woman was probably extra thoughtful to a newcomer because she was sort of starting over herself—focusing upon being an actress instead of just Fred Astaire's dancing partner, despite how much we all loved her in that part. (Though all these memories are clear as day, sometimes I think of this memoir as more of a biography, since the fellow I'm writing about has changed so since the Depression. For one thing, I was then so driven by naiveté, that wonderful trait that keeps you from realizing just what long odds you are up against.)

For a patriotic kid from the sticks, the topper to that magical 1937 was putting in an appearance at President Franklin D. Roosevelt's White House. Several well-received bookings that year at Washington, D. C.'s Capital Theatre had brought me to the attention of Roosevelt. But the President's fascination with the entertainment industry and its potential to aid charitable causes dated from at least World War I. In 1918, Roosevelt, then the assistant secretary of the navy, had joined movie stars Charlie Chaplin, Douglas Fairbanks, Sr., Mary Pickford, and Marie Dressler in a huge war bond rally in the nation's capital.

President Roosevelt, a later victim of polio, would subsequently turn his annual January birthday celebration into a charity fund-raiser for infantile paralysis. In fact, I would go on to act as the master of ceremonies at the President's Birthday Ball for four consecutive years starting in the late 1930s. Besides the "pinch me, I'm dreaming" state this put me in, I also made some special Hollywood contacts at these gatherings. To illustrate, America's top box office favorite at the time, Mickey Rooney, became my biggest supporter. Rooney was equally popular with the President, especially after his affectionately comic impersonation of Roosevelt in MGM's *Babe in Arms*, with Judy Garland. Anyway, as Rooney's and my paths kept crossing during these D. C. charity activities, the young actor loved what he called my "casual comedy style," such as interrupting a White House birthday toast with the warning, "Careful what you drink, Mr. President. I once got rolled in a joint like this!" Consequently, Rooney promptly told his MGM studio boss, Louis B. Mayer, "There's a guy [me] at the White House, funny as can be. You ought to get him."

I know revealing testimonials in one's favor might take away the mystery, like adding electricity to a haunted house. But no matter how solid your notices, life is often about who you know. Still, unlike the low point in my life—and there was strong competition here (let's just call it surviving childhood)—Rooney's push to get me signed by MGM is one of my fondest memories. Another major booster to get me on at the studio was the sexy, tempestuous Mexican dancer/actress/singer Lupe Velez. The title of one of her later popular pictures, *Mexican Spitfire*, perfectly captured her persona for period fans.

Velez's support, however, was a more complex scenario. First, she also got a kick out of my comedy. Additionally, Lupe was especially appreciative of my helping to flesh out her rather thin vaudeville act. When we both appeared at New York City's Paramount Theatre in early 1940, my emcee duties enabled me to stooge for her, and we worked well together. The two of us were held over for six weeks of record-breaking audiences. But the third reason she was so supportive was tied to us briefly being lovers. Now, this says nothing special about me in the Romeo department. Lupe was simply, and I say this affectionately, Hollywood's greatest nymphomaniac. Of course, even with a brothel-running grandmother, Lupe's sexual aggressiveness took me by surprise.

I know that sounds like a married man's excuse, but autobiography is often spelled a-l-i-b-i-o-g-r-a-p-h-y. Yet my relationship with Edna had always been more about our mutual workaholic push for success. Like that early billing that credited us with being siblings, our teenage marriage contributed to a sort of growing-up together brother-sister act. Still, that continues to smack of a male cop-out. Okay, Lupe was another case like Mary Ann back in chapter 3 (I hope I won't have to keep prompting you like this.) But she was more than easy. The woman was a track star in her chasing technique.

Between shows, when I wasn't in costume, I used to lounge around my dressing room in long underwear—the kind with the "open window" in back. Well, Lupe dropped in one day with a riding crop, and I asked, "What happened to your horse?" She said, "You'll do," and proceeded to chase me, using the crop to unflap my underwear's back window. Well, it wasn't long before she was, indeed, riding me three times a day—also the number of shows we did. But the woman was insatiable. She would have been happy to do it a dozen times, if I had been up to the task. While today I need eight hours sleep and two bowls of Wheaties between rolls in the hay, back then I was proud of my stamina... until spending time with Lupe. I don't know if the rumor was true that she had once "serviced" the whole USC football team (some subjects are just hard to work into a conversation), but it would have been consistent with her amazing appetite for sex.

Consequently, Lupe was also very supportive of my potential for pictures. She was going with two-time Oscar-winning MGM director Frank Borzage at the time, though, as you might imagine, she was happy to briefly go with anything in pants. Regardless, she got on the phone to Borzage and said, 'There's a guy here that looks like a turkey [with his red hair]. You got to put him in a movie!'" With such strong support from Lupe and Rooney, I was able to shoot an MGM screen test later that spring (1940), with Borzage overseeing the production.

Personally, I now refer to the test as my "greatest hits," since it included everything of note in my repertoire, from the career-making donut-dunking sketch, to the then new "Guzzler's Gin" routine, where I play at getting drunk during a television commercial. (Yes, I know this was early for a *television* sketch. But if it hadn't been for World War II delaying the small screen revolution, television would have been in most American homes much earlier.) Borzage was a tough audience, despite the film crew fighting the laughter during the shoot. He wanted something different, more edgy. This was the catalyst for yet another demonstration of what Edna and I did best—comedy brainstorming. Better than sex... well almost, she had the ability to endlessly pitch ever-more inventive sketch ideas to me. My contribution was comic improvisation—given her imaginative suggestions.

Naturally, however, we had to do a "W. C. Fields" [scam] on Borzage, playing our game as if Edna's many pitches were actually old routines of ours. But in fact, she was merely trolling for something groundbreakingly different with which to prompt my ad-libbing abilities. She hit a home run with her suggestion that I do my parody routine of how various film heroes die. Ever helpful, Edna then pretended to further remind me by noting some rich scenarios with James Cagney, Edward G. Robinson, Errol Flynn, Lionel Barrymore, and others. Given this instant comic outline, I was lucky enough to improvise myself into a movie career. (But I was so shocked by the quick turnaround in becoming an MGM player, that if you had set me down and revealed that not everyone worshipped Charlie Chaplin, you would have gotten the same impact.)

The best screen test bits from the celebrity group involved gangster greats Cagney and Robinson. For the former, I spoofed his death scene in *The Roaring Twenties*, where Cagney, though fatally wounded, manages to stumble along for about forty miles. With Robinson, I drew from his classic *Little Caesar*, having him talking away forever, as if he, too, had not been mortally wounded. But I then segued my Robinson parody into another comically croaking gangster—George Raft, though still slowly tossing his iconic coin, à la the actor's pivotal role in *Scarface*. A later film historian, one of the few French intellectuals not to have written about Jerry Lewis, said this was some of my best stuff. Ironically, since tests are not released to the general public, very few people saw it—other than special groups visiting MGM. As Ella used to say, "The system isn't perfect, but the fleas come with the dog."

Anyway, my early film work for the studio was in strictly "B" pictures, like *Maisie Gets Her Man* and *The People vs Dr. Kildare*. One could liken "B" movies to the upper echelons of baseball's minor leagues—getting an actor ready for the "majors." Though MGM was the most prestigious of all the

Hollywood studios, famous for its tag line, "More stars than in the heavens," MGM's greatest source of income came from the "B" films. Plus, the studio did me a favor by casting me in the "Dr. Kildare" series. Though not quite in a league with the studio's phenomenally profitable "Andy Hardy" "B"-turned-to-"A" series (with Mickey as Hardy), the "Dr. Kildare" films had a large loyal following.

Though I seemed to register well in these pictures, MGM got on me for gaining weight. While one could still blame the donut sketch, which I had pulled out of retirement and performed as part of my act at the then mushrooming number of California military bases, a bigger culprit was simply fatty eating habits. Growing up in southern Indiana's Vincennes, close to the Kentucky border, meant I relished such tasty but rich Southern dishes as fried chicken, fried potatoes, pork chops, grits, biscuits and gravy, and fatback (Ella, who was definitely a large earth mother type, liked to say, "Fat people are usually good-natured, because it takes them so long to get mad clear through.") In addition, what is more common than a formerly impover-ished individual putting on weight once his metaphorical ship has come in?

An all-purpose film factory like MGM has a simple answer for fat—the studio gym. Though I did lose some weight, I also played the huckster—buy-ing pricey, slightly oversized clothing. Then, when the MGM powers that be would ask about my dieting/exercising, I would quickly show off the baggy pants and roomy sports jacket. It was an effective scam that I used through-out the 1940s, the heyday of my screen career. If I'd had to give up all my fried favorites, I might have turned into that angry guy that hates everyone and ev-erything, including dolphins. Though life is often a lot of should-have-dones and could-have-dones, I never had any reservations about either ducking that cockamamie exercise, or chowing down.

Oops, I neglected to add that during the 1940s the weight gain was also impacted by my being more of a party person. But I merely tack that on to address why I went from being such a social animal to almost reclusive. I simply got tired of the always "on" one-upmanship practiced by entertainers. Moreover, I felt this lack of sincerity was especially strong among comedians. Thus, I started to divorce myself from hanging out with most fellow funny-men. But I made an exception with my good friend Joe E. Brown. Fittingly, we were on the same page about this lack of comedian sincerity, and Brown had the perfect story to prove it. I first heard him share it with an appreciative audience back home in Indiana. His set-up for the story involved four film comedians who met regularly, but their conversation was merely an excuse to try to top each other. Brown then stated: "Mostly, they didn't listen to what anyone [else] was saying, for they were so intent on what they were going to say next. Well, one day one of them finished a story, there was automatic laughter and another said, 'You may wonder why I'm so quiet but today I had news that has just about knocked me out. My father and I were very close. We corresponded regularly until I came out here and then I sort of drifted away. Today I heard—he died last night.' The man paused for a second, and immediately another comic burst in with, 'If you think that's funny, listen to this.'" So, if I'm not exactly a loner, let's just say I choose my friends carefully, and Joe E. Brown is one of them.

Of course, let's be honest here. When one writes an autobiography, there is no one else there to refute what you say about your past. It's rather like that old vaudeville set-up line—"Things I overheard while talking to myself." Better yet, I am reminded of something sexy Veronica Lake, of the famous peek-a-boo hair style, once told me about memoir writing: "It's a strong temptation to lie, or at least embellish, which is probably why any autobiography is usually less true than biographies written by the impartial bystander." So when I scribble about comedians usually being so focused on self, I know I'm being self-serving, too, since I'm writing and hoping to hawk *my story*. You probably think I'm as self-centered as the last dodo. I merely bring this up to admit to some memoir hypocrisy. Still, if I manage to pepper this tale with assorted wisecracks, maybe you'll stay for my wrinkles—wrinkles as truthful as I can make them. Otherwise, I'll feel like I've fallen into a hibernation of the spirit—my comedy spirit. That's because a writer without readers is like a comic without an audience—a gift forced to shine at the bottom of the sea.

Memoir writing and shrinking from comedians was still years off when the movie arrived that made me a screen star—1941's *Whistling in the Dark*. This was a comedy thriller which borrowed liberally from two like-minded Bob Hope hits for Paramount—*The Cat and the Canary* and *Ghost Breakers*. I played a radio murder mystery expert kidnapped by real killers. The leader of a fake religious cult (Conrad Veidt, the eerie somnambulist from the German classic *The Cabinet of Dr. Caligari*) needs a perfect scenario for a murder his organization is about to commit. Naturally, my underdog character is elected for the job.

The headquarters for the cult is a spooky old mansion with sliding panels, secret passageways, and a creepy housekeeper—the same "haunted house" scenario as the aforementioned Bob Hope pictures. The formula upon which both Bob and I rose to film stardom was essentially clown comedy meets parody—spoofing a mystery thriller setting. While this combo had been done before, such as Laurel & Hardy having trouble *Way Out West*, what made Bob and me different was a new type of hyphenated hero. That is, a character who could fluctuate between the most cowardly incompetent of comic antiheroes and cool, egotistical wise guys. To comically paraphrase, we could talk the talk but we almost always tripped on the walk.

It had been my idea to tap into this dual focus personae, since I had long admired Hope. Besides, MGM's track record during Hollywood's Golden

Age repeatedly demonstrated that this was *not* the best studio for comedians. For example, when MGM took away Buster Keaton's creative autonomy at the start of the sound era in the late 1920s, the studio's actions contributed to self-destructive tendencies in the comedian's personal life. Paradoxically, MGM is credited with resurrecting the Marx Brothers' screen fortunes in the 1930s. But it was at a cost—the studio homogenized the team, taking away their goofy edge. Comedy connoisseurs, including yours truly, prefer the chaos-producing purity of the team's earlier Paramount pictures.

Regardless, the critics, members of a profession which normally pans for gold, were more than kind about *Whistling in the Dark*, with *New York World Telegram* reviewer William Boehnel, an early fan of my vaudeville work, waxing the most poetic about my breakout film: "Meet a new star... He's terrific, as those of you who have seen him in stage shows probably know, because it's been a long time now since the screen provided such a fresh, unaffected, bubbling clown."

Though I feel most natural doing slapstick, the *Whistling* script gave me the lion's share of the comic lines, which also doubled as examples of my antihero/wise guy character. For instance, at one point a cult thug growls at my radio sleuth, "Quit stalling... You get in my hair!"

My character's response is equally gruff, "Yeah, well, I'll tell you something!"

The mobster's comeback is an ever tougher, "What?"

I then meekly reply, "You could use a shampoo."

More frequently, however, my *Whistling* transformation, from smart aleck to coward, occurs in a single reading of a line, such as when a woman cast member asks if I'm a man or a mouse. I answer, "I'm a man... But tell me if you see a cat coming." On another occasion, I seemingly comfort a female co-star by observing, "To show you it's perfectly safe, I'll let you go first." And after some broad slapstick (a comic fall down a short staircase), I breezingly note, "Don't worry about me... because that's what I'm doing." Like a junior psychiatrist, my antihero/wise guy even coins a comedy credo grounded in amusing logic. The catalyst for this insight is a complaint from a co-star about me always making with the smart remarks. I reply, "If I don't crack wise, I'll crack up."

The *Whistling* script also worked in a variation of my "Guzzler's Gin" sketch. I play a TV announcer getting progressively more drunk while sampling the sales product during each live commercial break. In the movie the commodity is a liquid vitamin drink which, like Lucille Ball's later "Vitameatavegamin" TV sketch, is heavily laced with alcohol. My drunken actions exactly mirror what I do in the "Guzzler's Gin" routine—involuntary comic contortions of the face and upper body, wheezing, accompanied by an eye-popping countenance, and the transformation of my voice to a throaty whisper.

As a footnote to Lucy's "Vitameatavegamin" bit, now that she has passed on, I can confess how steamed I was that Lucy essentially stole my "Guzzler's Gin" routine. I felt as discombobulated as a 500-piece jigsaw puzzle turned upside down. We were old MGM friends, for crying out loud. You just don't do that to a comedy buddy—even if there had been a full moon or something…. But swiping material wasn't like her. Given the times, we can probably blame her TV writers. Still, she could have been a good egg and refused to do it. Otherwise, it makes you look as crooked as a dog's hind legs. Sadly, it was things like this Lucy incident that contributed to my later real life "Guzzler Gin" problems. But that's getting ahead of the story.

Despite *Whistling* becoming a huge hit, I worried that my success would soon disappear. Friends, like Veronica Lake, kidded me about not letting fame go to my head. But there was never any danger of that. I didn't yet feel like I fit in filmland. I might just as well have been an auto mechanic in Amish country. Consequently, I remained self-deprecatingly comic about my new Hollywood status. Skimming through another old scrapbook, I came across the following crack I'd made back in 1941, shortly after the star-making release of *Whistling*: "That must be somebody else, I thought, and I still think so, for, as I've often said, Edna and I came to Hollywood solely because she had a pair of slacks she wanted to wear under a mink coat."

As a Veronica Lake addendum, I must add that I never took her joking about fame without kidding her right back. And I usually keyed upon Veronica's signature sexy blonde hair in that peek-a-boo hair style, such as, "I opened up my mop closet the other day and I thought Veronica Lake fell out." Or, "Veronica Lake wears her hair over one eye because it's a glass eye." But I was not the only comic having fun with her hair. Legendary radio comic Fred Allen observed, "I was stopped by a cop the other night for driving with one headlight out. He looked at me and said, 'Hey, watta you tryin' to pull, a Veronica Lake?'"

While mediums exist as a kind of "spirited" customer service department, comics need a bit more direct contact with their customers (audiences). So, while I was proud to be making it in the movies, I missed not having that immediate feedback from an appreciative crowd. My remedy was to put together a radio program shortly after *Whistling* came out.

As luck would have it, my new program, the *Red Skelton Scrapbook of Satire*, proved just as popular as my *Whistling* movie. What gave this triumph on radio a certain consistency with my emergence as a movie personality was the presence again of a Bob Hope factor. Just as MGM saw the wisdom of applying Paramount's parody mix of the comedy thriller and Hope's antihero/smart aleck persona to my *Whistling* picture, NBC Radio had even more reason to accent the connection—the network produced both our programs. Moreover, to maximize the link, NBC put the comedy shows back-to-back on Tuesday nights, with Bob providing my lead in.

Thankfully, the notices for my *Scrapbook* show were excellent, such as *Variety*'s comments: "Much more costly entertainments would have been pleased this season to have done relatively as well on their inaugural program as did Red Skelton... it was a very enjoyable bit of comedy and music, if able to maintain the level, should find lots of listeners." Through lots of hard work, and the producing skills of Edna, we were more than able to "maintain the level"—generating solid Hooper radio ratings for our opening season (1941-42) and many more to come.

While the basic components of the program will be more fully fleshed out in the following chapter, suffice it to say this medium allowed me more creative control. Though I had many parallels with the Hope persona, radio (more than the movies) gave me a better platform on which to differentiate myself from the ski slope-nosed comic. Most specifically, there was my growing number of comedy characters, starting with an early variation of my seminal silly figure, Clem Kaddlehopper.

Along related lines, my densely packed psyche (all those comedy characters) encouraged my suggesting that I was a little crazy... but as long as I made money, I was safe from the people with nets! And that reminds me of the old Vegas routine about a star on a press junket upset that he did not receive a large luxurious suite in the hotel. Instead, he simply had a small bungalow on the grounds. But when he reminds the publicist that his co-star has one of those grand suites, he is told she has an entourage. The disgruntled actor's rebuttal: "I am a paranoid schizophrenic. I am my own entourage!"

Whether one sees me as a crazy comedy entourage or a single hard-working clown, *Whistling* and *Scrapbook* (both 1941) put me on the entertainment map. But while my first memoir musings would sometimes flirt with the apocryphal, the most amazingly honest thing about my early entertainment successes, was that I never portrayed a story more amazing than my own. But this fame factor would soon reconfigure my private life.

Radio & Multiple Changes: Movies, Military & Marriage

> My inventive ways with personal history might have been influenced by Grandma Ella's saying, "I don't necessarily agree with everything I say."

WORLD WAR II was probably the most volatile time of my life and career. So much was going on between 1942 and 1945 that I felt as goofy as another of Ella's favorite lines, "Thank heavens the sun has gone in and I don't have to go out and enjoy it." My state of flux would involve a divorce, a broken engagement, war service, a nervous breakdown and a new marriage. I'm going to key upon my greatest creative outlet of the time, radio, and the re-defining of my most significant and complex relationship with first wife and pivotal mentor Edna Stillwell.

Radio was special because I could exercise more control than in the movies. But it came with a built-in irony. With my rubbery face and gift for pantomime, I was at my best as a *visual* comedian. Of course, radio was full of such paradoxes. For example, one of my major radio rivals was *ventriloquist* Edgar Bergen and his smart aleck dummy Charlie McCarthy. Still, all my years in vaudeville made me more than comfortable with a comic line, and one naturally gravitates to the medium which gives you the most freedom. I'd rather be nibbled to death by ducks than lose my creative control.

The ticket for my radio success was my one-man band of comedy characters, with Edna as the conductor, since she doubled as both head writer and quasi-producer. She was a bit of a drill sergeant, both as a wife and as a producer. But that's what put us on top, and I'll always be beholdin' to her for that. So what happened to our marriage? We succeeded! It was time to lighten up, and Edna was stuck in fast-forward mode. Her comedy workaholic nature reminds me of something Milton "Uncle Miltie" Berle's son, William, once wrote about his dad: "[He] worked so hard and was so devoted to his work that he had no time to develop skills other than comedy. Like some mad monk in pursuit of everlasting perfection, who never leaves the remote monastery… [honing] his talent to get laughs. If there was a comedy god watching… Milton sacrificed his entire being to achieve communion with that god." That was Edna to a "T," too. Granted, this does not justify my straying eye; it merely helps to explain the phenomenon. As the old saying goes, "I'm frequently right, but when I'm wrong… my God." Super-stardom is a tough puppy to handle. It can, at least in the beginning, make you so self-centered you're a city of one.

The collapse of my marriage, however, was still in the future when the radio program became a hit during the 1941-42 season. My ensemble of zanies was still evolving at the time, but my two main stars were my "mean widdle kid" Junior and my cluck from the country Clem Kadiddlehopper. These two dominated, while a distant third figure in these early days was Willie Lump-Lump, a comic drunk, enabling me to recycle "Guzzler's Gin" shtick into the program.

Though most comedians depend, to a certain degree, on topical material, my stuff, whether character-driven or in monologue, often had a more generic universal component to it. For instance, here is a period bit from my joke file, which is almost as big as Uncle Miltie's: "The craziest things happen when you're jogging. There was a guy ahead of me running along, so I caught up to him and [nearly out-of-breath] said: 'Jogging? Health?' He said: 'Prison—escape.'"

Still, one could say Junior dominated the radio program—a character Edna had patterned after my child/man tendencies. But she was undoubtedly influenced by Fanny Brice's "Baby Snooks" and Edgar Bergen's Charlie McCarthy. Like these predecessors, Junior's extended tag line—"If I dood it, I get a whippin'.… I dood it!"—is grounded in a smart aleck mentality. Radio historian Frank Wertheim would later call me the most mischievous of the Snooks, McCarthy, and Junior trio. Wertheim's example was actually a routine I'd forgotten, though it was in my files. Here's Wertheim's evidence of Junior's extreme comic nastiness: "'Oh, I wish I had left you home,' his Mummie scolded. 'Oh, no you don't,' Junior replied. 'Because by now I coulda had three rooms *completely wrecked!*'"

Clem Kadiddlehopper, my oldest comedy character, was also central to my radio program, though he never got recycled into a description of any war missions. Initially, we used him as a singing cab driver on the program. Though he's rural and rustic, a stereotypical cabbie is nothing short of the proverbial magpie—gabby. Thus, I had the perfect excuse for Clem's nonstop verbal riffs and singing, especially when one could argue that his definitive line is his humming simpleton's anthem, "Du-du-du-du-du-du." Plus, by making him mobile (a cabbie), I could tap into a basic component of clown comedy—the road trip, which provides a non-stop supply of various funny locations and/or new comic characters. You exhaust one setting, and then move on. Of all my Looney Toon types, Clem's inspired stupidity most often represents the background "comic music" of my career—a throwback to my earliest Hoosier clowning.

I used to give my radio studio audience an added bonus after the broadcast. I enjoyed putting on a wilder, possibly more hilarious, post-program. Early on I had done a radio warm-up act, but as a full-tilt funnyman, I only succeeded in knocking out myself and my audience before we even got to the broadcast. Anyway, the post-program allowed me to do some material which couldn't be used on radio, from pantomime to the modestly naughty. What follows is an example of what played as provocative back in the 1940s: "A teacher took a class of first-grade students to a racetrack on a field trip. Seeing one tiny person squirming, she led him into the bathroom and started to help him unzip his pants. Astonished at what she saw when the job was done, she asked, 'Are you in the first?' The tiny person answered, 'No, I'm riding Black Bart in the fifth.'"

Speaking of the sexually provocative, my brothel-running grandmother Ella died just after my first radio season. Marooned now in old age, with a mind like a sieve, my memories of her remain surprisingly strong. From her gift of the dear sweet Artina, to just inspiring me to be an entertainer, I owe so much to Ella. When I was young I used to wish I could go back in time and save her from all the hurt. But with her death I could only save her memory.

Ella was a great reader. She said it gave her something to do when business was slow. Novelist Edith Wharton was a special favorite of hers. There was this one Wharton short story, "The Fullness of Life," that had a passage which especially spoke to Ella: "[A woman's life is like] a great house full of rooms, [most of which remain unseen] and in the innermost room, the holy of holies, the soul sits alone and waits for a footstep that never comes."

I can still hear her repeating those lines, sensing how important they were to her—though as a youngster I didn't have a clue as to what they meant. Only later, with my ongoing attempts at a tour of all the rooms in Ella's mansion, did I start to understand the pain behind her rough, joking earth mother exterior. In this light, Ella's large, imposing presence suddenly seemed sparrow-frail, delicately featured. I shed enough tears to float a battleship, though I never let on to her what all the waterworks were about.

Strangely enough, however, I didn't cry when I heard about her death, after a call from Murr. Somehow my thoughts of her in death reminded me of that wavy antique glass in her boarding house windows, where you could almost see the light bend—and for some reason I found comfort in that. Besides, being morose would have been the last thing she would have wanted. Though I hadn't seen Ella in some time, we'd kept in touch with letters, and she was a big fan of my radio program. I smiled to think she got her last wish, or as she once described it, "Old whores should die in bed." I also recalled her favorite tongue-in-cheek crack about her brothel background: "When the wages of sin are paid, I'll get time and a half." Ella's last photograph to me showed a creased-leather face that would not have been out of place in any Depression era scrapbook. But for me, I'll always remember her as the happy, bejeweled, feathered madam that briefly brought Artina, "golden like the sunshine," into my life.

Through the years I'd subsidized Ella's boardinghouse, since she largely operated it as a half-way house for vaudeville friends and former prostitutes down on their luck. She used to say, "Though a broken life might seem like a book without an ending, or a joke without a punch line, we should be glad for whatever, or whoever, we have." Thus, there was a great deal of laughter in the house, especially when the vaudevillians put on one of their impromptu shows. In fact, Ella was such a people person she would sometimes sort of hold on to you as she spoke, as if she was afraid you were going to run out on her.

Though Edna only got to know Ella later on, my wife was also charmed by this most provocative of grandmothers. But my more deep dish first spouse had insights on Ella which went well beyond my pure sentimentality. For example, she said the most fascinating thing about Ella was her ambiguous nature—attractive in so many respects, yet repellent (to some) in other ways. Naturally, this division left tons of wide-open spaces for interpretation. And since Edna's childhood had been nearly as sad as mine, she could also project her own damaged good feelings about life onto Ella's story, something, I guess I'd been doing for years myself. Of course, Edna could be brutally honest, too, like, "Sometimes when I claim someone is wise, I'm really just saying, 'I agree with them.' That's how I felt about Ella." Pencil me in for agreement there, too.

As they used to say on *Monty Python's Flying Circus*, "And now for something completely different." In the same amiable spirit as her observations about Ella, here are some Edna press conference comments during our divorce on, you'll excuse the expression, my infidelities: "Red reversed the usual order of behavior for wayward husbands. Most men leave home early and come home late. He went out late and came in early. Once I asked him to explain these absences, and he told me that he had been waiting at the corner of Sunset and Vine for the signal to change. Even the judge smiled at that one."

Do you see what Edna did there? By being comic about a rather serious subject for the 1940s, she managed to save our popular *family* radio show. Even though in private Edna was often as sober as an Indianapolis judge, she knew when to apply her comedy writing skills. That press conference might just have been her best "comic sketch." Not many soon-to-be ex-wives would be able to do that. For most wounded spouses, it would be easier to walk into hell and back with a quart of milk.

I am convinced that without this generosity on Edna's part, I would have entered some 1940s fold in time and vanished. So is it any wonder that I kept her on as my manager and head writer? Besides, she'd been taking care of me for years; why should I rock the boat. Moreover, keeping her on was simply applying a basic life lesson she had once taught me—surviving is recognizing that one's existence is merely like a series of comedy sketches, and it's important not to take any of them too seriously!

I later recognized, however, another darker factor about keeping Edna on in my professional life. I've already addressed the inherent parent-child factor in our relationship, from my being the model for "Junior," to her acting as my motherly caretaker. Consequently, consider the psychological ramifications of a then boy/man like me divorcing his surrogate mother. Even if she had not been so central to my ongoing success, it makes perfect psychological sense to keep her in the picture. A complete break might have been devastating. Indeed, I am convinced that the nervous collapse I later suffered in the Army was brought on, at least in part, by my separation from the woman I called "Mummy."

Our ongoingly friendly working relationship did fool much of Hollywood. For instance, I remember a plea from gossip columnist Louella Parsons that went something like this: "I hope Red and Edna are back together soon, for two people who get along so well should never have been separated." We further fueled such talk by performing our old vaudeville routines at Army camp shows during the war. The rousing topper to our show had Edna literally carrying me off the stage on her back to the delight of all hands.

I should add, of course, that Edna's generosity during the divorce was not just about saving the radio program, or even our ongoing friendship. I had given her the chance to shine artistically when her best other Depression-era opportunity was to be a mortician's assistant for her uncle. And though I was the star to the general public, within the entertainment community Edna the writer was nearly on par with me. So, as she confessed to me after one of our Army shows—and several gin and tonics, "Why should I sacrifice power and prestige to some sexy little starlet slut that caught your eye?"

The wannabe actress in question was Muriel Morris, also under contract to my parent studio, MGM. She was a leggy, beautiful blonde that had had small unbilled parts in several of my films. It wasn't just sex, though there was that. MM was just so attentive... and there was even a Hoosier connection. Her clan was also from southern Indiana –Evansville. In a more macabre coincidence, given Edna's mortician connection, Muriel's late father had made caskets!

Of course, MM was not the only one on my dance card. In fact, some columnist back then wrote of me, "He had a good head on his shoulders, a different one every night." I even doubled with Milton Berle a few times. But that could be sexually hard on a male ego, since Uncle Miltie was famous in the industry as the most well-hung fellow in Hollywood. If you'll allow me a provocative detour, here's my favorite story on the subject, courtesy of chronic gambler Chico Marx. Chico told me he once cornered Milton at the Hillcrest Country Club bar and asked, "Quick, come with me. I just bet a guy a hundred bucks you got a bigger cock than he does." To Berle's credit, he replied, "I'm not going to expose myself to a total stranger!" But a begging Chico won Milton over with the line, "Aw, c'mon Miltie. You gotta take out enough for me to win the bet!"

Regardless, Muriel and I almost tied the knot. The Los Angeles papers had me left waiting at the altar, which wasn't far from the truth. After that era's one-year waiting period before a divorce became final, MM and I had planned on an April 1944 wedding. But she underestimated my ties to Edna. Muriel threw down the demand—"Choose between your ex-wife and me!" Now sexually, Muriel had me. Why, her technique in performing what we used to call "speaking into the microphone" (use your imagination) was wonderful. But there was no way I could cut Edna out of my professional life.

So that ended it between Muriel and me. Poor girl, I don't know who was more surprised, her or me. Still, I managed to be most diplomatic for the newspaper boys. Here's the line I gave them; I even looked it up in one of my old scrapbooks: "I'm sort of a comic Frankenstein created by other people, like my first wife. But Muriel, who is really wonderful, and some others, find it hard to understand things which are absolutely necessary in show business. Politics notwithstanding, Hollywood is the real home of strange bedfellows."

Despite the end of a marriage, the divorce from Edna probably helped our radio program. Indeed, I still carry a funny little note in my billfold which she wrote me after we split: "We're both quick-tempered but quick to forget. It's different now since our divorce. If we argue, I can leave and go home, or you can say 'so-long' and shut the door. We don't have to live the pressure every hour of the day and night."

Because radio did not necessitate memorizing scripts, costume changes, and camera blocking, there was much less preparation time for each program—as opposed to the later overwhelming demands of TV. This gave us airway performers a chance to balance a film career with radio. While MGM was just not the best place to make movies, if you were a comic, the studio had done right by me with *Whistling in the Dark*. Fittingly, my best follow-up films during the war years were that movie's two sequels: *Whistling in Dixie* and *Whistling in Brooklyn*. As the titles suggest, my *Whistling* character took his shtick on the road, from the old South to the wacky world of Brooklyn.

My favorite was the latter, since it involved baseball and "dem bums," the antiheroic Brooklyn Dodgers. The movie was an excuse for a slapstick free-for-all at famed Ebbets Field—the home of the "Daffiness [Dodgers] Boys." A vaudeville friend and regular in the *Whistling* pictures, "Rags" Ragland, perfectly caught the spirit of this zany baseball land with the best line from *Brooklyn*, "I wanna git there [Ebbets Field] before they throw out the first umpire." I even got to pitch against three future Hall of Famers: Hoosier-born Billy Herman, Arky [Arkansas] Vaughan, and Joe "Ducky" Medwick.

I had the most fun, however, with legendary manager Leo "the Lip" Durocher, also now in the Hall of Fame and synonymous with the line "Nice guys finish last." We peppered his dialogue with quips at my expense, such as, "I never forget a face, but this time I'll make an exception." During the production, we also constantly played comedy one-upmanship, with Leo usually getting the better of me. For example, he gave me a joke book, the cover of which featured a picture of… BOB HOPE!

While things were going great professionally, my love life wasn't exactly panning out. Oh, I was seeing lots of women, but it was sort of a sexual revolving door, and I was ready to settle down. (I'm kind of quiet during sex… I'm just happy to be there.) I was definitely no Charlie Chaplin. About this time, he told me at a dinner party that he had slept with over 2,000 women! (Charlie was all of fifty at the time.) Still, even he soon found the love of his life in young Oona O'Neill, the daughter of Nobel Prize-winning playwright Eugene O'Neill. But Charlie and Oona notwithstanding, Hollywood, then and now, seems sadly allergic to old-fashioned romance. After Muriel called off our marriage at the eleventh hour, I had a brief but serious affair with starlet Lynn Merrick, whom I had met on a war bond tour. Ah, love on a train. (I am reminded of writer Ben Hecht's tongue-in-cheek definition of a starlet: "Any young woman in Hollywood under the age of twenty not actively employed in a brothel.") Alas, Lynn was not interested in marriage, and it had nothing to do with Edna continuing to manage my career. Lynn was simply out for a good time, and she immediately hooked up with another radio comedian after dropping me. To guarantee no one got serious this time, though, she picked a married star who specialized in "good times." It would be indiscreet to mention him by name. Of course, as the gossip loving Jimmy Durante might have responded to such discretion—"What a revoltin' development!" So I'll drop a couple vague clues; this mystery comic influenced my career and was often teamed with a famous singer nicknamed "der Bingle."

Regardless, about the time I'd given up on finding wife number two, I met a twenty-three-year-old MGM actress named Georgia Davis, whom the studio was promoting as the next Rita Hayworth. Some friends brought Georgia to one of my house parties in 1944. Unfortunately, my class clown tendencies had her hating me even before we were introduced. Overwhelmed by her redheaded beauty, I simply started kidding her, with my riff going something like this: "Look, I just had that sofa reupholstered, so how about removing your feet [one of Georgia's legs was curled under her]? Let's keep the seat neat. Are you a real redhead or can't you stay out of trouble? How about those freckles? Sincere or something out of a box of confetti?"

Well, Miss Georgia Davis arose to her full height, looked me straight in the eye and said, "Mr. Skelton, I think you are the rudest man it has ever been my misfortune to meet." And she stalked out of the house with most of my dinner party friends in hot pursuit to explain I was just a funny fellow who meant no harm but who had to play Bogart now and then. Such began the fiery relationship of two volatile redheads. It was to be a fairy tale relationship… without a happy ending.

Though I was immediately taken with this spunky auburn-haired beauty, my marriage proposal came a bit too quickly for Georgia. She wanted to take the romance ever so slowly; so we took it slowly. Unfortunately, my life at the time might be described as a crazy scene, with the emphasis towards crazy. See, while I was courtin' Georgia, Uncle Sam was courtin' me. Thus, Miss Davis was soon datin an Army private—when I could manage a furlough.

By opting to serve as a regular soldier (with field artillery duty at California's Camp Roberts), I inadvertently set myself up for double duty—a soldier constantly asked to entertain. I was a patriotic young fool; no easy commission for me. Eventually, the strain would be too much, and I entered special services as a performer. Still, my easy-going nature and desire to please resulted in too many one-man shows, with me suffering a nervous breakdown shortly after being shipped to the Italian war zone in early 1945. I should have seen the breakdown coming. After all, the exhaustion was there all the time. I think I know why the Army keeps you so darned busy all the time. If it didn't, every guy in uniform would be falling sound asleep. I've actually seen fellows so tired that they have gone asleep standing up. And that's no gag. Nervous breakdown or not, everything that ever happened to me or anybody else has happened for a reason… though I may never know it. Good is going to come out of it because out of everything springs some good.

I've always thought of myself as having a dull guy persona. For instance, to recycle an old gag, an exciting night for me would be to go to a department store and try on loud ties. But entertaining the troops was genuinely exciting—bringing joy to men and women in uniform, about to go into harm's way, gave this "sad sack" a real rush. Before my breakdown in Italy, I think I played every military camp in the United States… twice. Still, I pushed and pushed to be sent overseas. However, as the old axiom goes, "be careful what you wish for" because you might get it!

My subsequent Atlantic troopship crossing was an ordeal. I was so sick the face of my watch turned green. Yet, I somehow managed to do several shows each day. Plus, I didn't get much rest—my sleeping accommodations were with all the other GIs. Consequently, when I tried for some shut-eye, there were non-stop demands for autographs, solo and/or small group performances, and soldiers wanting to talk. I loved the guys, but the attention was never ending. But the real problem were the S.O.B. officers, and I don't mean "sweet old boys." They ordered me into more shows than I could handle. Thankfully, one of the ship's cooks came up with a brilliant solution; an extra pantry off the main galley was empty, and I had a secret hideaway. I would sleep double-time in my hole-in-the-wall.

After the war, one of my self-deprecating lines made all the newspapers, and in those days, there were a lot of newspapers: "Guess I'm the only celebrity who entered the Army as a buck private and came out the same way. I dood it." But this went beyond simply getting an easy laugh. Remaining a private was actually a point of honor for me. During my tour, officers had so overworked and underappreciated me, the last thing I wanted was to join their ranks.

Someone once wrote, "My memory, like a flashlight, its batteries half spent, conjures stray images out of the darkness." That's kind of what I retain from my nervous breakdown. But like a good historical writer, I'm now trying to see the past more clearly. I was entertaining like crazy in Italy, questioning President Roosevelt's actions towards the Soviets at the Yalta Conference (my politics were then slightly to the right of Louis the XV), and continued to be bone tired.

The next thing I know I'm being written up for a section eight—the ye old "crack-up" release. Now, while I never thought I was Napoleon, I did, for a time, forget I was Red. My stateside recovery took place at Camp Patrick Henry Hospital in Virginia. Edna, my former spouse, and my bride Georgia (we'd married shortly before I shipped out for Italy), made headlines when they traveled together from the West Coast to visit me. Much was made of their great friendship—a greatly exaggerated situation, which will be further addressed shortly.

Regardless, my behavior during and after this breakdown was completely passive. I was a regular Mr. Milquetoast. My future meltdowns were not so quiet. For example, when my television show nearly failed in the early 1950s, I actually took to drinking up in a tree in my backyard! Worse yet, as the proud owner of an extensive gun collection (I have over a million hobbies), I used my perch to shoot at shingles on my roof which disturbed me. Yes, wayward shingles can be especially irritating in times of stress. Moreover, once your gunslinger reputation gets known, it's also hard to get roofers over to the house.

There's an old axiom among mystery writers, that the audience for this type of story doesn't necessarily have to believe in ghosts but they should at least believe in shadows. This might have been a metaphor for my crack-up: — I didn't necessarily have to believe I had crazy tendencies, but I should at least expect to periodically jump the tracks. I remember thinking how ironic this was. All my life I had wanted to be like my comedy hero—Charlie Chaplin. But instead of getting his comic gift, I shared his greatest fear—losing my noodle. So with every meltdown, I would re-dedicate myself to being so successful that no one would ever consider locking me up. But I couldn't help thinking, in a normal society, outside of show business, I'd be in a padded room.

To try to remain centered, I did utilize a little mantra I'd learned from Edna. I always told her she should have been a football coach, because this three-part guideline would not have been out of place in a locker room. It went something like this: (1) Blame no one; (2) Expect nothing, and (3) Do something! Edna was always very good for me, and I regret deeply that I later minimized her influence on me.

Interestingly, after my marriage, which surprised a lot of friends who thought I'd reconnect with Edna, she suddenly married MGM's Frank Borzage, the director of my studio screen test. It was an impromptu decision on her part, to the point of the bride borrowing her mother's wedding ring, before a brief ceremony in Las Vegas—a four hour drive from Las Angeles. One Hollywood insider suggested Borzage was merely getting some sexual payback for my affair with the director's former girlfriend, Lupe Velez. But that was pure poppycock. Both Edna and I had hit it off with Borzage from our first moment in Hollywood. Besides, he was more than aware of Velez's sexual addiction tendencies, bedding anyone and everyone with a pulse.

Indeed, we soon confounded Hollywood by all living, both Georgia and I and Frank and Edna, in the same luxurious Los Angeles apartment complex—one of my money manager Edna's investments for me. This seemingly sophisticated Noel Cowardish lifestyle, including the occasional joint night on the town, was worlds away from that poor Vincennes boy struggling to find some affection. Despite these appearances, the ongoing working relationship between Edna and me would put strains upon both new marriages. But my immediate focus was jump-starting my career after the war years— life in the fast lane once again.

Buster Keaton—
Mentoring & Murder

"Filmmakers need to be like 'dirt dogs of baseball'—persistently hardy types."

– Buster Keaton

A WRITER FRIEND OF MINE, Janet Malcolm, once wrote me, "The working biographer is like a professional burglar, breaking into a house, rifling through certain drawers that he has good reason to think contain the jewelry and money." Well, as someone writing his autobiography, I have the keys to this metaphorical house and I'm still struggling with just what is the most telling and valuable "jewelry and money" of my life. But if I were to put my own spin upon this subject, I'd say that while biography is about what a writer happens to learn, an autobiography ultimately comes down to what the subject decides to confess. Of course, one could argue that for many readers, all writing (both non-fiction and fiction), is not so much about characters but rather curiosity about what a writer is up to. So what am I up to? Well, I'm a work in progress, struggling with my past—a comic symbol who also happens to be a man but who will eventually be reduced to merely a comic symbol… if I'm lucky. My hope is that these fragmentary scribblings will occasionally beam a kind of strobe light upon what passes as truth in a memoir.

Though I struggled with my film identity after the war, largely because of a conservative home studio (MGM), I managed to hit a proverbial home run with 1947's action parody *A Southern Yankee*. Ironically, the person never mentioned in either *Yankee* press clippings, or even the credits for the movie itself, proved to be the most significant contributor—silent comedy legend Buster Keaton. The comedian, famous for his unchanging "Great Stone Face," uses his minimalism as a defense against the absurdities of today's world. Consequently, beyond the laughter, his stoic deadpan made him a thinking man's comedian, too.

Paradoxically, one is more apt to link my work with the emotional Charlie Chaplin, both because I was prone to personally reference his "little fellow," and I patterned the pathos of my later pivotal television character, Freddie the Freeloader, on Charlie's Tramp. However, due to Buster's ongoing ties with MGM, he had a huge influence on my film career. Sometimes Buster was assigned to my movies as an uncredited gag writer—his fall from silent comedy grace, after the coming of sound, was to my benefit. Plus, several of my best pictures were loose remakes of Keaton films. Thus, even when Buster was creating inventive new material for me, my most memorable movie moments were often simply recycled Buster bits. This was certainly true of my earlier *I Dood It*, an updating of Keaton's *Spite Marriage*. The signature scene from both films involves a gentlemanly slapstick attempt to put a comically comatose bride to bed on her wedding night. Naturally, my one-way wrestling match with Eleanor Powell in *I Dood It* was closely patterned after Buster's tour de force bout with Dorothy Sebastian in *Spite Marriage*. (But if truth be told, both of these brides—with their inventively minimalist "performances" as so much dead weight—manage to steal these scenes, not unlike Terry Kiser's entertaining turn as a comic corpse in the darkly comic *Weekend at Bernie's*.)

Sadly, I never fully appreciated Buster at the time. I was often more interested in getting back to my dressing room so that I could write jokes for my radio show. Regardless, Keaton's contributions to *A Southern Yankee* made this my greatest picture. Buster's most inspired bit was what he called the "two-sided flag scene." But let me quote from Keaton's autobiography, *My Wonderful World of Slapstick*, my favorite show business memoir: "I contributed the gag in which Red was shown walking between the Union Army and the Confederate Army, with both armies cheering him madly. The reason was Red was wearing half of a Union Army hat and uniform on the side facing the Northern soldiers and a Southern hat and uniform on the other. In addition he had sewed together the flags of the two opposing sides so that the boys in blue saw a Union flag and the Southerners only the flag of the Confederacy. Both sides cheer him wildly until a sudden gust of wind reverses the flag, showing both sides the game he is playing. As Red turns around to straighten the flag they discover his half-and-half uniform [too]."

As a comic footnote to the scene, though it was initially conceived as having the flags sewn together, and was first even shot that way, the censorship office would not allow it—too disrespectful! Consequently, in the finished picture I carry *two* flags between the opposing armies, with both the Union and Confederate soldiers initially seeing only their own flags. Still, many viewers "remember" the sequence as having the flags sewn together.

For Buster, the absurdity of modern life is often triggered by natural forces, like the rock slide of *Seven Chances* or the wind storm of *Steamboat Bill, Jr.* But in *A Southern Yankee*, I love how a simple change in the wind wreaks comic disaster. Now, each army sees the enemy's flag, and as I struggle to control these symbols in the wind, the two-sided nature of my uniform becomes apparent, also. "A change in the wind"—what a wonderful metaphor for how easily man's grand plans are derailed.

Thanks to Buster, my *Yankee* reviews were all suitable scrapbook material, such as the *Hollywood Reporter* claiming, "Skelton, well on his road to becoming a really great clown, makes the most of every scene." One publication, *Cue*, even had an intuitive sense of the uncredited Keaton, noted: "With gags borrowed from old time silent movies, and slapstick stunts adopted from his [Red's] own and others' comedies, Red Skelton romps dizzily through this wacky Civil War comedy."

I only belabor these positive notices because of Keaton's unique contributions to the film, and the fact that my first biographer, Groucho Marx's kid, Arthur, claimed the *Yankee* reviews were "lukewarm." As a young man, Arthur was a great tennis player, though he had trouble escaping his famous father's shadow. Thus, even when he would win a major match, the newspaper headlines would invariably refer to him as "Son of Groucho." Still, he should have stuck to tennis. How Arthur ever came up with the "lukewarm" reference I'll never know. His "research," and I use the term loosely, must have focused on one rare *Yankee* pan that my clipping service somehow missed. Arthur's Achilles heel as a tennis player was a weak follow-through on returns, and it would appear that that flaw followed him into referencing film returns (reviews), too.

Regardless, Buster's comic genius would make all the difference on several other of my films, from *Bathing Beauty*, to *Watch the Birdie* and *Excuse My Dust*. In fact, for *Beauty*, he even resurrected a bit his father, Joe Keaton, had used in vaudeville. My *Beauty* character is in a girl's ballet class, with one leg horizontal to the bar. My comically martinet instructor commands me to seemingly defy gravity by lifting my other leg to a parallel position with said bar. Somehow, through the enthusiasm of Buster and the spirit of his dad, I briefly seem to defy the laws of science (with both legs horizontal to the ballet bar) before taking one of my patented pratfalls. Just as Joe Keaton's use of the bit was a wow on stage, my rendition is a tour de silly, and probably the best thing in *Beauty*. Thanks, Buster.

Unfortunately, I later did a great disservice to Keaton. In an oral history I did for the New York Public Library, I minimized this sweet man's memorable influence on me. Why? You might assume it was ego, and that was possibly part of it. As one gets older, you tend to take more and more credit for everything of importance in your life. It's sort of the law of aging. Time frequently turns former benchwarmers into all-state athletes, as distant events turn into the hazy soft-focus of history. Sadly, I did the same thing about both Buster's influence as well as Edna's—which I'll address shortly.

With Keaton, however, my minimizing of his impact on me had another ugly component—we had a falling out about an old Hollywood murder case! This involved the vivacious blonde comedienne Thelma Todd, who had been found dead in her parked car of carbon monoxide poisoning in late 1935. But there had been so many extenuating circumstances, that the police were reluctant to accept either a suicide or an accident as the cause of death. Indeed, the case had been re-opened in the mid-1940s, about the time Buster and I were re-connecting after my war service.

Todd was a popular good-time party girl nicknamed "Hot-Toddy" by her friends. She came to Hollywood in 1926 after winning a New England beauty contest. Quickly finding her niche in comedy, she would soon co-star with a who's who of film clowns—Charlie Chase, Joe E. Brown, Laurel and Hardy, Buster Keaton, Jimmy Durante, Wheeler and Woolsey, the Marx Brothers, Harry Langdon, and Ed Wynn. Her flair for comic timing and a sexy come-hither persona made her in constant demand, both in and out of the movies. For instance, when a Hollywood party was dying, the popular quick-fix was to invite "Hot-Toddy," and then the fun would begin.

Not surprisingly, the beautiful party girl often attracted controversy. Even before her mysterious death, Todd's name was constantly linked to bizarre news stories during the 1930s. At the height of the Depression, a wealthy male admirer offered her $50,000 in cash for a year of companionship! When she did not respond to the love letters of another fan, she received a series of notes threatening her life unless she paid $20,000. Eventually, this would-be extortionist was caught, but the messy trial which followed necessitated Todd take part in a high profile New York judicial circus. The man ultimately was placed in a hospital for the criminally insane. Todd was also nearly the victim of a kidnapping, shortly after Charles Lindbergh's baby was snatched, and most of Hollywood became an armed camp—ever fearful to leave their gated communities. Ironically, this was a catalyst for Thelma to open a Malibu beach cafe/bar, where she sometimes surprised patrons by doubling as the cashier. But trouble then followed her there, when a West Coast crime syndicate threatened her life, if she didn't okay gambling in her nightery. And on top of this, her cafe partnership with Roland West, a one-time United Artist director/producer, had once been a stormy love-affair, with numerous public fights.

Paradoxically, at the time of Todd's death, many felt her life seemed to have calmed down. She had gone to a party at the Tracadero Club on Sunset Boulevard. The festivities were in honor of English comedian Stanley Lupino, father of actress Ida Lupino. The fun-loving ex-school teacher left the party in good spirits, after telling friends she had a new love interest in her life. A chauffeur picked Thelma up between 2:30 and 3 a.m. and took her back to her Malibu café, arriving there at 4 a.m. Sunday morning. She had an apartment above the establishment, and the driver waited until she waved goodbye from her door before leaving. It was the last time Todd was seen alive.

At 10:30 a.m. Monday Thelma's maid opened the actress' garage door and found the comedienne slumped in the front seat of her car. Todd was still wearing the mauve and silver evening gown, mink coat, and jewels from Saturday night. The ignition key was turned on, and the actress had been dead at least 12-20 hours—seemingly of carbon monoxide poisoning. But there was a bruise on Thelma's forehead, and a cut inside her mouth. And the evening slippers on her feet appeared brand new, yet the garage was some 500 feet from the actress' apartment, up an endless flight of steps—steps which would certainly have scuffed the slippers.

Plus, an added macabre twist was soon to come out. Mrs. Wallace Ford, wife of the film star, and Thelma's close friend, had had an afternoon party the previous Sunday. With the festivities in full swing, she received a phone call from Todd, at a time the comedienne was supposed to be dead. Mrs. Ford, who frequently talked to Todd at length on the phone, was later adamant that this was her friend. Thelma said she was running late, and there was a hitch— could she bring a friend? Mrs. Ford had no problem with this, though she was surprised by Todd's response, "When you see who I am bringing, you are going to drop dead." Moreover, Mrs. Ford remembered her own response as having a certain ominous foreshadowing, too, "Okay mystery lady." But the comedienne and her surprise guest never made the party. Yet, Mrs. Ford's story was given added credibility when actress Jewel Carmen told police she had seen a car with Thelma and a foreign looking man on Sunset Boulevard that Sunday night. Still, the topper to the case was that a post-mortem showed that the actress' stomach contained food *not* eaten at the Trocadero.

Buster had related all this background material to me one night over supper, during the production of *A Southern Yankee*. The catalyst had been both a *Los Angeles Times* article the previous day that called Todd's death "a still unsolved murder," and the coincidence that found us dining at the Trocadero. For a man known as "the Great Stone Face," Keaton was unusually emotional when he discussed the life and demise of Todd, a name, he said, she enjoyed telling people meant "death" in German.

Like many of her co-stars, Keaton had fallen hard for "Hot-Toddy." The two of them had frequently partied together, on and off, during the early 1930s, when Keaton's personal and professional life was a shambles and alcoholism dominated his every act.

Despite Buster's past history with Thelma, I was actually the one to first bring up her death that night. I mentioned to Keaton that I had met her back in the 1930s when I was a vaudeville headliner and she was promoting one of her pictures, I believe with Joe E. Brown. As a historical footnote to vaudeville—this old show business format had by then been reduced to stage shows between movie screenings in large metro theatres east of the Mississippi. Vaudeville acts sometimes starred film performers whose appearances hopefully boosted a picture of theirs then in release, which is the reason Thelma found herself on my theatre bill.

Todd and I had late night suppers together several times during that run. Though nothing romantic occurred, what with Edna still being part of my act, I told Buster that I thought Thelma and I might have connected sexually, had the opportunity presented itself. Because this was strictly innocent "wink, wink" guy banter, I was really surprised to find that my comments had seemingly made Buster simultaneously angry and jealous.

This was what got Keaton talking in such detail about Todd's past history, and murky death—which was the basis for the rehash in the past pages. But the Buster bombshell I haven't noted is that he confessed to being Thelma's surprise guest for Mrs. Ford's Sunday party—the mystery person whose identity was going to kill the hostess, so to speak.

Though I couldn't get any more juicy details out of Buster that night, we did decide to form an amateur sleuth pact in order to solve what had happened to poor Thelma. While this is the first public disclosure of the Buster/ Red detective duo, our teaming up was a bit of a cause célèbre within the movie industry. In fact, writer/director Blake Edwards' later comic murder mystery, *Sunset*, in which the celebrated old cowboy Wyatt Earp joins movie cowboy Tom Mix in solving a Hollywood killing, was actually inspired by Buster and me tackling the Todd case.

Though Keaton was a "silent star," he ultimately was most talkative about Thelma. (I'm reminded of an observation by my close friend Marcel Marceau, "Never get a mime talking. He won't stop.") But Buster had major gaps in his memory, given that his affair paralleled the man's extreme blotto period. But one thing was certain; Keaton was convinced that Todd's business partner Roland West was responsible for her death. So, West became our focus. Yet first, I convinced Buster to fill in the blanks about his ties to Mrs. Ford's party.

Like this hostess, Keaton had also received a Sunday afternoon call from Thelma. According to Buster, this event had haunted him for years, like a movie freeze-frame—a sharp nagging memory. His eyes went all quiet before he explained. As with Mrs. Ford, Keaton felt certain the voice on the phone was Thelma's. But then again, he was still hung over from another all-night drinking binge. Regardless, Buster was to pick up Todd at her Malibu apartment, and she wanted him to wear something European—whatever that meant.

Unfortunately, Keaton's search for an "exotic" outfit, as he called it, took him to one of his drinking buddy neighbors. They started downing shots, and the next thing Buster knew, he was waking up from another hangover… on Monday afternoon. Before he could try to contact Thelma, her death was all over the late edition newspapers. Naturally, he was racked with guilt. If he had been with Todd, maybe she would still be alive.

Keaton never reported his conversation with Todd to the authorities, because he had immediately crawled back inside his bottle. The world never knew that his continued alcoholism during the 1930s was driven not by a lost film career but rather by failing Thelma. Eventually, Buster got past the guilt and the booze, and modestly re-entered the movie industry as an MGM gag writer and sometimes supporting player. But curiosity and some nagging questions about Todd's death continued to bother him.

First, as someone who had also been at the Trocadero Club party for Stanley Lupino, Buster felt Thelma's behavior was strained. Unlike most insiders at the time, who saw her in the standard "Hot-Toddy" mode, he remembered her repeatedly saying, "There needs to be a change in my life, and I'm going to pull out of here." But when Keaton pressed her on this she simply said, "Don't worry honey, my getaway plan isn't limited to one."

Was the Ford party on Sunday to have been some sort of unofficial Hollywood exit gesture by Todd? Or, was this "getaway plan" just a veiled reference to suicide? In pondering these issues for years, Keaton was starting to have second thoughts about whether it was really Thelma who called him that Sunday. Buster's questioning of this fact was tied to a little game Todd had begun playing with him. His greatest film was an epic Civil War comedy called *The General*, in which the title character (his giant steam engine) took precedence over the comedian's leading lady. Though now considered a classic, as well as a loose foundation for my later *A Southern Yankee*, *The General* was not originally a hit with the public. But Todd fully appreciated the uniqueness of Keaton's picture from the beginning, especially his ironic preference for a train over a lover, and she had taken to working a reference to the film into their everyday conversations, often as a silly tag line close. For example, she might sign off by saying, "Well, good night 'general,' take care of yourself," or "Whatever your 'train' of thought, I think women are safer."

Thelma had not, however, worked any such reference into their last alleged conversation. Between Buster's alcoholic fog and the shock of her death, this omission had taken years for Keaton to realize. But was it that big a clue? Might Todd just have been distracted and not gone there, or was it proof that an imposter, unaware of their private code, had called Buster?

Keaton then told me another long forgotten fact that had added to his second guessing the Thelma call. He vaguely remembered attending a party thrown by Doug Fairbanks in the early 1930s, where Roland West's estranged wife, actress Jewell Carmen, was in attendance. (This was the same Jewell Carmen that claimed to have seen Todd on Sunset Boulevard the night *after* Thelma allegedly died.) Carmen was quite the mimic and had a regular routine in which she imitated various sexy actresses of the day, from Mae West to Jean Harlow. But it now dawned upon Buster, that Carmen's take on Todd was the best in her repertoire. She nailed Thelma's throaty laugh, as well as her tendency to put pauses in unexpected places. Moreover, Jewell had even included in her impression one of Todd's favorite Hollywood stories. That is, early in Thelma's film career she overheard an actress (who will remain nameless) ask director William Wellman what her best side was. Wellman paused, and then said, "You're sitting on it." (I later heard the line attributed to Hitchcock, too.)

Buster began to think that Carmen had faked those Thelma calls to both Mrs. Ford and himself, as a cover for an estranged husband she reconnected with after Todd's death. See, Roland West had initially been a police suspect, since Thelma had told her driver on the way home that she had a late night business meeting with her partner—having even called him from the night-club before leaving. Moreover, given this West appointment, his adjacent apartment, and access to both the death garage and the cafe—didn't it seem strange that West had not checked on her at some point during the weekend? After all, he had admitted during questioning that the victim and he spoke daily, usually over brunch in their cafe/bar. But Carmen's suggestion that Todd was alive Sunday and calling friends defused the case against West.

Buster's lengthy tutorial on Thelma had taken us well into the evening. We decided to meet again in a few days, after doing some homework on West and Carmen during the intervening years since Todd's death. A week later a weather break in the shooting of *A Southern Yankee* gave us some down time to compare notes. Because West's and Carmen's careers had pretty much dried up after sound came to the movies, they had both clung to the cafe/bar as a steady income. Within a week of Thelma's death, Roland had opened the business to gambling, something Thelma had always strongly opposed. It proved so profitable for West and Carmen that they would never again need for money.

Buster said he found it ironic that the silent films the couple were best known for were some atmospheric horror film collaborations that often showcased stylized death scenes, even one including a corpse in a car! Had Thelma's death actually been unwittingly scripted years before? Unfortunately, both West and Carmen were now in poor health and not readily accessible. So Buster had made an appointment for us to meet with Todd's closest friend and former co-star in a series of popular short subjects, ZaSu Pitts. (Keaton's determination was impressive: "an old man still full of beans," to borrow a line from my grandma Ella.)

We met with the character actress the following week, and just like her movie persona, ZaSu was an entertaining study in helpless gestures and ever so comically expressive hands. She was our first break, since many of Thelma's possessions had ended up with her. The most tantalizing item was a trunk that included two journal-like diaries. Amazingly, ZaSu claimed to have never read them. Indeed, she had not known they were even there until recently, when a casual inventory of the truck's clothing revealed the diaries in a small false bottom compartment.

ZaSu—don't you love that name—said we were welcome to the diaries. (ZaSu was taken from the last two letters in the name of her Aunt Eli*za*, and the first two letters in the name of the actress' Aunt *Su*san.) ZaSu then confessed she'd tried to read the diaries, but her memories of dear Thelma had opened the floodgates, and all she could do was cry. The loss was still too painful, even after all these years. More than a little excited over this gift, Buster and I hurriedly drove back to my Wilshire Palms apartment. We then sat down with a large pot of coffee (black enough to dye your socks!) and started reading.

Mae West once said, "Keep a diary and someday it'll keep you." This sentiment more than applied to the Todd journals ZaSu had given us. They were part tell-all, and part sexy axioms befitting the witty West. For instance, Thelma wrote, "Gentlemen may prefer blondes—but who says that blondes prefer gentlemen?" Or, when she discovered a song had been written about her called, "If Those Hips Could Only Speak," she wrote, "Whatta they mean 'if they could only speak'? I can make mine talk anytime." And when she was once told a dozen men were waiting outside her vaudeville dressing room door, Thelma wrote that her response had been, "I'm tired; send one of them home."

Though highly entertaining, there was little befitting a murder mystery until the tail end of the second diary. A suddenly very somber Todd had countless questions about her business partner Roland West, including: was he trying to squeeze her out, had he already made an agreement with the gamblers, and how far would he go to take over? These and other telltale Todd concerns fed into Buster's hunch about West. But there was no smoking gun, except for a tantalizing aside on the last page—"Check the lining of my coat."

When Buster and I later asked ZaSu about this, she matter-of-factly said that Thelma sometimes hid things in the lining of her prized mink coat. Assuming it was lost to the world, we still asked ZaSu if she had any idea where that coat might now be. She thought a minute, with those helpless hand gestures fluttering about, and then said, "I think I gave the mink to Patsy Kelly." This was another comedienne Todd had teamed up with in a second series of comedy short subjects. Dynamic Patsy was an inspiredly comic loudmouth, a great partner for the more sexually poised Thelma.

Patsy was an old friend of Buster's, so the following evening we were at her tiny bungalow in the Valley, discussing Todd and her filing cabinet coat. Patsy vaguely remembered getting the mink from ZaSu, but couldn't recall what she had done with it. Finally, she decided it might be in a storage unit she had, not far from the old Hal Roach lot. We made a date to meet with her that weekend, giving Patsy time to sort through what she said was "a lot of stuff."

Visiting her that Saturday, we excitedly checked the mink's lining. We found a $10 bill, a grocery list, and some mascara. But no murder mystery clues. Still, all these items were in a portion of the lining that was so openly worn that it might have doubled for a pocket. Patsy ventured the idea that there might be a more elaborate hiding place in the coat, with what we had found merely serving as a high profile distraction. Thus, we gave the mink a more thorough going over. Nothing. Now it was my turn to brainstorm. I suggested literally cutting the lining out. So Patsy got out a pair of scissors the size of a horse's leg. I thought she was going to do a comedy sketch, or maybe shish kebob Buster and me. But in totally cutting the lining out we finally got lucky. We found a small stamped lavender envelope addressed to Buster. The handwritten note inside read:

> Dearest Buster,
>
> I hope I'm not one of those cases where the juice ain't worth the squeeze. I think I really love you, and if we can get past all the drinking, maybe we can have a life together.
>
> Yet, there are some things going on in my business life—not films but the cafe—that have me stunned. I believe Roland is playing fast and loose. And despite his old sophisticated, silent director demeanor, I think he's capable of anything. Don't laugh, but I'm really rather frightened of him.
>
> We're going to have a sit down after the Lupino party, and I'll know more then. Don't think me too melodramatic, but I'm mailing this Saturday, because if anything strange was to happen to me—I know it sounds silly—I want you to know about my suspicions.
>
> Well, General, I best sign off. Remember, even with all the booze, you're still the best swordsman I've ever known. And remember, opportunity knocks for every man but you have to give a woman a ring!
>
> As always, Thelma

Well, there it was. Patsy looked puzzled, Buster was near tears, and I had the Cheshire Cat grin of a detective whose homework had finally paid off. After filling in some loose ends with Patsy, we swore her to secrecy, and then Buster and I again retreated to my apartment. I was bouncing off the walls, ready to bring in the authorities, call the newspapers, and declare myself a mix of Sam Spade and Philip Marlowe. I figured it was only a matter of time before I put up my detective shingle… or should I join the ranks of Raymond Chandler and Dashiell Hammett as a film noir/tough guy detective novelist?

As I rattled on about all my murder mystery ideas, Buster remained quiet. Finally, I put a sock in it, given the lack of any response from Keaton. Trying to engage him, I asked, "What's our next move?"

Shockingly, Buster said, "We walk away."

Incredulous, I asked, "Why?" Actually, I think I fairly shouted it.

Buster took a deep breath, slowly exhaled, and then said, "I'm just a little man with a frozen face who made people laugh a bit long years ago. If I were to do a memoir, there would be several chapters I would hate to write, none more so than on dear, sweet Thelma. But her letter convinces me that Carmen faked that call—meaning I did *not* contribute to Thelma's death…. If I could live a hundred years, there would be no sweeter music this side of heaven."

"But we have to get her justice," I pleaded.

The Great Stone Face actually smiled, patted my hand, and said, "Even though we know Roland was behind her death, Thelma's letter wouldn't put anyone in jail. Besides, Carmen's dying of cancer and West is suffering from dementia. What's the point? We now know the truth, and that's enough."

"But—" I sputted, trying to form a rebuttal.

"Let it go, Red. Despite some sad detours, I really feel I've had the happiest and luckiest of lives. Maybe this is because I never expected as much as I got. The best thing that ever happened to me was marrying Eleanor, who brought me back from a personal abyss. If we went public with this Thelma business, it wouldn't prove anything, but it would be awkward for Eleanor."

Knowing and liking the much younger Eleanor, Keaton's greatest fan, I told Buster, "She would be supportive of anything you did."

Ignoring this comment, Buster gave me a philosophical answer: "Let me tell you a capsulized version of my favorite mythological story. 'When the Greek gods were bored, they created human beings. But the gods were still bored, so they created love. Now, this was definitely *not* boring; indeed, the gods tried it, too. Yet, the gods soon found they then needed to create laughter so that they could stand love.' Let's just laugh this off, Red, and move on."

This was the end to the Buster-Red detective business. But oh, my sainted aunt, I was upset about this development. Yet, it's one thing to read the Buster writing on the wall. It's another thing to accept it. Ultimately, I honored his decision. However, I'm embarrassed to confess that it caused me to hold a grudge against Buster, despite all he had done for me, and would continue to do. This anger later manifested itself in my minimizing his sizeable influence upon my movies.

While I still feel Thelma died like a stone sinking without a ripple, I now fully appreciate what Buster was trying to tell me. I abhor my follow-up behavior, and I can only hope this admission balances the books. Buster actually saved me from an embarrassing situation—my trying to be a Sam Spade or a Philip Marlowe would have set the tough guy detective format back years. Bogart I'm not, except for the Walty Mitty moment we all occasionally have. Let me close with my favorite comment about Buster, from the great critic James Agee. He described the comedian's minimalist mask of a face: ranking "almost with Lincoln's as an early American archetype, it was haunting, handsome, almost beautiful." I couldn't agree more. Thanks for everything, Buster. (Who knows, with Keaton now gone, too, maybe "Hot-Toddy" and a young Buster are once again trading laughs in a better place. I like to think that's possible.)

Edna Still Waves the Career Baton

"First they said, 'Practice makes perfect.' Then they said, 'No one's perfect.' So I quit practicing."

– Edna Stillwell

DESPITE THE ABOVE CRACK FROM EDNA, my first wife never stopped practicing to make everything perfect. While I was now married to Georgia Davis, Edna managed my money and produced my radio show. But I can now confess our relationship was much more complex than that. I felt that I owed my career to her, especially because of such inspired routines as the donut-dunking sketch. I was also professionally insecure without her advice on all major decisions. Mix in my divorce guilt over leaving this still dedicated disciple, and one has a lot to cope with, not to mention the potential stress for the second Mrs. Skelton. Sometimes I felt like a second-story man in a one-story town.

Regardless, I needed Edna ever present. In fact, the Wilshire Palms apartment where Georgia and I lived was not only owned by both Edna and me—she also lived there with her second husband, Frank Borzage, my former director. If you think this was a bit sophisticated, even for Hollywood, a lot of my Hoosier relatives were downright scandalized. I later heard rumors that the Borzages and the Skeltons had some sort of group marriage going on—switching partners nightly. It seemed sort of ironic, given my Indiana brothel baby background. Is it any wonder why I concealed or prettified so much of my early life? Even when things were totally innocent, like the Wilshire Palms living arrangement, people would talk—members of my own family! Sometimes I just wanted to wander the streets and cemeteries looking for a different family history. Understanding this sort of gossip is as difficult as looking at the murky surface of a river and trying to see the dangers below.

Anyway, while many people seem to wait for some invisible gear to catch and move their lives along, I always had Edna to make things happen. Of course, that brings us back to Georgia's stress factor. That is, the driven Edna would often come by my apartment unannounced, what with her and Frank being just down the hall, to discuss business and/or radio material. Georgia found the whole arrangement peculiar, as did both of our extended families. In Edna's defense, there was a great deal for her to confer with me about in the post-war forties, especially with television on the horizon. Plus, Hollywood has always been about mixing business with pleasure. For instance, one of my radio program rituals was taking everyone out to the Brown Derby restaurant following a broadcast. Since this extended family time involved staff and spouses, I regularly dined with producer Edna and wife Georgia.

On the surface everything seemed fine, with the *Los Angeles Times* and the *Hollywood Reporter* frequently running smiling pictures of me and "the two Mrs. Skeltons," as both papers like to phrase it. But underneath, both women had issues, especially Georgia. By the early 1950s, Edna's poor health and pressure from Georgia had resulted in my pushing my ex-wife out of the picture. Yet, until then, I caught hell all the time from Georgia about my "other wife," or the fact I used to call Edna "Mummie." (I know, I know, "Paging Dr. Freud!" And people wondered why I had a drinking problem during this period.) But I hoped, if the dreamless dead could wait endlessly for the doomsday horn, I could weather Georgia's anger until this thing worked itself out.

Unfortunately, I did some really stupid things that contributed to the conflict. For example, in the late 1940s I made the mistake of giving both women identical mink coats for Christmas, each in the $5,000 range. I never heard the end of that. *Look* magazine even found out about the minks and kidded me in print—"This sort of thing is not recommended by marriage counselors." It all seems funny now, but at the time I often flirted with taking enough sleeping pills to make Rip Van Winkle quiet for a very long time.

The mink business was probably more galling for Georgia because Edna controlled the purse strings on big purchases—purely as a safeguard against my susceptibility to hucksters and hard luck stories. She had to co-sign every check I wrote. Though this made good business sense, having your husband's ex sign off on your Christmas present—which she was also receiving—further defused the magic. Boy, was I in the doghouse a long time on that one. But I don't hold grudges... especially when I'm wrong.

Still, Georgia never quite understood my connection to Edna. She saw it as an ongoing threat to our relationship, which it never was. Like an early vaudeville billing, Edna and I were more like siblings. Maybe I can better relate this with an incident back when Edna and I were working the Walkathon circuit. She wanted to stop at a fortune teller's on the way back to our boarding house—I think we were in St. Louis. Well, the swami told her it was impossible to tell Edna's fortune, because the lines in her hand were too jumbled. She smiled, looked at me, and said, "If they're mixed up, the lines probably just lead to Red." When the fortune teller then checked my palm, darn if it wasn't equally jumbled, too. Let's just say Edna encouraged me to go outside my comedy comfort zone, and I was a better entertainer for it.

Differences with Georgia, of course, were hardly limited to battles over Edna. Living with me, your basic insecure boy/man, was no piece of cake. Georgia, in one of her more charitable moments, wrote of me at this time: "He still is highly changeable in his moods. I can never be certain of them but I know they are caused by a [child-like] lack of a long-run view, by subconscious fears that persist. I know I have to be six jumps ahead in awareness of how he's about to feel." Let's just say my comic philosophy of life was "live in fear," or as I sometimes abbreviated it, "cling to the wreckage."

When Georgia couldn't circumvent my depression, things could get ugly. Heavy drinking by both of us in the late 1940s and early 1950s only made things worse. My standard topper during these battles royal was to storm out of the house and check into an area hotel for a day or two. Sometime during the later make-up sex we embraced a shaky idea often tried by battling couples—starting a family. Valentina Marie was born in 1947, and Richard Freeman arrived the following year. I was also named Richard, but the color of my hair pre-empted it. In fact, even before I found out I was a brothel baby, my red hair was a definite clue that something was amiss—there had never before been a Skelton with locks of that hue.

While both Edna and Georgia tried to protect me from myself, my ex was still the one handling public damage control for my kid/adult tendencies. As I noted earlier, back in 1947 there was a ton of articles over my claim that I would pay MGM $750,000 to release me from my contract. Though this is still a major chunk of change, back then it was a king's ransom. However, while everyone in the media debated my offer, I was soon really "red" in the face. A week after my Daddy Warbucks pitch, at an Edna orchestrated press conference, I had to confess to "knowing more about jokes than high finance."

Unlike most women, Edna was more hammer and nails, instead of the stereotypical glue and lace. I used to kid, "I'm a self-made man… who else would help?" But Edna was always there, picking up the pieces. I've repeated all this to set up a pivotal revelation in the previously mentioned press conference, where I inadvertently gave my most revealingly honest public statement… ever. As this embarrassing event wound down, a *Los Angeles Herald Examiner* reporter asked me if I had any final thoughts. Without thinking, my normal state of affairs, I blurted out, "If you want the facts, talk to Edna. If you want a good story, I'm your man." Out of the mouth of babes, as they say. Still, that was a very honest appraisal of our relationship, as well as my tendency to always want to tell a better story—with apologies to the truth.

Thinking about Edna again makes me soul sick. Just as I later minimized Buster Keaton's influence on me, I would eventually do the same with Edna. It seems that sometimes my "better story" had to only focus on me. And the murder mystery caper with Buster I chronicled in the previous chapter also has an indirect tie-in with Edna. That is, I think all stories are actually "detective" pieces—trying to learn the why behind a character's motives. In this case, I'm dedicating the book in hand to shedding some light on my dark side. But I don't want it to be either psychobabble or a searing memoir, just an honest take on "my life and hard times," to borrow a phrase from one of my favorite humorists James Thurber. Oh, and it needs to be entertaining, too. Like the great Hitchcock once said, "The arts should reflect life, but with all the boring parts cut out."

Regardless, in the late 1940s Edna was not yet out of the picture. We had a hit radio program and I was turning out popular movies, like *A Southern Yankee* and *The Fuller Brush Man*. But my focus was to get a television series. This new medium offered me what they used to call the "blank page phenomenon." When one mixes talent with being *first*, you not only establish the quality standards, you also write the rules. Historical timing (a window to immortality) and a gift allowed Charlie Chaplin to forever become screen comedy's gold standard. It was my hope that if I entered television early I could achieve a comparable status on the small screen.

While I am embarrassed about my later neglect of Buster and Edna, I did do something positive back then, concerning my relationship with Chaplin. My comedy hero was constantly being attacked by the conservative press for his controversial private life and liberal politics. In fact, Chaplin was about to be barred from re-entering America, after he had left for England and the London premiere of his last great movie—*Limelight*.

Well, while my own politics were often conservative, too, I also recognized a raw deal when I saw it. And Chaplin could have been the poster child for raw deals. So every time I was interviewed about my plans for television, and Edna saw to it that this happened a lot, I would always find a way to include a positive reference to Chaplin in my comments. But this wasn't just about me being a nice guy, though I do read to orphans every Tuesday and Thursday. I firmly believed all I was saying about Chuck. For example, I praised the universality of his "little fellow," the Tramp, and posited my own hope that I could create a comparable figure for the small screen. Thankfully, I was later to do just that. During my second season I invented my own tramp—Freddie the Freeloader. Initially, he was also silent, though in later years I gave him a voice, too. I figured if Chaplin could let the Tramp-like Jewish barber in *The Great Dictator* talk, so could Freddie.

Another Chaplin reference I made in interviews involved the legendary comedian's short subjects—films roughly twenty minutes in length. As a pertinent point of reference, I reminded readers that if one subtracted commercials from my forthcoming half-hour time slot, what you had was essentially a twenty-minute short subject. So I would be creating in a framework comparable to that of my pioneering hero. Yes, I found lots of ways to plug Chaplin.

Since I frequently find myself returning to the subject of Chaplin, I'd like to include a quote that gets at the core of my fascination for this comedian. But given my general dislike for rock 'n roll, the source of the words will be surprising—Credence Clearwater Revival's lead singer John Fogerty. He and his group guested on my 1960s television show, and we struck-up an unlikely friendship, though I prefer to think of his music as country. Anyway, in comparing career notes on heroes, I found out "his Chaplin" was John Lennon. So here's Fogerty's take on Lennon, and it applies equally to my feelings about Chaplin: "When you really love someone's creativity you let them into your heart in a very personal way."

The summer before I debuted on television in 1951, two events occurred that made me feel almost bulletproof. First, I survived a potential airliner disaster. In Europe for a booking at London's famed Palladium, I had taken a side trip to Rome. Flying over the Alps, we nearly bought the proverbial farm. Three of our four engines caught fire, and well, it did not look good. A Jesuit priest on the flight turned to me and said, "Okay, Red, you take care of your department, and I'll take care of mine." While he gave last rites, I played the clown for over thirty frightening minutes. And with it being an international flight, my pantomime skills were never better utilized. This resulted in maybe my proudest "notice"—the title of a *Los Angeles Herald Express* article on the near accident—"Red Skelton Hailed For Averting Panic on Crippled Airliner Over Alps."

I followed this unscheduled show with a very successful run at the Palladium, despite a rocky beginning. Oh, it wasn't anything I did. Danny Kaye was the star that proceeded me at this heralded setting. Tradition dictated that the performer in residence introduce the next headliner from the stage. Kaye not only didn't do this, he added a drunk routine his final night that pre-empted my signature "Guzzler's Gin" sketch. To this very day, I still don't know why Danny did this. Years later, we got to be real friendly. But at the time I was madder than a junkyard dog. There I was in the balcony waiting to take a bow after an intro that never came. Georgia cried and I steamed. Even the custom-conscious crowd recognized the slight, which was only compounded by Kaye stealing my drunk act.

The only thing that I can figure out about Kaye's behavior is that my anticipated popularity might have seemed a threat to him. Kaye took his favored American performer status in Britain very seriously. He also had a huge ego. When Bob Hope later played the Palladium that season, he brilliantly skewered Kaye's English-tinged vanity with one of his jokes: "Danny Kaye visits me when he comes to America. You should see his dressing room here [in London]—two mirrors and a throne."

That fall my television program mirrored the hit status of my Palladium show. It seemed that I could do no wrong. As in everything I did before an audience, Edna's mark was all over my material. First, there was a parade of my comedy characters, with the period critics most enjoying a sketch involving Clem Kadiddlehopper. Second, my routines that opening night and throughout the first TV season were generously peppered with both "how to" bits (à la the Edna-authored donut sketch) and tipsy shtick, again borrowing from her writing of the "Guzzler's Gin" routine. Edna's comic mind had created countless variations of these two pivotal bits during our vaudeville years, and we drew upon them for years in both radio and television.

Despite a mountain of acclaim and two Emmy Awards for that first season, the wheels came off the bus the second year. The transition reminds me of an old comic line by my neurotic friend Oscar Levant. When an apparent stranger once asked him, "Do you remember me?" He replied with a certain ruthless joy, "Fortunately, I'm suffering from amnesia." Audiences seemed to turn on me just that sharply during the second season. Actually, they had reasons. First, we ate up a lot of classic material that initial year. As I noted earlier in the text, we used to call TV the "glass furnace." By the follow-up season the program sometimes felt like a rehash. Second, the first year we were "live," but the second season we filmed the program, and I seemed to lose my comic edge. Third, Edna had health issues the second year and eventually bowed out of my life completely—I was suddenly flying blind for the first time in over twenty years, going back to when I was an underage burlesque comic. Fear came back to me in ways I thought I had managed to forever eliminate. Even now, just revisiting this event, I feel a sort of night sweat coming over me.

I think another factor in my later purging Edna from my life was a sense that she had somehow deserted me. I know that wasn't true, but it still hurt a great deal when she walked away. Of course, it wasn't all a health issue, either. Her marriage to Borzage had failed, in part, because I was still making major demands on her. Can you believe I even had Edna carrying pictures of my kids, so if the odd interview came up, and they wanted a family slant, I was covered. No, she needed to break away for her own good. I'm just sorry that I refused to recognize it at the time.

I will blame my self-centeredness, however, on my suddenly failing television series. The bad press for this second season was devastating to me. After the amazingly unmitigated run of successes I had experienced, I was close to shock mode. Keep in mind that entertainment was all but a religion for me. The field of laughter, to paraphrase my favorite poet, Donald Hall, was my

Bible, Plato, Aristotle, Euclid, Thomas Aquinas, and *Boy Scout Handbook*. I not only felt like a loser, Hollywood columnists like Louella Parsons suggested my failure was due to Edna's absence—fueling more anger on my part.

Ironically, even with Edna's exit, she also continued to surface in the press' fascination with the by now messy nature of my second marriage. Georgia and I were constantly fighting. My concerns over the show were the catalyst for one domestic donnybrook after another. Several industry columnists, including Parsons and her arch rival, the equally influential Hedda Hopper, felt my arguments with Georgia were caused by my desire to bring Edna back in order to save the sinking series. This was all a bunch of poppycock, but it sold papers. Meanwhile, I got more angry—since I was always sensitive to the claim that Georgia wore the pants in the family.

My excessive drinking at this time only made matters worse. The father I had never known had essentially drunk himself to death, and for a time, I seemed to be on the same path. If that wasn't bad enough, I took to playing cowboy when I was drunk. One of my hobbies was collecting guns—which I always kept loaded. I figured, you always heard about someone getting shot with a seemingly "unloaded gun." Thus, my weapons would be safeguarded by being *loaded*. I know, crazy. Regardless, when I drank I took to climbing a tree on my estate, firing away with an old-fashioned six-gun at whatever caught my attention.

How something bad didn't happen, I don't know. Maybe my old friend Robert Benchley was onto something when he said, "God always protects little children and old drunks." Sadly, just as I had once treated Edna like a "whipping boy," I now turned my anger on Georgia in the same way. But this was my second wife's finest hour. She said something in an interview at the time that so moved me I've kept a tattered copy of it in my billfold ever since: "Red gets difficult because he's artistic. He's a high-strung genius and he gets emotionally upset so he tees off on the person nearest him, and that's me. Such is the hidden cost of art."

I quote this not as an excuse for my negative behavior towards Georgia, or Edna before her. No, this is a belated thank you to a woman with the patience of Job. Remember, the typical comedian has less accountability than a carny. Yet, I've been blessed with some amazingly understanding women. I'm glad to finally acknowledge this. Like a splinter under the skin, it was something that eventually had to come out. Of course, the cynic might add, "Skelton was just emulating another facet of his comedy hero—the brilliant but mercurial Chaplin."

My comeback came in the summer of the following year (1953), when I wowed a SRO audience at Las Vegas' Sahara nightclub. An old vaudeville friend of mine, Marty Rackin, had convinced me that a trip to America's gambling capital just might be the ticket to saving my career. Moreover, when

I then followed up his faith in me with more binge drinking and unstable tendencies (another frightening chapter with my gun collection), Marty essentially kidnapped me to Vegas. His tough love went so far as to then police my every moment and almost will me into being a hit in the desert—a comic force one paper kindly likened to an atomic blast. (This was, after all, time when atomic testing was still going on near Vegas.)

All I did was essentially my greatest comedy hits—thank you Edna— from the donut-dunking routine to my "Guzzler's Gin" sketch. But the audiences responded like it was all brand new. Suddenly, the fortunes of yours truly, a struggling television comic, were revived. CBS representatives were even moved to request I jump from the NBC peacock network, all because a sober me was knocking them dead in Vegas. Granted, I wasn't totally back. Alcoholism is a day-to-day thing. But I had turned a corner. One of the sweetest congratulatory notes I received was from Buster Keaton, who definitely knew what it was to struggle with the bottle. Paradoxically, I kept thinking how lucky I was—while most people pay big bucks to go into rehab, I was working my way through cold turkey... and earning $12,000 a week!

As a footnote, let me add two quick Vegas stories from this comeback trip. One of the local reviews of my Sahara opening was overly fascinated with my apparent gum-chewing during the act. But I don't know what kind of funny cigarettes the critic was smoking, because I can't remember the last time I chewed gum during a show—especially when my routine involved eating, à la the donut sketch. What's more, I've never been a big fan of the habit, and my reasoning is a bit provocative. In my Grandma Ella's Indiana brothel, chewing gum was forbidden during sex. The reasoning behind this unusual rule was that a gum-chewing patron could supposedly use it as a distraction to delay his coming—which would lessen the number of customers Ella's girls could handle. Actually, I'm not convinced gum could be used in that way, unless it was amazingly tasty gum. (On a personal note, I always think about baseball when I'm trying to delay the big sexual homerun. In fact, I once so got into my imaginary game that I yelled "Slide!" right in the middle of sex, and really scared the young lady I was with.) Anyway, Ella's standing rule, or should I say, "horizontal rule," somehow soured me on the gum-chewing habit.

The second Vegas story from this pivotal 1953 desert trip involved Frank Sinatra. Friends from the early 1940s, I hadn't seen much of him lately, as my MGM film work had taken a backseat to the television series. Well, we were up in his suite watching a college football game. Frank had a lot of money on the game, and his team was about to score and guarantee him a big payday. But everything depended upon his All-American passing quarterback. On what should have been the go-ahead touchdown, this back was flushed out of the pocket and decided to be a runner. Big mistake. Sadly, he didn't realize that once a giant linebacker is about to crush you, it's perfectly acceptable for a quarterback to protect himself by sliding to the ground. Instead, this Joe College got creamed and had to be carried off the field on a stretcher. His replacement immediately threw an interception and Frank lost a fortune. But the comedy payoff for me was what a shell-shocked Sinatra repeatedly mumbled at the screen during and well after the star quarterback made his unfortunate choice to not slide: "We're not birthing a baby here—feet first is ok."

The best thing about my move to CBS was eventually getting a new head writer—Sherwood Schwartz. Kiddingly referred to as "Robin Hood's rabbi," he was my new Edna. After surveying my past shows, he concluded they were 80% verbal and 20% pantomime—numbers he thought should be reversed. The program would be more about me doing pantomime. This writer with a name that sounded like refugee from a Mel Brooks movie also felt I should appear as just one of my characters each week—a simple but brilliant change. Trying to parade my whole comedy cast through each weekly episode had been overkill. He also wanted me to focus on a single theme each show, which worked well with keying on one character.

Schwartz was a modest but insightful man, calling himself a "facilitator." He would always say, "We didn't make you any funnier—we just created a format to maximize your possibilities." Robin Hood's rabbi was with me for eight seasons, and he brought my ratings back to those unique first year numbers. Schwartz later created such hits as *Gilligan's Island* and *The Brady Bunch*. Though both of these shows were miles away from anything lofty and poetic, they perfectly demonstrated what he brought to my program—an uncanny ability, like Edna, to "read" public tastes. Ironically, I once inadvertently called him Edna. Schwartz gave me a quizzical look and said he'd take that as a compliment, especially if it also included some accidental alimony.

Schwartz always felt my comedy characters were in a comedy middle ground, between the realism of Jackie Gleason's Ralph Kramden and the zany, almost surrealistic Ernie Kovacs, with his cockeyed poet Percy Dovetonsils and the Nairobi Trio—the three men in ape masks, trench coats, and bowler hats miming the strange musical number "Solfeggio." Two apes pretended to play instruments (piano and drums), while the nominal leader conducted. Given that leadership counts for little in the absurd modern world, the "crowning" achievement was that in a moment of distraction, the drummer would pound on the conductor's head. After several subterfuge-driven repetitions of this darkly comic drumstick violence, the ape conductor wraps the routine with a vase to the head of his musical nemesis. Compared to such Kovac characters, my comedy caravan was basically a slice of real life. While I especially enjoyed the comic oddity of the Nairobi [ape] Trio, they always frightened my children. In fact, after my daughter Valentina had an ape-related nightmare, Georgia kept the kids from watching poor Ernie's show. I continued to watch Kovacs in my TV den, which had three screens mounted on the wall, so I could check out what were than the three major networks simultaneously.

My favorite small screen comedian during the 1950s and '60s, however, remained Gleason. I even enjoyed recycling some of Jackie's signature lines at home, like "And away we go," "How sweet it is," and "Boom-zoom to the moon, Alice." Valentina especially liked my take on "How sweet it is," and my son Richard took to saying, "Boom-zoom to the moon, Alice" all on his own.

The bottom line for what I liked about Gleason goes all the way back to something George M. Cohan once said: "If you can get an audience to laugh, you might run a while. But if you can get them to laugh *and* cry, you'll run forever." Jackie was that way for me. For all of his Ralph Kramden bluster, when he would tell his small screen wife Alice (Audrey Meadows), "Baby, you're the greatest," he had me every time. And when Ralph would say, "I haven't done one thing right since I have been married," there's a real touch of pathos in his performance. I may be old, but I'm not dead—Cohan's insight still applies.

This sentimental slant reminds me of something F. Scott Fitzgerald once said. While I'm embarrassed to confess I have never read any of his novels, he moved me with the statement, "Show me a hero and I'll write you a tragedy." As in the Cohan quote, entertainment at its best is a mix of laughter and tears. That's why Chaplin is at the top of my entertainment list. As in life, art at its best is a roller coaster.

Some Highs and a Tragic Low

"Like many successful comedians, Red developed his distinctive persona by becoming his own material."

– Edna Stillwell

AFTER MY HEAD WRITER SHERWOOD SCHWARTZ brought me back from the dead on television, I had an extended successful run on the small screen. With that in mind, I'd like to relate some of my favorite stories from the 1950s. The first is about a young talent on my show who went on to become one of the video giants—Johnny Carson. He started out with an inspired local show in L.A. called *Carson's Cellar*. With no budget to speak of, Carson got by with wit and moxie, such as an episode on which he announced that "Red Skelton was the show's special guest star." A lone figure then raced across the stage. That, Carson said, was Red Skelton. Well, as luck would have it, I just happened to catch "my appearance." I was charmed. This was the kind of inspired comedy I had practiced in my old vaudeville days.

I immediately called Johnny and offered to really be on his show. Soon a whole parade of major clowns, funnymen like Groucho Marx and Fred Allen, were doing the same thing. Like a sign I once saw in a bar, "Happy Hour—any waking moment!," *Carson's Cellar* was a joy to watch. But its Sunday afternoon time slot was less than ideal, so when it was cancelled, I immediately signed him up for my program. He was both a monologue writer and a sketch participant.

The next season, I believe it was 1954, I was rehearsing a routine shortly before airtime which involved crashing through a breakaway door... which did not break away. Though I was once compared to football bruiser Bronco Nagurski, I'm afraid that door did what no linebacker ever did to Bronco— knocked me cold. As I was unable to go on that night, Johnny subbed his way to stardom. Calling himself "the poor man's Red Skelton," he combined his talent for ad-libs with some of his nightclub material, including a tongue-in-cheek Robert Benchley-like "lecture" on the economics of television. Between some wonderful notices, and great plugs from Jack Benny and myself, Johnny soon had an exclusive contract with CBS. While Carson's *Tonight Show* days at NBC were still almost a decade off, he had definitely made it onto the public radar.

Though our comedy styles were somewhat different, with Johnny more into the dry understated tradition of Benny, there were some parallels between Carson and myself. His troupe of comedy characters was often reminiscent of mine, especially the parallels between our two hucksters, my San Fernando Red and Johnny's Art Fern—the Tea Time Matinee Movie host. Plus, with both of us coming from the heartland, there was generally an amicable tone to our humor.

On a personal note, Johnny and I both had trouble getting to bed back then—too many distractions. But while he was just getting his first taste of the nightlife that had so fascinated me in the early 1940s and derailed my marriage to Edna, by the early 1950s I was simply obsessed with writing material for my show. Consequently, for a time, I was eating sleeping pills like candy. In fact, I was downing so many that I stole Dorothy Parker's response to the question of whether she took knockout drops: "In a big bowl with sugar and cream."

Conversely, one of my most quoted comments from this period would suggest that I was anything but a night owl. Georgia and I had gone to some boring Hollywood party. At one point I was overwhelmed by a monster yawn. My wife said, "I hope I'm not keeping you up." I replied, "I wish you were."

Speaking of my writing, author Gene Fowler was a huge influence during this time. The former newspaperman turned screenwriter and best-selling biographer became my mentor. When he discovered that I, in a very primitive way, took a blank sheet of paper and wrote daily, he was more than surprised. 'Course, I was more surprised than he when he sat me down and calmly said, "You have talent in the writing field, but God knows you have a lot to learn." So I tried. We went from a casual friendship to a teacher-student relationship. His lessons and criticisms were a mix of love and fun. The most serious of all subjects, life itself, became an entertaining exercise in writing.

Interestingly, Gene's style also reinforced my predisposition to mix fact and fiction in pursuit of telling a better and often more sentimental story. Fittingly, he had started out under the sponsorship of legendary writer Damon Runyon, whose stories were famous for colorful, slant-filled New York and/or Broadway characters with big hearts, strange names, and an imaginative style of speech. Fowler definitely followed this path in his writing, especially his early creative (can you say fairy tale?) biography of Mack Sennett, with the most appropriate of titles—*Father Goose*.

Granted, Fowler's later biographies are more anchored in fact than his Sennett book. But Fowler still had a tall tale component to his profiles. This made a big impression on me, given my "creative" autobiography tendencies, and someone who peppered his fiction with real people and places. Sadly, neither one of us got around to writing projected biographies of each other. Given our free-wheeling tendencies, readers might not have recognized us anyway.

Fowler was yet another father figure for me, and his writing advice often doubled as life lessons. For instance, when I would complain about my latest short story, he would remind me, "You're still in the race [Keep at it]." Fowler also had this great line, "Save it for the hill," which simply meant hold your best stuff for tough times. Before Fowler, I had often felt dull, with all the deep dish thoughts of the typical sophomore. This veteran writer simply gave me more confidence in myself. Oh, I know that this memoir is more historical trail mix than real history. But expressing myself keeps me from going nuts, or as Ella used to describe losing it—"going off the reservation."

Like my old Vincennes mentor, Clarence Stout, Fowler was also color-blind when it came to the races. I remember someone once asked him, "How can we get rid of racism?" Here was his no nonsense response: "Stop talking about it. I'm going to stop calling you a black man and I'm going to ask you to stop calling me a white man." Because of Stout, I really knew and appreciated who Fowler was; I knew how his whole song was sung.

Another favorite story from this period involved my children, Valentina and Richard, and Walt Disney's new television program—*Disneyland*. The episodes which really launched the show were from the anthology's "Frontierland" segment and featured the adventures of real-life frontier hero Davy Crockett (Fess Parker). It became an overnight sensation that spawned a merchandising bonanza, from coonskin caps to comics, and everything in between: fringed leather jackets, shirts, shorts, pajamas, soap, dolls, lunch boxes, tents, bedspreads, and so on.

Like most baby boomer children, Valentina and Richard were dying to meet Davy and his sidekick George Russel (Buddy Ebsen). But if truth be told, I was an even bigger fan of the duo. So under the cover of being a good dad, I arranged for these TV heroes to make an appearance at a joint birthday party for my children. Obviously, Crockett and Russel were a hit, but one of the Los Angeles newspapers affectionately blew my cover the following day with an article entitled, "Kids Can't Get at Davy; Skelton Monopolizes Him." But the piece did allow me to amusingly spread the blame: "It was like the new electric train at Christmas—the kids couldn't get to Crockett because of the parents." Yes, more evidence that I had never fully grown up. Plus, like the non-fiction fiction tendencies of my writing mentor Fowler, Crockett was a real figure whose life had been re-configured by legend.

Another wonderful 1950s adventure occurred whenever I took my television show on the road. I love real people and the only way to meet them is to get out of Hollywood. My favorite such excursion took us to the Fontainebleau Hotel in Miami Beach. It's a great city and, with all the tourists, a crossroads of America. In fact, one of the program's better jokes involved tourists. There had been a news story about the dangers of Miami driving—what with visitors stopping on major highways to snap pictures of seagulls Given my seagull "team" of Gertrude and Heathcliff, it was easy to come up with a sketch where I pitched a solution to the city council—residents should adopt a seagull and always include the bird in any car trip. That way, the traffic flow is maintained, the tourists are happy, residents are happy, and more seagulls get a chance to see Busch Gardens.

Ironically, two of my funniest bits from that trip never made the show—too dark. One involved seeing my first bumper sticker—"Drinking and Driving: A Deadly Mix." My perverse sense of humor had me pulling up beside this car, rolling down my window, and randomly suggesting, "You should also try ammonia and Clorox."

The second comedy catalyst on that Miami trip involved another news story—some poor shmuck tried to kill himself by downing battery fluid. The hospital, which must have been run by bartenders, came up with a special treatment which involved industrial strength vodka! This hello coma approach was administered through a slow drip process that worked out to approximately three drinks an hour. The happy "victim" was on this for three days! Well, one of my associates—"yes men," if truth be told—said, "Wow, what a treatment." Now, you have to remember, I was boozing really heavily at the time. So this was my casual response to the "wow" comment about this "medical" cure: "Just sounds like another Labor Day weekend to me." Naturally, I couldn't share this sort of habit with the public, but the crack was big among my crew for months.

As an addendum to Florida and the Fontainebleau, my television program so showcased the hotel—I even drove up to the entrance in a Model-T Ford decked out as my Hoosier hayseed character Clem Kadiddlehopper—that it influenced another major comedian. Jerry Lewis, who has always treated me like an honored king of comedy, later told me that when he saw the Fontainbleau show a light bulb went on. Sure enough, when Lewis directed his first film, *The Bellboy*, he set it at the Fontainbleau. And as a further bow to me, the movie was a nod to my preference for visual shtick—one sight gag after another. Of course, I had to hassle Jerry about his featuring a Stan Laurel-like character (another of his comedy heroes) in the movie. Jerry said it was just a little gift for Stan, who felt forgotten in retirement. But I was merely fooling with him; I didn't care. I felt honored that Jerry credited me for the movie idea. You know, as one gets older, simply being remembered means more and more. Regardless, like me, Jerry also loved Miami, though he would kid about the place, saying that on some visits he felt like he'd "died and gone to Jew heaven."

Over the years I had a lot of great guests, but during the 1950s, former heavyweight champion Rocky Marciano was close to being my favorite. The only undefeated heavyweight champion in history, Marciano had retired with great fanfare earlier the year (1956) he visited our show. Boxing was much bigger back then, second only to baseball in popularity with the public. And with Major League Baseball not yet then having reached the West Coast, boxing was huge in Hollywood.

The sport's prominent place there even predated the arrival of the movies. Director Leo McCarey's father was *the* promoter of the time, bringing in many high profile fights, one of which even inspired my favorite scene in Chaplin's *City Lights*. The sequence has Charlie's Tramp as a reluctant boxer who manages to get knocked out just as the little fellow's lucky punch has also flattened his opponent. This delightfully funny but seemingly unlikely event was actually based in fact. One of Tom McCarey's bouts really ended in a double knockout. Fittingly, one of Leo's later film principles was that no matter how exaggerated comedy gets, it should have one foot in reality.

Personally, I also subscribed to that same philosophy of comedy, with my comic character boxers, Cauliflower McPugg, being a composite of several real fighters. One of my favorite sources was the British boxer faking Phil Scott, whose signature move was to drop like a stone in the second round, forever holding his privates. Another colorful character was New York fighter Joe Benjamin, whose sense of humor was greater than his boxing skills. Once in a bar a customer critic came up to him and berated him, "I've seen you fight three times and never win." Joe replied, "You're going to see me win one now," and immediately dropped the boob.

Since the retired Marciano was only thirty-three, Rocky comeback stories frequently peppered the sports section of newspapers across the country. Consequently, that was the comedy slant taken for his visit to the program—a comeback against Cauliflower McPugg.

In a *Los Angeles Examiner* article "Rocky vs. McPugg," Marciano played it straight and said, "If I can get on my bicycle, you know, keep moving away from McPugg, and last the distance, then I'll be happy to retire for good this time. All those stories about him having a glass jaw are patently false… you don't get a name like "Cauliflower" by going down too quickly! It should be a good fight. If I were a betting man, and let me assure the boxing commission I'm not, I'd put my money on McPugg." Marciano was a class act, and I dearly enjoyed working with him. We were also on the same page about a lot of basic values. For example, I knew I was going to like this man when he said, "Hollywood tends to underestimate the middle states. But it's where this country was formed." His 1969 death in the crash of small plane was hard to accept. And I actually wept when his widow later told me that Rocky had included an autographed Cauliflower picture I'd given him on his den's wall of celebrated fighters. Wow, McPugg rubbing elbows with Jack Dempsey and Joe Louis.

Boxing represents a natural transition to the mob, what everyone used to call the wiseguys. They had a stronghold on boxing back then, just as they did nightclubs and Vegas. I remember Jerry Lewis and me agreeing that through the 1940s and '50s it was impossible for any entertainer not to deal with them. And while I have to choose my words carefully here, they were a type of men who, within their own set of rules, could be honorable. But I think my friend Frank Sinatra romanticized them to an extreme, even coining the later popular phrase, "Wiseguys were like movie stars with muscle." Of course, Frank's career had been given a boost by the mob. If you saw the first *Godfather* movie, you'll remember how the Sinatra character got out of a bad big band contract by a wiseguy friend making Frank's bandleader/boss "an offer he can't refuse"—threatening to kill him. That really happened. The bandleader Frank was under contract to was Tommy Dorsey, and the gangster who put a gun to Dorsey's head was none other than Frank Costello. I got variations of the same story from both Frank and Tommy, friends dating back to our MGM years.

I remember Jerry's old partner, Dean Martin, one of the most underrated comic personalities to grace our profession, once sharing about how poverty often forced young people into crime and/or close associations with the mob. Dean was from a tough section of Steubenville, Ohio, and he constantly heard around the old neighborhood, "Learn to steal, learn to deal, or go to the mill." Unlike Frank, or even Jerry, Dean would never cozy up to anyone, be it the mob or his television sponsor. His philosophy of life was perfectly encapsulated in an x-rated Italian term "menefreghismo," which might best be translated as a "what the fuck" attitude. Eat, drink, and be merry, because who knows what tomorrow will bring. Yet, Dean still felt that you treat people the way they treat you—regardless of what society might say about certain elements, such as the mob. And since most mobsters admired Martin's moxie and talent, they all got along fine.

Well, let me include one exception to that statement. Dean loved the ladies, and since he was just as cool and unfazed by everything in real life as in the movies, the ladies loved him, too. Thus, he had a habit of spotting a pretty woman sitting ringside in a nightclub audience and flirtingly performing entirely to her. One night in a Miami club he pulled this on the most gorgeous woman imaginable, with legs up to her ears and breasts to die for. Jerry, who told me the story, said she was so lovely every man in the place had a community erection.

What Dean had not taken into account—what he *never* took into account—was her date. According to Jerry, he was a wiseguy in the mold of Joe Pesci's loose canon in *Goodfellas*. You know, the kind of character that roots for the bad guys in the movies. This gangster pulled a gun on Dean backstage and it was touch and go there for a while. Thankfully, Jerry came to the rescue. Granted, he was telling the story, too. But here's Jerry's take on this misadventure with the Florida hood Freddie "Nostril": "I stepped between my partner and the man's gun and proceeded to do the verbal tap dance of my life. I said, 'Mr. "Nostril," you have to understand something. People make mistakes—that's why they have erasers on pencils. Now, I'm going to admit to you that my partner made a mistake. I know Dean did what you said he did, but I'm going to offer you my hand, to give you my word of honor, that I know my partner, and I know that out of respect for you, out of the same respect I have for you, he would never have done this if he had known who this young lady was.' I was lying through my teeth. But I had no alternative, because Freddie "Nostril" was very serious. Eventually he put the gun down and left. Thankfully, we could breathe again. Yet, for once even Dean seemed rattled… until he caught me off-guard with some comedy: 'I've never seen a more stupid son of a bitch—you could've been killed.' As Ella used to say, "You're greatest asset [in this case, Dean's sex appeal] can be your greatest weakness."

Unfortunately for me, singers have it all over comics in the flirtation department. Even if I had been foolish enough to ignore this Martin and Lewis lesson, how does one make time with the ladies while performing a "Guzzler's Gin" routine, or my donut-dunking sketch? Indeed, the way my comic chewing of those "sinkers" ended up "broadcasting" donut chunks all over the stage, I was simply pleased when no pretty patrons got sick! In contrast, as a young comic protégé of mine, Flip Wilson, liked to say, "Why, those bandstand groupies don't even mind when the singer inadvertently spits all over them." Yes, my latent lover tendencies would have been much better served as a crooner. Of course, the fact that my singing voice often frightened folks, especially small children, made it easier to accept comedy as a career. After all, what else could I expect, given my tendency to be sort of a divining rod for all things antiheroic. Naturally, there are some hip—read sexy—comics, such as Mort Sahl or the young Johnny Carson. But I've always been sort of a comic saltine: same make-up, same square design, same product, year after year.

Before I sign off on Martin and Lewis, I must say I've always had a soft spot for film's last great comedy team. However, my connection to Lewis goes beyond our everyman clown tendencies. We're both also loyal disciples of Chaplin—to the point of being obsessed. For instance, after Charlie left the country I ended up buying his old studio—something I could neither afford nor use—for my television program. But buy it I did. Along similar lines, Jerry tried to replicate Charlie's total control approach to production: writing, directing, producing and starring in his films. It proved too much for Jerry to handle, though he was hardly alone in the attempt. So many other comedians have tried and failed to wear all the production hats, à la Chaplin, from Harry Langdon to Eddie Murphy, that some academic type recently called the fixation the "Charlie Disease." I never succumbed to this disease, despite my love of all things Charlie, because I had played on the same vaudeville bill with Langdon in the early 1930s. His attempt to be another Chaplin had ruined his silent film career, and he was quick to advise me, "Don't try to do it all. There's only one Chaplin."

With regard to Lewis catching the "Charlie Disease," Martin diagnosed the problem early in his patentedly x-rated fashion, "He thinks he's Chaplin's fucking little fellow Tramp." Jerry would have been better served by staying with Dean. Martin had a way of convincing audiences he was a cool version of themselves—which complimented everyone with which he was teamed. For example, he softened Jerry's comedy craziness, and took the edge off the ego of his Rat Pack buddy Sinatra. Everything went down better with Dean.

You're probably thinking, "What the hell in a hootenanny is all this rambling on about Martin and Lewis?" Well, I guess I've belabored my Dean and Jerry stories because my friendship with both men represents another of my favorite 1950s memories. But Dean's provocative "menefreghismo" philosophy is also a perfect transition to the decade's dark side. Just when my television series had rebounded, and my second marriage was in a better place, we found out our 8-year-old son Richard had leukemia. Like a lot of comedians, I'm superstitious. Until recently, I even got nervous talking about why something was funny—maybe I'd jinx whatever comic gift I had, and it'd just leave me. Thus, shortly before little Richard's diagnosis, I was already feeling a little uneasy about just how good my life was then going.

Like those works of tragic literature my writing mentor Gene Fowler was always encouraging me to read, I now think of this personal calamity playing itself out in five acts. First, there was simply shock—how could this happen to my little namesake, who everyone called "a carbon copy of his father, and a comedian in his own right?" Act two might be called the "See It All Tour," where Georgia and I tried to pack a lifetime of adventures for Richard into an extended summer vacation.

The tour had innocently begun with some visits to East Coast historic sights, such as Philadelphia's Liberty Bell and New York's Statue of Liberty. But the little guy got such enjoyment out of these American stops—and with no ill effects—that we decided to show him other parts of the world. He was in remission at this time, and the medical specialists gave us the green light. Our subsequent trip to Europe had many highlights, from a private audience with the Pope, where Richard was given a medal (the boy asked if that made him a hero), to a visit to the ruins of Pompeii.

When we stopped in Paris, Richard asked me why the *Mona Lisa* was smiling, and I replied, "Because everyone's looking at her." But given the attention our tour was generating, I think everyone was looking at us. We felt a little like some of the Edward Hopper paintings we saw that summer, such as *Nighthawks*—four people viewed through the window of a diner after dark. That is, like Hopper figures, we felt sort of trapped behind glass. (Among the Hollywood crowd, Hopper is celebrated for paintings which often resemble a scene in a film, such as his *House by the Railroad* being the inspiration for Hitchcock's spooky old Victorian mansion in *Psycho*. As a painter myself, maybe I should have sent Alfred some of my stuff. But back then clowns were not yet considered potentially scary.)

Act three arrived just as our tour was winding down in London. Ironically, it started off well at the airport, with Richard showing his dark sense of humor by dryly asking a reporter, "I say, how is the Skelton boy?" But that was the trip's last bit of levity. There was a press conference at our London hotel, the Savoy, and one of the attending columnists, the *London Daily Sketch*'s Simon Ward, bitterly attacked both the conference and the tour as nothing short of a publicity stunt for my career.

Though this perspective was an aberration, I was furious. Calling the trip a PR play was like acid poured on wounds in the heart. Many reporters came to our defense, but all the coverage of the sudden controversy soured things, and we soon came home. I tried to take the high road and put a positive spin on everything with my first comments to journalists back in the States: "The kids had a lot of fun. Probably we would still be there but both of them are anxious to see their little friends back home."

Paradoxically, while little Richard remained in remission, Georgia and I soon suffered from stress-related illnesses. She was hospitalized for exhaustion, and I nearly died from a severe asthmatic attack. Still, with Richard sailing past the original five-month prognosis, my wife and I dared to hope. But shortly after a year, in April of 1957, Richard's condition started to deteriorate. We practically started living at the UCLA Medical Center, with Georgia and I taking a room next to Richard's.

The final day's activities included watching one of his favorite morning cartoons, *Mighty Mouse*, and trying to talk about his upcoming birthday. Georgia, my 9-year-old daughter, Valentina, and I had briefly left for supper, only to be immediately called back when Richard took a turn for the worse. Fittingly, for a little boy who was a "carbon copy of his father," Richard managed to impart his minutes with a darkly comic comment. Sensing his death was near, he requested a final kiss from each of us. When little Valentina was slow to respond, having to pull up a stool for added height, he told her, "Hurry up, Valentina, I haven't got all day."

The fourth act, the death of Richard, left our family inconsolable. A sense of our extreme guilt is caught in a telegram from good friend Oscar Levant: "Please bear up for our sake. My deepest sympathy and love." But we did not bear up. At the Forest Lawn Funeral three days later, none of us could walk without assistance, and we spent most of our time in a room adjacent to the main chapel. But our tragedy touched a nation, and the cards and letters poured in. Mamie Eisenhower wrote, "The President joins me in sending our heartfelt and deepest sympathy to you both. Having lost our first little boy, we also know the empty place it leaves in your heart."

Several letters thoughtfully praised our special travel tour for Richard. For instance, J. Edgar Hoover, head of the F. B. I., even provided a first-hand memory of the trip: "I recall so vividly your visit to Washington, D.C. last year. He was such a happy and courageous child and a regular little trouper. I deeply regret this tragic loss to you." General George Marshall, architect of the post-war "Marshall Plan," was even more poignantly sensitive: "Richard was such a brave little boy and, as parents, you did a most noble thing by pouring into his life all that time would allow."

As luck would have it, Steve Allen's card also serves as an unintendedly ironic segue to act five—life after one's loss. Allen's note said, "As a writer I could think of some appropriate words to say to you at this difficult time but as a father I know that words in themselves couldn't bring you any comfort. Only time can do that."

Time could not bring comfort to Georgia. She would commit suicide 18 years later, on the anniversary of our son's death. For a time, many held the same fear for me. Life had taken on a sudden unreality, like trying to walk under water. I was so submerged that the light of the world, which had always seemed forever young to me, and joyfully unsupervised, had turned darkly old. In an instant, I slipped back into being that frightened insecure little kid from Vincennes. But, as the following chapter documents, I finally was able to recover.

Palm Spring in the 1960s: Desert Recluse

"Our lives are not determined by what happens to us, but how we react to what happens."

– Edna Stillwell

WHEN LITTLE RICHARD'S DEATH had brought me so low that all the songs seemed without words, I received the above note from my first wife. She always had a positive way of reframing a bad situation. Edna riding to the rescue here reminds me of a related game we used to play during our marriage. Calling ourselves the "Miserable Artists' Club," we had nonstop conversations about how personal pain often shapes art. Though I most liked to focus on sad clowns, our discussions included anyone whose artistic hair shirt seemed extra scratchy. For instance, given my interest in painting, Edna included this Van Gogh quote in one of our "Miserable Artists' Club" sessions: "The more I am spent, ill, a broken painter, so much more am I an artist." Fittingly, Van Gogh wrote this shortly before he decided to trim one of his earlobes!

Though Edna and I were both aware of many creative types who had what my friend George Plimpton once comically called, "Non-unhappy childhoods," it is more fun to chart train wreck foundations to art. Plus, we were both convinced that this romantic perspective on the suffering artist let people off the hook as far as creativity. That is, most folks don't want to believe that the average Joe could just sit down at a piano or a typewriter and create something for the ages—art needs to be the product of a lot of misery and angst.

In fact, you could compare this to conspiracy theory types, of whom I am a proud member. But if the truth be told, we're in denial here, too. One does not want to believe in the randomness of evil. For example, take the JFK assassination. It's just hard to believe that some shmuck could go into a building and shoot the president.

Returning, however, to the "Miserable Artists' Club," my favorite candidate was the great pantomimist Joseph Grimaldi, whose praises and chronic depression I've already noted, including his ironic visit to a medical specialist. The doctor advised him to see the brilliant clown Grimaldi—this would be his salvation. The patient sadly shook his head and said, "Doctor, I am Grimaldi."

Apocryphal or not, I love that story... and I relate to it. From a prostitute mother to stepbrothers who enjoyed terrorizing me, I had my fair share of black days even before my mental breakdown in the Army. Only in performing could I escape my periodic depressions—a responsive audience meant I was briefly loved. I think my long-time arrested development, locked in adolescent self-absorption, was a defense mechanism against further hurt. Let's just say it took me a long time to become a human being. Even now, my dear daughter Valentina will occasionally remind me that I often seem more open and animated with fans than family.

I should add that, like myself, there are many *mainstream* artists who fight depression through their work. One does not need to only focus the "Miserable Artists' Club" on darkly deep dish types, like Beethoven, who went deaf at the height of his musical gift, or Frida Kahlo, a painter whose near fatal accident as a young woman sentenced her to a lifetime of chronic pain. In contrast, I am reminded of my cartoonist buddy Charles Schultz, whose *Peanuts* strip is about as mainstream as it gets. Yet, Chuck has been fighting Gloomy Gus tendencies his whole life, and it's comically reflected in his strip. As he once told me, "Red, all the loves in the strip are unrequited; all the baseball games are lost; all the test scores are D-minuses; the Great Pumpkin never comes; and the football is always pulled away."

Now to come full circle to Edna's chapter opening comments about my grief over little Richard's death. She was merely playing a variation of our old "Miserable Artists' Club" game—reminding me to creatively use the pain instead of being brought down by it. The way I turned the corner on my grief was to realize that Richard's death gave me a better understanding of pain and a feeling for other people who were suffering. Ultimately, I also found new joy in the simple things of life, from a beautiful sunset to painting my clown pictures. Edna further assisted my private evolution with another comment that would now be called tough love: "You can crash and burn, or you can crash and learn."

Sadly, while I managed to rise from the ashes, Richard's mother, Georgia, never got over his death. I partly blame myself. In my initial grief over his death, I felt the need to turn parts of our Bel Air home into a memorial for our son. I also decided that everything in Richard's room had to remain exactly as it was when he was alive—wherever the toys were last played with, or discarded. Indeed, even bags of fan mail to Richard, received during his long struggle with leukemia, remained on the floor of his room. And here's the topper: I also had a glass cabinet full of Richard mementos placed in the hall outside the boy's room.

Call me crazy, but I needed these artifacts to help communicate with my son. Like in a movie by my favorite Western director, John Ford, in which the grave of a loved one frequently becomes a comforting catalyst for regular monologues with the deceased, I often talked to Richard in his room.

But, while this unconventional grieving process helped me, it was disturbing to Georgia. Worse yet, while I would daily leave this sad setting for the studio, my poor wife stayed home with Richard's mementos and drank. Georgia had been fighting alcoholism and an addiction to prescription drugs for years. With Richard's death, she simply gave up the fight.

Unfortunately, my behavior here was also less than sensitive. Since I used my son's loss to stop my own heavy drinking, I showed little sympathy for my wife's addiction problems. I even discouraged Georgia from seeing a shrink. I used to believe that getting better necessitated doing it all yourself. And a composer friend, Arthur Rodzinski, was always telling me, "Psychoanalysis is bad. I tried it. They open the wound and then it remains open and there's endless bleeding." Amazingly, I also preached to Georgia, via my daily love letters to her, about using will power over the pills and booze. I realize now that was totally unrealistic. In all honesty, I'm afraid those love letters I was always mentioning to the press were just as likely to be about my daily pet peeves, instead of romantic pledges.

The letters to Georgia began in 1962, after we moved to Palm Springs—an attempt to put miles between us and the sad memories of our Bel Air home. To me, things seemed to straighten out with the move to the desert. But our Palm Springs paradise sometimes seemed like a prison. Years after Georgia's suicide I gave a bitter interview to the *New York Times*, where I blamed the move on her assorted demons. But once again, I was being unfair, as well as terribly simplistic. Yes, we partly relocated because of Georgia's instability. Yet, we also wanted to get our daughter into a healthier environment, too. Plus, I was becoming increasingly reclusive, and I just wanted a private getaway. I even made arrangements that enabled me to rehearse and shoot my television program in two intense days, freeing the rest of the time for desert painting and writing.

Before, however, I explore my attempt to be some sort of Palm Springs Renaissance Man, I'd like to address what might seem a strange development in the selection process of our house in the desert. The home in question was along the 16th fairway of Palm Spring's Tamarisk Country Club. But it was neither the setting, nor the house's U-shaped architecture that drew us to the place. When Georgia and I first looked at the house we both simultaneously saw the ghost of little Richard playing and laughing on the grass in front of the place. As my daughter likes to say, "My dad is very psychic." But no matter what you think, I know what we saw.

Granted, there's more than a little irony involved in leaving one home, in part, because it has become too much like a memorial shrine to a dead son, only to select another house based upon seeing that son's ghost. But then, I've done lots of things that made less sense. Besides, I've been seeing ghosts my whole life. Not a week goes by that Ella doesn't drop in on me. Usually she's laughing in that old brothel rocker of hers, with the house motto over the fireplace: "God is happiest when his children are at play."

Along related "spirited" lines, sometimes just before I go on stage, the ghost of the great Grimaldi whispers in my ear, "Make 'em laugh son; ours is the grandest profession." None other than Stan Laurel had told me that Grimaldi periodically visited him, too. But the old pantomimist always appeared in Stan's dressing room mirror and gave him a good luck wink. I should add, Laurel also believed in reincarnation. That's how he explained the unaccountable inspired gift of little Shirley Temple. You know, he even half convinced me on that one.

Of course, when you confess stuff like this, you get kidded. Steve Allen once wrote, "I have never known a successful comedian who was not somewhat neurotic. The unsuccessful ones must be in even worse condition." Steve didn't mean anything by it; he's a comedian, too. Personally, I think the secret of life is to stop thinking… without falling asleep. But since I'm a clown with eccentric ideas, I play to expectations—I'm nuts and I know it. But as long as I make them laugh they ain't gonna lock me up.

Regardless, I think it's past time for me to explore how Palm Springs became a creative retreat for me. By physically getting away from any and all distractions, I was able to devote increasing time to my many hobbies. But this most benefited my painting. Though I had been dabbling in this medium since the 1940s, I really became serious about painting during the Palm Springs years.

While Edna had always encouraged my artistic interests, it was Georgia, a former art student, who became my teacher. Georgia's original goal was to just use painting as a way of getting me to relax. She even gave me my focus on clowns. I had originally struggled, and Georgia encouraged me to paint what I knew. Sadly, my eventual success as a painter was also negative for Georgia. I became so obsessed with it, and so needy of her feedback on each canvas, that I now think it had a smothering effect on her. Georgia was losing her identity. And then when the trained artist, my wife, was passed by me with the clown pictures, I had overshadowed her once again.

Unfortunately, I would later treat Georgia's influence on my painting in the same manner I dealt with both Edna's and Buster Keaton's impact upon my comedy—I would eventually erase it. After my 1970s divorce from Georgia, I was much more likely to rewrite my background with "facts" that pre-dated my second wife. For instance, I was fond of telling an alleged tale from the 1940s, just after Jackson Pollock hit it big with his abstract poured paint-ings. I claimed to have wandered into a modern art exhibit in a department store—a major clue that I was just making this up. Anyway, I asked the price of one prominent painting. When the clerk answered, "10,000 wouldn't buy that one," I comically replied, "And I would be one of the 10,000."

This was spun out of thin air, both to be funny and to give me a pre-Georgia connection to painting, because I have since claimed this "incident" is when I got interested in art. That is, if a goofy abstract painting could bring in $10,000, why wouldn't some representational art be even more valuable? And while this is a fabricated footnote to my past, I do stand by my anti-mod-ern art, profit-driven comments. As the greatest photographer of all-time, Edward Steichen, once told me, "I don't know any form of art that isn't or hasn't been commercial. After all," he added with a wink and no small im-modesty, "Michelangelo also liked to be paid well for his work." (I should add, photography is yet another of my million and one hobbies.)

In time, however, I even pushed my painting roots back to childhood. I made the claim that my boyhood poverty forced me to fashion a brush from a lock of my hair, which I somehow attached to a pencil. Paint was scrounged from discarded school supplies. My canvas was any discarded piece of card-board. I was nothing if not a good storyteller. But again, it was all made up, though the Lord knows I was that poor. I'm embarrassed to say that I further "documented" the fib by gifting my daughter with a painting I credited to my teen years. But it had been done much later.

One thing that wasn't a lie, though, was the amazing success my art-work brought me. After two years at Palm Springs painting, I had my first art show in June of 1964. The exhibit was at Las Vegas' Sands Hotel, where I was entertaining. The public seemed charmed by a clown painting clowns, and a color photo spread in *Look* magazine didn't hurt the publicity, either. Even the manner in which I decided to showcase my art brought praise. The upper portion of a wall covered by rows of my clown paintings included a window-like opening that allowed me, made-up as a clown, to pose from the other side, as if I were yet another painting.

I knew that I had arrived when major art collectors in show business, legends like Maurice Chevalier and Frank Sinatra, wanted a "Skelton" origi-nal. But to keep my hat size down, I attempted to be self-deprecatingly comic about my painting, such as the following widely quoted comment of mine: "I work on two paintings simultaneously until I can figure out what's wrong with the first one. Sometimes I don't find out for weeks. Sometimes I just don't find out." Trying to stay cool in the desert heat, I also periodically enter-tained reporters with the trials and tribulations of painting in the shallow end of my pool, given that oil and water do not mix: "You ought to see the pool after one of my painting sprees. It's an Olympic-sized palette."

Besides my full embrace of painting during the Palm Springs years, I also divided my free time among several other hobbies. My interest in gardening resulted in buying vacant lots on either side of our residence. They were soon transformed into formal Italian and Japanese gardens, with my favorite activity being the care and maintenance of countless bonsai trees—those small ornamental shrub-like plants whose size and shape are severely restricted by the grower.

I got into the bonsai habit after several trips to Japan in the 1950s. Along related lines, I had an elaborate teahouse constructed in the Japanese garden. This building became hobby central for me, where I worked on everything from musical compositions and short stories, to more painting. I spent so much time there that I added a bath and a bedroom, and it might have qualified as a guest house. This was where I composed such published sheet music as "The Kadiddlehopper March" and "Red's White and Blue March," not to mention my children's book, *Gertrude and Heathcliff*, about my two comic seagulls.

Despite enjoying all these hobbies, I've sometimes wondered if my Midwestern work ethic was a blessing or a curse. I turned these things into sort of a daily grind—every twenty-four hours I needed to produce a new short story, another musical composition, a love letter to Georgia, a painting, and so on. Moreover, all my entertainment heroes through the years had worn many creative hats, from my dear Vincennes mentor Clarence Stout, to the ultimate in multitasking, Charlie Chaplin.

Sadly, this was another cruel trick I played on Georgia. We escaped to the desert, and then I abandoned her for my teahouse hobbies. Georgia's plight reminds me of something Chekhov once wrote: "If you are afraid of loneliness, don't marry." My old writing mentor, Gene Fowler, was always repeating that line, since his obsessive scribbling often left his wife feeling like a widow, too. But in Georgia's case, she retreated even more to her pills and liquor. As a footnote to Fowler's interest in Chekhov, an author he encouraged me to read, I found a certain darkly comic realism in his tales that mirrored my life with Georgia. That is, we're all taught that stories should have a tidy beginning, middle, and end. But Chekhov's work unfolds like life—random, inconclusive, seemingly meaningless, and sometimes absurdly cruel. Though I never developed Fowler's intellectual taste for Chekhov (after all, I'm just a simple clown), I now recognize that my life in the desert with Georgia did have a certain Chekhov-style sadness to it.

I don't know why I was so blind to this at the time. I'm only just now connecting the dots and filling in the blanks, uncovering things I refused to acknowledge back then. While Georgia remained my biggest cheerleader throughout the Palm Springs '60s and early 1970's, the wheels were essentially coming off the bus for her. The wake-up call should have been her "accidental" shooting. But I'm getting ahead of the story.

For now, I'd like to explore my television side to the 1960s. Like most of America, I was a regular small screen junkie. But this went beyond research for my show. More correctly, I was simply mesmerized by the phenomenon. After all, this pop culture development had even changed America's eating habits, introducing such new terms (and customs) as the "TV dinner" and "TV tray"—which unfortunately probably eliminated a lot of family small talk at supper.

My obsession with TV back then reminds me of Ella's boarding house and a regular named Alice Sebold, who used to talk about "The Almost Moon." I never found out if Alice was one of Ella's brothel women or just another down-and-out stray my grandmother was fond of collecting. But Alice was a beautiful, fragile redhead of indeterminate age, who had these long showgirl legs to which I'm so partial. She would sit on the rag rug floor near Ella's pot belly stove, with those wonderful gams drawn up under her, and relate, "The moon is whole all the time, but we can't see it. What we see is an almost moon or a not-quite moon… We plan out lives based on its invisible rhythms and tides." Well, back in the 1960s, I saw television as having the same invisible pull on me. Those magical broadcast waves were always out there, and they seemed to dictate that I not only contribute to their production with my own show, but that I also watch as many other programs as possible.

With my bank of three television sets on the wall, for yesteryear's three main networks, I would monitor all programming simultaneously… for hours. Given my long-time interest in gadgetry, I was also taping shows years before that technology became standard fare in American homes. All this viewing pushed me into a sort of video unreality, where my dreams sometimes even had television credits. It was sort of like having Lucy and Ricky chasing Fred and Ethel around nonstop in your noodle. Everything became slightly twisted in a comical manner, like an old burlesque joke of mine which Georgia sometimes repeated as her favorite drunken mantra during our desert days: "Oedipus, schmedipus, as long as they love their mother."

Surprisingly, given that I had reduced my own television work load to a hectic, two-day schedule, my Nielsen rating numbers from the 1960s were amazing. After struggling for much of the 1950s, I was in the top ten for most of the '60s, charting as high as #3 in 1962-63 (behind *The Beverly Hillbillies* and *Candid Camera*) and #2 in 1966-67 (behind *Bonanza*).

I now sometimes wander how I managed that success. Comedians have a regular ritual called "getting in the bubble," when you take a few moments of pre-showtime calm to get in the killer mode for an unpredictable live audience. But no matter how many times you've done it in the past, an act/routine has to be polished or it goes away—it just packs up and catches the next boat, like MacArthur leaving the Philippines. Thus, I often worried that my two-day television work "week" was not enough time, but the ratings seemed to suggest otherwise. (As a closing comment on the killer mode—my best ad-lib involved the lovely Marilyn Monroe. She arrived late one night at the Sands, swathed in white ermine. With a hush coming across the crowd, I immediately cracked, "Marilyn, I told you to sit in the truck.")

Maybe my two-day schedule worked because I was so focused during this time. I slept little and ate less. Except for an occasional candy bar or 10-cent package of soda crackers, I would consume nothing except hot peppers—which killed my desire for food. See, there was no use in my eating, since I could never keep anything down. After endless rehearsing and then taping, I was an exhausted, beat man. With clothes wet enough to wring out, I would rehash the program with my producer, get a bite to eat, clean up, and drive back to Palm Springs from Los Angeles.

The only real fun time during this grueling two-day period was what came to be called the *Red Skelton Dirty Hour*, when I got a chance to do one rehearsal with some blue material. Naturally, I flirted with a certain degree of hypocrisy here, since I'm famous for always advocating clean humor. But the *Dirty Hour* was a nice release for me, and it wasn't open to the general public—only to CBS personnel and special guests. Plus, to be honest, I'm drawn to bawdy humor in private. As I noted before, this is a legacy from my earthy, brothel-running Grandma Ella.

My most often cited provocative crack, however, occurred at a Beverly Hills party hosted by John Wayne. Georgia and I were standing with Humphrey Bogart when an extremely sexy actress passed by. This woman could have caused cardiac arrest in a yak. When I asked Bogart who she was, he answered, "I don't know her name but Tyrone Power says she's the best cocksucker in town." With that, I patted Georgia's head and told Humphrey, "Aw, now you've gone and hurt Georgia's feelings."

Bogart dearly loved that line, and must have repeated it to half of Hollywood, because through the years countless movie insiders have asked me about its authenticity. I know it's disrespectful to Georgia, and part of me feels sorry about that. But my second wife's promiscuity, which I'll address more in the next chapter, would often cause me to be rather biting in my references to and/or about her.

Regardless, while I was sometimes criticized for hypocrisy on the *Dirty Hour*, such as in a nasty mid-1960s piece from *TV Guide*, most people just saw it as another example of my quirky nature. Personally, I was more offended with some of the things that passed for humor by the late 1960s, such as the political satire of the *Smothers Brothers Comedy Hour*. Any time you have to publicly shock people into a laugh, or to get their attention, you're wrong. It's not advanced humor at all. Still, maybe I was just getting long-of-tooth. My own teenage daughter, a fan of the Smothers Brothers, ironically quoted one of my own jokes back to me: "You know how to tell when you're getting old? When your broad mind changes places with your narrow waist."

On a happier note, my 1960s television program gave me a great deal of pleasure, especially the mid-'60s show "Concert in Pantomime," which co-starred my internationally acclaimed mime friend Marcel Marceau. Hosted by Maurice Chevalier, we performed before a black-tie studio audience of prominent guests. Marceau and I alternated with four solo sketches before combining for a mimed version of *Pinocchio*. This was the first time most of America had seen the French mime—something of which I was very proud. Several critics had thought it would be over the general public's head, but the ratings were great. (That reminds me of a Minstrel show I was in that bombed. One of my fellow players said it was "over their heads." But my old Vincennes mentor, Clarence Stout, who produced the show, had the perfect comeback: "It wasn't over their heads—the audience ducked!")

My "Concert in Pantomime" had Marceau appearing as his clown-tramp character Bip, with white face and pants and striped tight shirt. He performed the signature routines, "The Tug of War," "Bip the Dice Player," "Bip the Skater," and his show stopper—"Bip as a Mask Maker." The latter sketch is about the removal of a hideous mask… and the revelation of the true person underneath. The *New York Times* described it as "Genius." I couldn't agree more. Compared to Marceau, I feel like a pair of brown shoes at a formal.

For the record, my poor man's pantomime was applied to "A Girl Dressing in the Morning," "Mixing the Salad," "The Drunken Doctor in Surgery," and "The Old Man Watching the Parade." With the exception of the last routine, which has become one of my most popular and universal everyman bits, I managed to add some broad humor into the other pantomimes, such as sneezing into the salad. Each of these sketches had been honed during what I saw as the highlight each week of my television program—the "Silent Spot."

As you might suppose, I most enjoyed my 1960s television program when the comic focus was keyed to silence, from Marcel to a 1962 visit from Harpo Marx. The mad Marx mute played the guardian angel to my hen-pecked character, George Appleby. Paradoxically, while my favorite comedy figure remained the originally silent tramp Freddie the Freeloader, by the '60s I had him talking a bit. As much as I liked pantomime, I didn't want to wear out my welcome with general audiences.

Though I often had a rather prickly relationship with my writers—pure jealousy; I hated to admit I got any assistance—I did always admire something one of my writers (Larry Rhine) once wrote about the tramp: "Freddie was our favorite. There was depth to this lovable rogue. Chaplinesque. A have-not but in his mind a have-everything. A soul in a discarded tin can. Whereas Clem is one joke, a bonehead, Appleby a henpecked spouse... Freddie is a poet, philosopher, make-doer." Yes, I really liked that, especially the "Chaplinesque" comment.

Fittingly, Larry was also a huge Chaplin fan, a fact that helped cement a friendship with a young Woody Allen, when the comedian made some early films on the West Coast. I mention this as a segue to including a great Chaplin insight Woody had once shared with Larry, concerning the Tramp costume/persona: "I'm sure there was no calculation with Chaplin [over Tramp symbolism], even though people would say, 'Well, the moustache represents vanity, and the oversize shoes this, and the walk that.' I believe what was going through Chaplin's mind was, 'Hey, I bet this will be funny: I'll wear these big pants and these big shoes and a moustache and I'll look silly.'" Years before, Chaplin had shared with me a story remarkably close to this brilliant Woody assumption.

Despite all Larry's attention to pantomime, one of my most memorable programs from the decade featured a special monologue—my take on what the "Pledge of Allegiance" meant. Though inspired by one of my Vincennes educators, I think my "Pledge" struck a responsive chord with contemporary viewers distraught over the then recent assassinations of Martin Luther King, Jr. and Robert Kennedy, as well as the controversy associated with the Vietnam War. Ultimately, the "Pledge" became a resume item for me, spawning a minor hit record, sometimes being included in my comedy concert material. I was equally troubled by the chaos America was then experiencing, and the support generated by my interpretation of the "Pledge" meant a great deal to me.

Just as the "Pledge" was born of my Vincennes days, my most favored Palm Springs neighbor was also from Vincennes—Ida Mae Skelton, the woman the world mistakenly believed was my biological mother. Murr, as I called her, had done her best to raise me under the most adverse circumstances—not to mention murderous step-brothers, and I returned the favor in her later years. My early film success had first allowed me to bring Murr to Hollywood. And when Georgia and I relocated to Palm Springs, I moved Ida Mae down, also.

She was a funny old gal that liked to drink beer and have a good time. Though Murr's mother-in-law, Ella, was the woman that most impacted my young years, Murr was a last link to that past, and I spoiled her. But she didn't care about material things; Ida Mae was just happy to have a nice home. When Murr died in 1966, she still had a closet full of my unopened gifts. Plus, there were stacks of $100 bills I'd given her taped to the bottom of her bathroom floor mat! I repeat, she was a funny old gal that liked to drink beer and have a good time... and I loved her dearly.

Murr also kept me grounded. For a short Hollywood time, I became full of myself. I guess my defense, beyond the multiple follies attached to being young, was that no one had ever made me the center of the world—so I took it upon myself to briefly become that egotistical center. But this wasn't good for my comedy, not to mention there's always hot new competition. As some columnist once wrote, "Hollywood breeds stars like minks." Thus, my creative process works best when I maintain a humble frozen rope of memory back to my Vincennes loser childhood—mining it for the pathos-orientated humor which became my signature.

Stormy Weather

We're a species with amnesia, or as my profane Grandma Ella used to say, "We're victims of CRS—'can't remember *shit*.'"

IF THE ABOVE QUOTE IS TRUE, and I think it is, amnesia also doubles as a form of self-protection. The person who spends too much time with his memories flirts with relocating to crazy town. This makes writing an autobiography a decidedly dangerous vocation. So even when one is dropping that plumb line to the past, painful events can sometimes only be revisited through selective memory. To paraphrase a line noted earlier, "It might not have occurred exactly in this manner, but that's how I choose to remember it."

Still, this book has been my first attempt to address a host of painful events with as much honesty as I can muster. This continues to be a difficult task for me, since I've always tended to exaggerate and embroider the incidents of my life. This was done to both psychologically protect me from my embarrassing brothel beginnings, as well as not wanting to disappoint the expectations of my audience. Ella, a most "creative" spinner of allegedly true tales herself, liked to translate the phrase: "He gave colorful accounts of his exploits" as: "He was a liar." Be that as it may, as a born storyteller, it was fun to create an imaginative alternative to my dysfunctional real life. So my alcoholic grocer father suddenly became a world famous clown, and the brothel birth disappeared. I belabor these facts again—confessions I've shared previously—because I'm about to wrestle with some of my most painful past inventions. Having said that, I promise to still pepper this account with as much humor as possible—like Groucho Marx on Red Bull.

Before, however, I go down my confession path, let me discuss something that no amount of creative tweaking or bald lying could make go away—the 1971 cancellation of my television program after 20 consecutive years. I was really canned twice. CBS dropped me in 1970, with NBC then picking me up for a final season. But given my long history with CBS, this was the cancellation that hurt the most. I was a pioneering victim of demographics. Despite high ratings, the network felt my Nielsen numbers were too small town/rural and old. CBS was out to attract a younger, urban-based audience. For someone whose mantra could be: "I only come to life when there are people watching me entertain," the cancellation felt like a death sentence. Also, like an old Mafia don, I am all about *respect*. You only get respect in this world through your own creative ability. I had given CBS years of "creative ability," and huge profits, yet they had unceremoniously fired me. For me, it doesn't get anymore disrespectful.

To this very day, I cannot seem to let go of my anger about the cancellation. Sadly, this bitterness has indirectly resulted in the negation of my television legacy. I own the rights to my programs, and because of CBS' action, I've never allowed the shows to be rebroadcast in syndication. Thus, while television historians often link me with Lucille Ball and Jackie Gleason as pivotal small screen comedy pioneers, my programs have been off the air for years. In contrast, *I Love Lucy* and *The Honeymooners* have remained on television in nearly continuous reruns since the 1950s. The mix of high quality comedy and familiarity has cemented the unique pop culture status of Lucy and Ralph Kramden. Meanwhile, I've shot myself in the foot by keeping Freddie, Clem, and all the rest of my comedy characters off the air. I'm currently flirting with changing that—maybe dusting the old episodes off. We'll see. But the bitterness lingers.

Now, I told you that story in order to tell you this one. The death of my television life contributed to the end of my second marriage. As often happens in all walks of life, when the career is in crisis, so goes the personal life, too. Almost twenty years before, when my television program last struggled, my marriage to Georgia had gone through its most publicized problem period. This time neither the show nor the relationship would survive. Naturally, there was another woman; there usually is. But as Ella used to say, "One cannot, nor should one try to, impose conditions on love. The heart wants what the heart wants." Yet, I'm getting ahead of the story.

As I look back on a long life, Georgia was my great love, even more than my first wife, Edna—my inspired muse and loyal, insightful advisor. In the beginning, Georgia made me feel like a schoolboy. Our dating days, in wartime Hollywood, filled me with such passion I seemed to float like a balloon figure in the Macy's Thanksgiving Day Parade. Given my entertainment successes, we were two redheads who had the world by the tail. Then she gave me our beloved Valentina and little Richard, and my joys knew no bounds. But I was a driven man, and I slowly began to ignore her for the sake of my comedy and assorted creative hobbies. I still needed her around, but only as my supportive audience of one.

When she complained about our nightclub days being over, that we never went out anymore, I comically alibied that if one tried to maintain the level of fun of attention consistent with early courtship, one would have a heart attack. Georgia gave me a funny, sad smile, nodded, and walked to the liquor cabinet. After mixing herself a stiff drink—she knew no other kind—Georgia turned and said, "We'll see."

"We'll see" soon translated into periodic affairs, and an ever escalating amount of drinking. Little Richard's death seemed to be as low as it could get for Georgia, but I later discovered her pit was bottomless. As my friend Oscar Levant, another victim of depression and various addictions, once wrote, "There is no such thing as a lowest point." But our son's death made Georgia even more dependent upon alcohol and various prescription drugs, and more promiscuous. Like a bad "B" movie, I once even caught her in bed with our gardener. She was always sorry, and I always forgave her. Then Georgia would drink some more and be on to her next affair. I paid her back by occasionally straying myself, but mainly I just became more self-absorbed in work. However, my anger sometimes came out by trashing Georgia in public. For instance, whenever I needed something retrieved from home, if there was a crowd around, I'd yell at my studio errand boy, "Remember to knock first at the bedroom; Georgia might have a customer." I know it was a heck of a habit to get into, but somehow it helped me cope. Instead of a married couple, we just happened to be two people living under the same roof.

Because Richard's death brought us so low, the move to Palm Springs seemed to help for a time. A reclusive life brought us together more, as well as reducing sexual temptation for Georgia. But again, my own addiction to creative hobbies soon had me once again cloistered away from her. Even the daily love letters to her, which I initiated after our Palm Springs relocation, probably added to Georgia's stress. I expected her to immediately read and compare them to past letters. Love somehow became drudgery. But I didn't realize how desperate she still was until my summer 1966 booking at Las Vegas' Sands Hotel.

During my midnight show Georgia "accidentally" shot herself with a .38 caliber handgun in our suite. Valentina and her college boyfriend, Art Coleman, who had accompanied us to Vegas, were the first on the scene. They had been preparing something to eat in the suite's kitchen when they heard Georgia moaning in one of the bedrooms. Art investigated and had Valentina call the hotel doctor. Though I managed to get it treated as an accident by the authorities, we all knew it was a suicide attempt. A decade later Georgia would take her own life with that same pistol—one of many from my gun collection.

Though she suffered from chronic depression, the triggering device for this attempted suicide was an argument we had. I was upset over a low-cut dress she planned to wear that night—one of those gravity-defying things, sort of a negligee negligently worn. So I bawled the hell out of her, cracks like, "You're always dressed to the teeth, assuming your teeth are situated in you abdomen!" But my excessive anger was really tied to having just found out she was sleeping with the president of the Sands. Flash forward to the ten o'clock show and my insistence about introducing her. Georgia was unhappy about this, feeling she had gained weight (all that drinking) and did not look her best. But introduce her I did, and still livid about this latest affair, I not only made a crack about her weight, I think I might have made another trampish comment, too.

Years later, I rehashed all this and more with Valentina—what she still calls her parents' "screwy marriage." Her take was that Georgia had no life of her own with me. She reminded me that I would even wake her mom up with all my attention needs, such as the daily love letters or the latest clown painting. And since Georgia had trouble sleeping anyway, that got her into more pills. Valentina feels that I had broken the spirit of an initially very spunky woman. My daughter says she even told Georgia, "You've lost your identity doing everything for Dad!"

As hard as it is for me to accept this assessment, and Valentina offered it with as much love as possible, I'm afraid she is right. Shortly after this heart-to-heart with my daughter, I had been going through a file of private papers. I came across a memoir Georgia had written back in 1934, when she was all of 12 years old. Valentina's comment about her mother's initial spunkiness is more than documented in Georgia's childhood autobiography. For example, just listen to all the piss and vinegar she brings to the following passage: "My father is always telling me what to do and I fly into him like a fox after a chicken, then the fight is on. All of a sudden my mother appears and I pity my dad. That's the way it goes. I boss my younger sister Maxine and Daddy around and Mother bosses us all. Maxine and I have grand fights together and sometimes she gets a bloody nose. It seems like one of us ought to be a prize fighter. Maybe this is because I like to be noticed like other children, so I'm always trying to attract attention, either by my fists or my wisecracks. Mother smiles and blames it on my red hair—she has red hair, too."

It's sometimes hard to deal with my guilt over Georgia. Maybe if there had been something like a Betty Ford Clinic back in the 1960s, things could have turned out differently. But sadly, as noted before, I never put much stock in outside help—I always felt the individual had to do it all. Georgia did see a psychiatrist once or twice after her 1966 suicide attempt. But then I cut her off. I think my excuse was something like, "She'll just fool them anyway."

I also remember reading one of Oscar Levant's humor books about this time, *The Memoirs of an Amnesiac*, and he painted a pretty grim picture of most treatment programs for depression and/or chemical addictions. In fact, it reminded me of that old joke about hospitals, "If you don't want a nurse, ring for one." So I had my reasons. But I should have paid more attention to another section of Oscar's book, where he talked about addiction. In recently revisiting that text, I was touched by how his comments sounded like Georgia. For instance, "I remember the never-ending desire for those drugs which would give me instant oblivion, the wild and neurotic quest for unconsciousness."

Even when Georgia had disappeared into her booze and/or ill oblivion, when she would sometimes ramble on assorted subjects, what she called her "drunkalogues," there was an aura of wit and sweetness about her. I once overheard her tell our cook, "We're a family just like yours... if you lived in a movie." That reminds me of something an AA friend once told me, that addicts are often overachievers with a bad self-image. That was Georgia, and I made it worse by demanding so much attention for all my projects.

I should add, that for all the dysfunctional scenes I've described, life with Georgia during our final decade of marriage was still sometimes wonderful. In going back over my bound love letters to her, I'll cite just one example of this. The following 1969 note was inspired by our watching a late movie on television: "We were safe in our beds, free to talk, laugh and grumble a bit, to read and have a cold glass of milk with an oatmeal cookie. My, we sure live it up! If anyone says we are hokey, they had better add 'and healthy, too.' You have never been more understanding, more loveable, more kind. When we go over our notes to each other we will find not one cross word. How we are blessed with love. It's like love should be, not talked about or read about, but lived."

One of the hardest things in life is to just enjoy it. For a long time I've had so many positives going for me that I work at absorbing all the good. So when time with Georgia went well, I tended to wax poetic. But the bad times often found me with my head in the sand, or writing nasty "love letters" that I never shared with Georgia. I was in as much denial as she was, with my "drug" of choice being nonstop creative activity. There's an old saying that goes, "Wise men avert their eyes and move on." But one might substitute "cowardly" for "wise" and apply the motto to me. I sacrificed a great deal for the creative process.

Ironically, my attempt to socialize more for Georgia's sake resulted in me meeting the woman who became my third wife. Georgia and I were members of the Palm Springs Tamarisk Country Club, with our home being adjacent to the club's golf course. But we had never really taken advantage of the organization's fine dining services, or socializing with the other show business people that frequented the club. We then started dining with composer Frederick Loewe, who collaborated with lyricist Alan Jay Lerner on such hit Broadway musicals as *Brigadoon*, *Paint Your Wagon*, *My Fair Lady*, and *Camelot*.

Now, the 60-plus Loewe's constant companion at these dinners was a secretary/girlfriend half his age—Lothian Toland. Georgia nicknamed Lothian the "nymphet," because as my second wife was fond of telling anyone who would listen, "You wouldn't believe how that girl went after Red." At first it seemed quite innocent, though I was obviously flattered by the attention of a younger woman whose appearance reminded me of Edna. After that, as they say, it was what it was. We were soon meeting on the sly; we even had a secret phone code—three rings meant it was Lothian, or Lothy, as I nicknamed her.

Georgia's health issues, often related to and/or exacerbated by her alcoholism, meant she was frequently hospitalized, providing numerous rendezvous possibilities for Lothy and me. In addition, I practically had a separate residence with my teahouse/office. Eventually, any pretense was dropped, and I began spending most nights at Lothy's nearby condominium. But during the day I would return to the teahouse and play at my various hobbies. I became an expert at ignoring my flawed behavior, or I alibied by saying, "We're all flawed." And for a time I even used the loopy excuse that comedians were somehow attracted to addictive types, and that justified our moving on. My evidence was the marital track record of my comedy gods, Charlie Chaplin and Groucho Marx. Of their collective seven wives, six ended up being alcoholics. It now seems so obvious that living with comedians *causes* these problems.

Though I had obviously stopped writing my daily love letters to Georgia, she kept writing to me. I never read them at the time. But given our habit of having everything bound, I am still in possession of those letters. And for some perverse reason, all these years after our divorce and her subsequent 1976 suicide, I'm drawn to this sad correspondence. Let me quote briefly from a 1971 note, the year I filed for divorce: "I would be honored if you kept my letters. Perhaps ten years from now you may see the blinding brilliance of my love and respect for you down through our lives together. You dwell now on only the unhappy days and forget our joyous ones. You say your daughter believed we gave her no proper childhood, yet our home movies and remembrances of happy times prove her wrong. These surviving letters to you, dear, dear Big Red prove my deeply sustained powerful devotion, admiration and respect for you all this time."

As gut-wrenching as this reads, I'm not ashamed to say that I can somehow live with it today. I'm not proud of what I did, but I have worked through the guilt. However, I could not have handled reading Georgia's love letters at the time. Indeed, I eventually fabricated a whopper of a tale to cover my guilt. I implied to new friends and contacts that Georgia and I were still married at the time of her death. Plus, I claimed that Georgia was dying of cancer. Those words which I had spoken at that long ago press conference had never been more true: "If you want a good story—talk to me. If you want the facts—talk to Edna."

young new cheering section, my special audience of one. I realized that I only had a limited amount of time, and if this was to be the best it's ever gonna be, I needed to get back to real "live" audiences. So with Lothy's blessing I started playing a lot of college dates. (I also wanted to show CBS that I was popular with young fans.) And the joke was on the network, because I soon won a college "entertainer of the year" award.

Ella used to tell me, "You can never win an argument with a woman." Wiser words have never been spoken. But I should be quick to add that I had no real complaints with any of my wives. All three were loyal to the point of being Skelton watchdogs, ever protective of my creative time, even when it hurt the various relationships. Oh, Georgia did some really desperate things near the end of our marriage, like taking a lover of her own, or even sexually experimenting with lesbian liaisons. But that was just a payback response to my carrying on with Lothy.

Naturally, all this was hard on my only surviving child, Valentina. But even before my divorce from Georgia, my daughter and I were often at odds. As a teenager in the hippie 1960s, she had some issues with our wealth. And I had also made some rather nasty public comments about the counterculture. Ironically, I now realize that the artistic life I was then leading in Palm Springs was very hippie-like.

While Valentina and I eventually worked through all this, her mother and I were more than a little unfair about her love life. We basically attempted an almost arranged marriage, as Victorian as that now sounds. Our candidate for her was millionaire oil man Ed Pauley. We wanted Valentina with someone well-established *outside* of show business. But she was just as spunky as a young Georgia; Valentina married someone we were totally against, Carlos J. Alonso, a bouncer at a private membership-only nightclub called the "Climax." Even that title offended me, especially since Valentina also worked there part-time. I did eventually get Carlos a job at CBS' local film department. Their marriage did not last, but it did produce my beloved granddaughter Sabrina.

Sadly, I all but ignored Valentina for years during the 1970s and 1980s. What an awful confession for a father to make. My divorce from her mother, and Valentina's from Carlos, had both occurred in the early 1970s. But just as we were starting to get past these events, Georgia committed suicide in 1976. Oh, there were still the occasional cards and letters, and I sometimes sent money. But our only official "family" activity was at Thanksgiving, and even that was always in a restaurant.

As my previous track record with wives and Buster Keaton has demonstrated, when I move on I tend to erase the past. Georgia and I used to have a little ritual where we actually washed offending parties from our lives—a practice I continued with Lothy. While I never did this to my daughter, for too long I treated her like the proverbial black sheep of the family. Isn't that rich? Me, the son of a prostitute, getting superior with my only surviving child. Ella would have read me the riot act. She had this saying which is so applicable here, "There's no pixie dust or anything. There's no magic formula. You just have to do the right thing!" Or, she might have hit me with the line she often used when someone close disappointed her, "You'd make a perfect stranger!"

Eventually, I tried to help Valentina out by making her manager of a store selling my art work. But I even managed to screw that up. Because she didn't have any experience in sales, my organization didn't allow her to sell the original clown paintings. And you can only make so much money selling prints and Red Skelton coloring books. Unfortunately, I didn't keep close tabs on the girl, and poor Valentina had trouble getting in touch with me. See, I still avoid the phone—always have. Edna always handled everything in the early years, and I saw no reason to change with the passage of time.

Remember my old phone story? When I first signed with MGM, studio chief Louis B. Mayer became upset that I would never take a call. Finally, he cornered me on a sound stage and asked, "What did you do before Edna?" Though my answer was dead serious, it was one of the few times I ever made the old S.O.B. crack a smile, "Before Edna started managing me, nobody ever called."

By the time Valentina was trying to track me down, Lothy manned my phone. Though she was a very devoted wife, she was also my most controlling spouse, and she insulated me from any and all distractions—including both Valentina and later my granddaughter Sabrina. But I don't blame Lothy; I'm the one that set up this privacy system. Lothy was merely orchestrating my wishes. Consequently, I wasn't always there for my family. Undoubtedly, the situation was probably made more awkward by the fact Lothy wasn't much older than Valentina.

Sometimes I wonder how I could have let such things happen. It's like I'm a poor imitation of myself. I look and sound like Red Skelton, but I've done stuff that doesn't register as me. I'm reminded of a story Chaplin once told me. At the beginning of his amazing screen career, "Chaplinitis" had so swept the country that there were Charlie Chaplin look-alike contests being held in film theatres across the country. As a lark, Charlie actually entered one of these competitions in a neighborhood theatre in West Hollywood… and finished third! Like my not acting as myself towards Valentina, Chaplin had been shocked that not one but two impersonators out-Charlied him. It's all rather frustrating, or as the Irishman shouted outside the pub, "Come out and fight while I'm in a temper."

I think I lost my way with Valentina, for a while, for reasons that probably went beyond my ongoing needs for artistic privacy. The much younger Lothy was my fountain of youth, *My Picture of Dorian Gray*. Just before I got involved with her, I had one of those funny/sad mirror moments that come to everyone over forty-five or fifty: "I'm not going to die young." Anyway, this is one of those compromising moments I mentioned earlier, where more autonomy is given the new, much younger wife than you would have imagined possible just a few years earlier. Oh, to have the romantic ego of Bob Hope's screen persona. I think my all-time favorite Hope line is the following warning he gave to one of his leading ladies: "Never leave me, Baby, you'd only suffer!"

Regardless, we all have regrets, and sometimes we play mind games to avoid them. But as a philosopher once said (or maybe it was my plumber), "The people that try to live two places at once (figuratively or literally) end up no place." Thus, in the next/last chapter I will attempt to share some closing thoughts on a shaky life finally anchored—thanks to this book—in one place. I'll try to avoid any heavy memoir messages, like a learning soufflé made with lead. Given my background, all thee references to summing up remind me of a comic line from my pantomimist friend Marcel Marceau. He enjoys saying, "You know, my last words will be my first."

Exit Laughing

> "I think Americans were fond of my humorist father, Irvin Cobb, because he was Mr. Average Citizen. He was themselves, grown famous."
>
> – Elisabeth Cobb

I STOLE THE TITLE OF THIS CHAPTER, and the subtitle of my memoir, from the autobiography of a neglected humorist I loved as a child—Irvin Cobb. The above quote from his daughter is also an Everyman philosophy I've tried to apply to my own success. Cobb was a populist but not in the naïve, idealistic manner of Frank Capra and *It's a Wonderful Life*. Oh, Cobb believed in the people like "Mr. Capracorn," too. But instead of the common man always doing the right thing automatically, Cobb felt, as I do, that the normal Joe sometimes needed herding to get down the correct democratic path.

This more realistic approach to populism was also the hallmark of Cobb's close friend and celebrated humorist Will Rogers, as well as famed director John Ford—with whom both humorists worked. Indeed, my favorite example of this more calculated populism comes in a Ford film without either Cobb or Rogers—*Young Mr. Lincoln*. Like many Americans, I'm a huge fan of Lincoln, with many biographies of the 16th president in my library. Regardless, the *Young, Mr. Lincoln* scene I dearly love finds Henry Fonda, as the title character, calmly talking an angry lynch mob back to their senses. These are not normally bad men, and Fonda's Lincoln uses humor and an appeal to the group's innate goodness to save them from themselves. That, to me, is a moving, true-to-life take on history. The wise guidance needed by the populist common man, as demonstrated here by Lincoln, is also winningly summarized in the name of Cobb's most famous character, Judge Priest.

Though my interest in Lincoln goes back to my Hoosier childhood, fueled by the fact that Abe also spent his formative years in southern Indiana, I have experienced other connections through the years to this beloved president. For one thing, Georgia's father was the spitting image of Lincoln, which tended to minimize arguing with the man. I always half expected him to wear a stovepipe hat, too. Like Lincoln, I'm an insomniac easily troubled by injustice. And sadly, my third wife now seems to be acting rather like Abe's provocative spouse Mary Todd. Let's just say I've recently received some notes from my wife which wouldn't pass for love letters. I wonder what would happen if they ever found their way into some sort of Skelton university archive? [Editor's note—they briefly did. Please see the Bibliography.] Regardless, my philosophy has always been, if things don't make you bitter, they'll make you better.

As a final footnote to this interest in Lincoln, what follows is my favorite comic story from *the* populist president. Lincoln had trouble finding a Union general capable of winning any Civil War battles. Just when he was finally having some success with Ulysses S. Grant, critics started complaining Grant was a drunk, and offered proof. "Well," said Lincoln, with just a trace of a twinkle in his eye, "you needn't waste your time getting proof; you just find out, to oblige me, what brand of whiskey Grant drinks, because I want to send a barrel of it to each of my generals." That finished the crusade against Grant. Lincoln once also offered the best take on this crafty form of populism I so admire: "They say I tell a great many stories; I reckon I do, but I have found in the course of a long experience that common people, take them as they run, are more easily informed through the medium of a broad comic illustration than in any other way, and as to what the hypercritical few may think, I don't care."

I know this is probably taking the long way around the barn as far as a chapter opening, especially a *final* chapter. But including this Cobb/Lincoln connection is important to me; since one's memory is often faulty and always changing, I'm merely adding these things as they come to me. Grandma Ella used to say, "To remember is to misremember." Well, while I've never wavered about my Cobb/Lincoln thoughts on people, this attempt to pen my memoirs reminds me just how much I've forgotten. Adding such important material so late in the book merely underlines that fact. Though there will undoubtedly be additional late additions of memory-delayed material to this chapter, I won't overdo it. There's nothing worse than staying too long at the fair. Plus, it's probably best to not reveal everything about myself, always maintain a little mystery, I say. Naturally, after my tales of being a brothel baby with a red light madame for a grandma, one might assume I've simply penned a tell all. But you'd be surprised. What I've shared has not been for shock value. This late-in-life memoir has been an attempt to finally come clean with myself on a host of events I either invented and/or prettified.

Since the last chapter so focused on the personal, I'd like to add some closing comments on what I used to affectionately call my career. If legends write their own stories, clowns like me have to cobble together whatever passes for an autobiography. Life isn't simple—it should be, but it isn't. Anyway, after I entered television in 1951, I let my movie career slide. Truth be told, I'd lost interest in films long before that. Poor Buster Keaton, my MGM mentor, learned this the hard way. As I noted earlier, I was more focused on staying in my movie dressing room and writing gags for my old radio program—the foundation of my later television show.

With 1950s TV demanding 39 new episodes a season, even if a small screen star wanted to double as a movie actor, it was hard to maintain a career in both media. However, MGM simplified the process by firing me after my alcoholic meltdown in 1953—when the ratings for my television program went into the toilet. Oh, there would be occasional other films, but I eventually turned into Mr. Cameo, including a comic turn in Sinatra's Rat Pack picture, *Ocean's Eleven*. But my favorite cameo was also the last movie I ever appeared in—1965's *Those Magnificent Men in Their Flying Machines, or: How I Flew From London to Paris in 25 Hours and 11 Minutes*. Ironically, the title was funnier than much of the film, but the critics were more than kind about my opening prologue. I represent early man in a series of pioneering attempts at flying—all spectacular failures.

The *Los Angeles Times* said, "It is more than a coincidence that the chap who inspires the most merriment—and in the briefest time—is Red Skelton." The *Hollywood Reporter* credited my occasional brief other appearances in the film "shrewdly inserted" running gags on man's frustrated attempts to fly, while the *Hollywood Citizen-News*' "only gripe" was "over wasting the talents of Red Skelton" through under use.

The aforementioned inserts had been inspired by humorist Robert Benchley's comparable use in the Bob Hope-Bing Crosby picture *The Road to Utopia*, the best of the "Road" series. I had been a fan of Benchley's since his 1930s "How To" short subject series had given Edna ideas for many of my best sketches. But admiration for Bob in the entertainment community was common. For example, Alfred Hitchcock so enjoyed Benchley's comically professorial persona that he cast the humorist as a drunken reporter in *Foreign Correspondent*, a political thriller released on the eve of our entry in World War II. But Bob's influence on Hitchcock didn't end there. When the master of suspense later hosted his own television series, he patterned his dry, tongue-firmly-in-cheek opening and closing remarks—the best part of the series—on the great Benchley.

Though I will always feel that 1948's *A Southern Yankee* is my best starring feature, *The Clown* would take the cigar as the most memorable 1950s vehicle in which I was top-billed. It holds a special place in my heart for a couple of reasons. It was my most Chaplin-like movie, and my daughter Valentina called it her favorite. I had taken her to a re-issue of the film during my son Richard's fatal bout with cancer in the late 1950s. Georgia and I had been showering so much attention on our son that I made a concerted effort to do some special things with Valentina—just the two of us. Of course, my dying at the film's close came as a bit of a shock to her at the time—she would have been ten or eleven. Even then, she had a grip like a vice, and I feared for my fingers.

The Clown was a loose remake of *The Champ*—a sentimental 1931 tale about a washed-up, self-destructive boxer, played by Wallace Beery (who won an Oscar in the part). His only ongoingly loyal supporter is a young son, a part effectively played by 1930s child star Jackie Cooper. My version follows the same sad pattern, only I'm a comedian down-on-his-luck. Tim Considine, a later regular on television's *My Three Sons*, is the devoted son. This updated tearjerker (my character dies after a successful television comeback) still manages to showcase a great deal of comedy. For instance, when my agent in the movie reminisces about our early days in the business, the film cuts to actual footage of my Keaton-created inventive ballet sketch in *Bathing Beauty*, from the drill sergeant-like instructor, to the sticky paper passed among the dancers. I also reprise one of my early "How To" bits from the feature—*Having Wonderful Time*, a comic tutoring session on how different people go up and down steps. This routine seemed to especially charm little Valentina.

My *Clown* reviews were so positive that I thought lightning would strike twice, that like Wallace Beery, I would also win an Oscar for this rich part. The *Los Angeles Examiner* critic wrote, "This is Red's greatest acting triumph to date, and it makes one wonder if there is anything the irrepressible master of nonsense cannot do in the realm of the theater." The *Hollywood Reporter* added, "Skelton's performance compels recognition of his genuine acting skills, demonstrating that he is a consummate artist as well as a great comic." But just when you start scribbling an Academy Award acceptance speech… you don't even get nominated. Still, the kind notices meant a great deal to me at the time, since I had been going through such a difficult time with my TV show.

Drinking heavily at that time, when I wasn't climbing trees and shooting guns, I retreated to my painting. In fact, it wasn't until I was drunk that Picasso's Cubism started to make sense to me. After some study—for no better reason than a distraction from my troubles—I also enjoyed Picasso's insightfully comic take on Cubism—"Traditional perspective and illusion are abandoned in favor of analysis of a subject from all perspectives… simultaneously." Granted, I still didn't like modern art. To me, form should never be more important than a representational subject, but I do appreciate an artist with a sense of humor. Earthy comic Buddy Hackett once told me, "Picasso's a fuckin' comedian. Look at his pictures. Every broad has six tits and seven eyes. I half expect to see him in Vegas any day now!"

To carry Buddy's analogy a bit further, some of Picasso's interviews are pretty comical, too, once you get past the fact he talks in the third person, and elevates himself to god-like status. Here's Picasso critiquing his own work: "If you note all the different shapes, sizes and colors of models he works from, you can understand his confusion. He doesn't know what he wants. No wonder his style is so ambiguous. It's like God's work. God is really only another artist. He invented the aardvark (I think God got bad advice on that one), the giraffe (another goofy one), the elephant, the cat, and other assorted misfits. He has no real style. Why, even last night's sunset was a little flat...."

Picasso and my late movie accomplishments notwithstanding, during the 1950s and 1960s, I largely focused on television. Thus, the 1970s cancellation of my program made me bitter towards CBS and its chief of programming. The day he dies what I'll do on his grave won't pass for flowers. But my anger towards CBS, the network I now refer to as the "Crappy Broadcast System," didn't stop there. I totally rejected the small screen medium.

I went from a man who watched eight to ten hours of television a day on a tier of three sets (so I could see each network's programming at the same time), to a steamed old comic who just stopped viewing. Anger doesn't start to cover it. The situation completely colored my views toward some really progressive new programs, such as *All in the Family*. Since I was off the air, I tended to rain on everybody else's parade. My ongoing tirades against TV soon made me the longest-winded bastard you ever listened to. For a host of reasons I'm too embarrassed to go into right now, I rejected anything that was popular after my cancellation.

It's funny, even when the job's done, the routines of a lifetime refuse to stop. For years I'd been sort of like a chef of comedy in a non-franchise joint. And to extend the metaphor, I daily went to the market (watched the real world) to see what looked good (funny). Despite the loss of my program, the comedy ideas kept coming. I always tell people I hit the road with my one-man show to prove I was still popular with younger viewers, after CBS' numbers claimed my audience was too old. While this was part of the catalyst for my continued performing, I usually neglected to add that I also needed an outlet for the nonstop sketch material that kept coming to me. Yet, this was par for the comedy course. Stan Laurel once told me he was still writing routines for himself and Oliver Hardy five years after his partner died.

Unlike my old days on the road in vaudeville, I no longer traveled with a spouse and an animal menagerie when I entertained in my post-TV years. Lothy, my third wife, usually stayed at home—she tended to feel neglected when my fans were around. And they were around a lot, since I enjoyed people and generally made myself very accessible when I was on the road. For example, many of my concert dates were at college campuses, such as

Indiana's Ball State University. In that sort of setting I invariably stayed at the student center hotel, and wandered about campus. Interacting with young fans is always fun, and frankly, it's good business. One sells a lot of extra tickets. During my last visit to Ball State, this casual sell-promoting resulted in the university actually adding a second show. Like Will Rogers, "I never met a man I didn't like," especially if he also doubled as a paying customer.

It's sad to say but, as my daughter Valentina noted earlier in the text, I was often more open and outgoing with my ever so loyal fans than my own family. While I felt like I owed everything to these affectionate and attentive audiences, I sometimes falsely believed my family was taking advantage of me. For instance, just as I had once made cruel jokes about second wife Georgia's promiscuity, I later made unfair cracks about Valentina being lazy. One such joke had me telling friends or colleagues, "We just had an earthquake out in California." When they would show concern and request more information, I would deadpan, "Yeah, Valentina just got out of bed."

I know, what was I thinking? The poor girl was anything but lazy. When I all but cut her out of my life after marrying Lothy, she had to scramble to get by. Valentina did everything from waitressing to driving a school bus. A millionaire pop, and she's working for tips! I wasn't the best dad to her. I guess it might have been fitting for someone whose opening TV monologue once included the joke, "The best advice for minimizing stress is on any aspirin bottle, 'Take two tablets and keep away from children.'"

Regardless, my previously stated self-therapy reasons for writing this memoir might be questioned when this book appears, given that a young Hoosier scholar is currently working on a biography of me. The author is a professor from Ball State University named David Caine. Thus, some folks might think my book is merely a defensive preventive strike against anything provocative David might turn up. I call him David because I've met and talked to this writer several times on my various visits to Ball State—my favorite home state college, given all the times they've booked me for concerts.

David is a conscientious fellow who helped orchestrate an honorary doctorate for me a few years ago. But obviously, my memoir has nothing to do with any fears I might have over his biography. The guy's one of my biggest fans, for crying out loud. Moreover, I knew nothing about his plans until he recently shared them with me in a letter. Poor boy, his other biographies all deal with long gone comedians, including such favorites of mine as Chaplin, W. C. Fields, and the Marx Brothers, or as David comically phrased it, "the safely dead." I think he's worried about what the consequences of me still being around would be—you know, feeling like he might have to whitewash something to please me.

I wrote him back that I would help where I could, short of dying. I appreciated the doctorate, but there are limits to my vanity. David might also

Club in Los Angeles just a few weeks ago. Like many artists, I have gotten into the habit of taking a photograph of each painting before it's sold or given away. So I asked Jack if he'd send me a picture of my Blacksburg landscape, done so many years before. As a thank you for the trouble, I promised to send him one of my clown lithographs. Well, my copy just arrived, and I have to brag—it isn't half bad, especially given my condition. But I was most amused by my inscription—"To Jack and Julie. Best of luck to real folks. May you always be happy and successful. You doodit, Red Skelton, nut ward 1945."

Despite the humor, that had been a pretty dark time for me. Had this memoir dwelt more on Blacksburg, I think I might have stolen my book title from Woody Allen instead of Irvin Cobb. I've always enjoyed Allen, because so much of his comedy shtick is borrowed from Bob Hope, something Woody readily admits. Anyway, Allen's best picture is his bittersweet romantic comedy *Annie Hall*. But the working title for that film was *Anhedonia*— which means the inability to feel pleasure. That's often an apt description of me, even in seemingly good times. So I would have been comfortable using *Anhedonia* as a title, too.

After I'd largely recovered at Camp Pickett Hospital, I did my first closed-to-the-general-public show, just for troubled GIs, that included racy material. Like my later *Dirty Hour* television rehearsal show at CBS, the comedy was pretty tame by today's standards. But my justification was that these poor patriots desperately needed a comic wake-up call, and I would do whatever it took. So I recycled a few bits from my burlesque days, like "Don't keep a man guessing too long—he's sure to find the answer somewhere else," or "I'm like a lotta men, I want a good woman. But history teaches us good women are no fun.… The only good woman I can recall from school lessons was Betsy Ross. And all she ever made was a flag." Given my lapsed Catholic background, I also had a bit about "spotting two priests dining in a nightclub where I was performing. Just for luck, I couldn't decide whether to send them a bottle of wine… or a Cub Scout."

Peppered among this suggestive stuff was my more basic observational material, the comedy approach I learned from Edna. Since I've always had dogs, I remember one of my Camp Pickett routines was about an old collie of mine that always kicked its hind legs when it had a nightmare. I used that premise for comic riffs, like: "What could ever generate a nightmare in a dog? Maybe drinking from the toilet, and having the lid fall on his head?" Besides the observational stuff, I used to have a library of joke books, from which I recycled my favorites. Though rarely suggestive, I included a few samples in my Camp Pickett show, too. For instance, a rabbi walked into a bar with a frog on his shoulder. The bartender asked, "Where'd you get that?" And the frog answered, "In Brooklyn, there's hundreds of them."

One of the young men in my Camp Pickett psychiatric ward audience had been a closet homosexual taunted into a nervous breakdown by his fellow soldiers, the kind of story one seldom heard about in what has come to be known as the good war (World War II). At the time I saw myself as liberal along these lines, part of the legacy of tolerance I had learned from my Vincennes mentor Clarence Stout. Plus, I had several gay friends in the business, such as comic Rip Taylor and Indiana-born actor Clifton Webb, who actually played a witty homosexual columnist in Otto Preminger's best film, *Laura*, the year before I "went nuts."

I belabor these facts because I later struggled with the subject when my only grandchild, Sabrina, told me she was a lesbian. My daughter Valentina's one child, Sabrina is a documentary filmmaker of whom I am very proud. Still, her lifestyle initially threw me. Isn't it funny how one's tune can change when controversy hits close to home? Lothy had an even bigger problem with homosexuality than I did. But then, so did a lot of people in the recent past. For example, remember all those gay-bashing comments President Nixon made on his once secret tapes? I think something about Leonard Bernstein and the Kennedy Center had set the president off. I had performed at the Nixon White House, and he always treated me with great respect (being a big fan of my "Pledge of Allegiance" sketch). But just between me and you and a fence post, I think Nixon jumped the tracks a long time ago. Like many people, the main thing standing between him and greatness was himself. Still, I shouldn't knock someone who gave me a special award for my mix of entertainment and patriotism. (Personally, while such recognition is flattering, part of me feels that the President should only honor people who discover things like cures for diseases... or at least Tupperware.)

Regardless, given Lothy's natural protectiveness towards me—all three of my wives had plenty of starch in their corsets when it came to screening me from distractions—I was not able to reconnect with Sabrina for some time. This is yet another regret I'm happy to confess here, especially given how generous Sabrina was with how long it took me to come around. She had written me a note which I put in one of those safe places I now can't remember—don't you hate that?! Anyway, to paraphrase, it went something like this: "You were born in a small conservative town just a few years after Oscar Wilde was sent to prison for being gay. I understand and appreciate how hard this must be for you." Even if I hadn't then yet come around, that magnanimous—a big word for me—spirit would undoubtedly have changed the thinking of this old clown.

Though the subject of being a "switch hitter" never came up in conversations with my beloved Ella, I'm sure she would have scolded me about my initial issues over Sabrina's gayness. Ella's earthiness was anchored in a libertarian's belief that what went on behind closed doors was nobody else's business—a philosophy also most convenient for a woman running a brothel. Because she was always so entertaining on the subject of sexuality, such as her description of my early "romantic" needs ("Every so often a young man has to let the badger loose"), I regret never asking Ella about this other subject.

As this memoir is also a chronicle of forgotten moments later remembered as memorable, I must document my fascination with iconic silent actress Louise Brooks, the sexual siren with the black helmet hair and those sensual sexy lips. As a Vincennes youngster working as a movie usher I was captivated by her striking beauty. Then, as I noted in an earlier chapter (I hate to keep prompting you like this), when Ella arranged my first sexual encounter way back in my teens, I almost chose the brothel girl my grandmother had made to resemble Brooks.

After Louise dropped out of movies in the 1930s, much of the world forgot her, but not me. When Brooks was rediscovered again during the 1950s, no one was more pleased than this old clown. Yet, I was most charmed by Louise's later autobiographical essays about the movies, particularly the piece she did on her friendship with one of my heroes, W. C. Fields. Moreover, when these articles were collected in the book *Lulu in Hollywood*, I began thinking again about doing the book in hand.

Beyond this inspiration, however, I keep going back to the raw sexuality that attracted me to Brooks as a boy. Like those old hand-tinted silent movies that seemed to almost pulsate with color unevenly applied to the random object in the film frame, the screen Louise gave off a sort of sexual aura. Plus, now that I've become a student of her life, I find she was just as hedonistic off the screen. In fact, her take on writing a memoir is most provocative: "The history of a life can only be really understood by looking at the individual's sexual nature." Sadly, after Brooks applied this theory to her own life in another book-length manuscript, she had second thoughts and destroyed the memoir.

Like many workaholics, I'm fascinated by, and attracted to, a sexy hedonist like Brooks. Conversely, there's also fear of her—unbridled passion for such a person will lead to self-destruction. I'm reminded of the classic picture *The Blue Angel*, in which Marlene Dietrich's cabaret singer, a part for which Brooks would have been perfect, destroys the life of a professor (Emil Jannings) who has fallen blindly in love with her.

I think my second wife, Georgia, was my personal hedonistic Brooks. She was the love of my life, and the passion of our dating days would have made a censor blush. But while she wanted to continue these good times forever, I started going AWOL for my work. This wasn't always easy, especially when her sexual come-on included the throaty line, "Let's take this party upstairs." Still, my many creative interests won out more often than not, and she started inviting other men upstairs to the party. Naturally, this tore me up and I often made with the cruel whore-type cracks noted earlier—and me being a brothel baby, too! Yet, I still loved Georgia, and felt guilty that I had also abandoned her—since I was no longer that hedonistic lover who had married her.

I guess this is just another example that there are two sides to me… but has the good side won?

Epilogue... or, "Paging Dr. Freud!"

My daughter Valentina tells me that a man with a pierced ear is a good bet for a woman—because he knows pain, and how to pick out jewelry.

AT MY AGE you shouldn't make promises; you don't know when the ball will roll off the table. But I'll keep trying to defuse all the yarns I've spun since the world was young. Still, it wasn't like everything was a lie. Well, maybe close. Yet, if you play a bit with reality, the story might not be exactly factual, but it can still get at the truth. For example, when I fibbed about my father being a world class clown, I flirted with growing a Pinocchio nose. But my dad had done some amateur clowning for various Vincennes men's clubs, like the Odd Fellows. So there was an inkling of truth there, and I used it to help me *really* become a world class clown.

If what follows seems rambling to you, there has simply been a flood of final things I need to cover before I close. Whereas, I've attempted to be chronological prior to this, I now feel rather like the boy down to his final fifteen minutes at the carnival—in a rush to not miss anything.

Grandma Ella once said, "Doing your best doesn't always mean you're doing your best every darn day!" Though I've long tried to maximize every moment, writing this memoir brings home to me anew what she meant—I could have done so much more. I'm reminded of a joke from my last television monologue: "A fellow stops at a 24-hour convenience store and is surprised to see a checker locking the door. When the potential shopper asked, "Aren't you open 24 hours?" he received this reply, "Not in a row!"

I've yet to address herein my thoughts on superstition—no small topic with regard to entertainers and athletes. As the average goes, I'm not as superstitious as I used to be. There was a time that I always had to wear a maroon tie. (My actor friend Van Johnson had a similar need. He was obsessed with wearing red socks. I could never get a straight answer on just why. At first Van said it had something to do with his mother, but on at least two other occasions I heard him mention a woman. However, since Van recently came out of the closet—to the sorrow of an army of blue-haired former bobby soxers fans—I'm betting on mother.) Anyway, my maroon tie obsession is an outgrowth of a smash New York vaudeville engagement back in that memorable 1937. Conversely, I still can't wear casual and/or old clothes. I did enough of that as a child. Naturally, this can get expensive, especially since I'll do anything for a laugh, which frequently jeopardizes whatever I have on. One ritual I have maintained since the death of my little boy, Richard, is to always request, when I appear in concert somewhere, that one seat remain empty in his honor.

Of course, I have already mentioned my oldest superstition or bugaboo—not talking on the phone. But in all honesty, I'm not so bothered by that now. I only cling to the fear of phones story because it both makes for funny copy and allows me to avoid potentially boring conversations. But some of my fellow performers have real issues with superstitions. I once doubled up with pianist, composer and all-around wit Oscar Levant at Philadelphia's Warwick Hotel. It was late and Oscar called the front desk for cigarettes. Because the bellboy who brought them up had the number 13 on his uniform, Oscar decided we needed to relocate to the Ritz Hotel. Oh, and he had to pitch the cigarettes, too. We also had to carry all our luggage on foot, since the first cab we tried to hail was again the dreaded number 13. Poor Oscar could be spooked by anything, and he would fold quicker than a cheap tent. Still, he was fun to be around. I remember Oscar prefacing some remarks by saying to a cocktail party group, "You've heard of Plato, Aristotle, and Socrates?" When there was a general acknowledging murmur Oscar fairly shouted, "Well, they're morons!"

Surprisingly, I've neglected to note a basic superstition common to many comedians—a reluctance to discuss why something is funny. There is a fear, which I used to share, that the magic of producing laughter might somehow go away if one analyzes the joke. Sometimes my fellow comedians feel so strongly about jinxing the process that they comically mock any analytical efforts. One of the most inspired takes along those lines comes from my old favorite, Robert Benchley: "In order to laugh at something, it is necessary (1) to know *what* you are laughing at, (2) to know *why* you are laughing, (3) to ask some people why *they* think you are laughing, (4) to jot down a few notes, (5) to laugh. Even then, the thing may not be cleared up for days."

Personally, I've grown okay with comic dissecting. But still, I'm sympathetic to the forgotten funnyman who said, "Attempting to define comedy is like trying to nail jelly to a wall." (If I have any anxiety now, it's probably concern on how this memoir will be received. Hopefully, the publisher won't send me a rejection letter along the lines of something Oscar Levant once did as a joke for a publisher friend: "You worthless, pill-popping piece of illiterate. Don't ever send me this kind of silly swill ever again. We know where you live.")

Regardless, I best return to the more traditional basics of memoir writing—addressing personal controversies. For instance, I generated a tidal wave of shock when I stated in more than one interview that when I died all my television programs would be destroyed. This seemed to especially upset my old small screen writers, who filed a court-ordered injunction against me. But this was all so unnecessary, since I had never planned to torch my shows. Once again, I had mistakenly expected people to somehow "read" my true intentions.

I was simply angry, angry like my stay back in that Army nut ward in 1945. I had claimed I was going to commit suicide, but I didn't mean that either. With regard to my TV programs, I was still bitter over CBS' cancellation. Since I had never let the shows be syndicated, my threat to destroy them seemed to carry more weight. I borrowed the idea from silent actress Mary Pickford, who was always making noises about burning her old pictures, given her fears that the movies were no longer appreciated. But whereas Mary was serious, I was just blowing smoke. (Nothing came of her threat; American Film Institute scholars convinced Pickford of the movies' historical and cultural importance.)

After my bluff was called about destroying the TV programs, I suffered through a series of newspaper interviews where I tried to explain I had never been serious about it. But this just made me sound like even more of a boob. Eventually, I just gave up and refused further comment. You'd think I'd learn to say what I mean. I'm trying to do that here, but after eighty-plus years, old habits die hard. Bitterness over all this did fuel my nonstop negative cracks about television, the medium with which I was once so obsessed. For instance, when someone would ask if I "missed television," I often replied, "As often as possible." Or, if the subject did not come up with a reporter, I might venture, "TV gets worse every year and they're ten years ahead of schedule."

Still, in rereading the early portions of this book, and based upon other memoirs in my library, I think the most interesting part of any autobiography is before the person makes it. After that, it's often, "I wrote this script," or "I made this film." I tried to avoid that trap, but I don't know if I was always successful. It's the difference between someone writing, "Then I played the Palace, the Valhalla of vaudeville," and the reader saying, "Stop the presses! How did you ever get to the legendary Palace?" Of course, given my background, part of me even feels funny talking about having read memoirs, let alone writing one. In the Vincennes of my youth, too much reading and thinking was often considered potentially dangerous. I can remember one of Ella's girls saying, "If you read too many books, your head will fall off."

Again, forgive me if my reminiscing seems to go all over the autobiographical map. But I find the process so freeing, sort of a literary healing. Thus, I'm embarrassed to admit that this writing might also be likened to therapy—a chance for a cathartic rehashing of the past. The shame comes from the fact that I denied my second wife, Georgia, the opportunity to go the traditional therapy route (a psychiatrist), after her mid-1960s suicide attempt. I'm haunted by the question: would such therapy have kept Georgia from taking her own life a few years later?

Still, what long life is without regrets? After a certain amount of time, everyone becomes a casualty of life. The secret to happiness comes in trying to reframe the process—celebrate survival and make an adventure out of a sermon. I've always felt that man's greatest gift is persistence. We can't all be smart and strong and handsome. But we can all fight the good fight.

Fittingly, I also think persistence is at the heart of clown comedy. That is, the wacky world of film and television comedians has them struggling with life even more than their fans—which helps fuel the resiliency reflex. For example, if Laurel and Hardy (or the designated comedian of your choice) can somehow muddle through, there is hope for real people. Even given all the loopiness associated with clown comedy, there is often an inherent truth to be found there. I'm reminded of the scene in the Marx Brothers' *A Night at the Opera* where Groucho explains to Chico the various taxes to which his singing protégé will be subject: "You know, there's a federal tax and a state tax and a city tax and a street tax and a sewer tax."

Chico asks, "How much does this come to?"

Groucho replies, "Well, I figure if he doesn't sing too often he can break even."

Obviously, clown comedy has been good to me, and in recent years I've been flattered by the attention my long career has generated, from the Golden Globe's Cecil B. DeMille Award for "outstanding contributions to the entertainment industry," to a lifetime achievement Emmy. The honorary doctorate from Ball State University was fun, too, since I dropped out of school fairly early.

Being remembered, however, comes in many ways. I was charmed by a recent Steve Martin interview someone sent me. The author had asked Martin if he remembered the first time he was funny. Steve replied, "Probably in the third grade. I would watch Red Skelton the night before I came in and do his bits at recess, always including Red's comic sea gulls, Gertrude and Heathcliff. The pay-off was often a harmless pun, just right for a little kid audience:

Gertrude: 'Did you hear Henny Penny got arrested?'
Heathcliff: 'No. What did they charge her with?'
Gertrude: 'Using foul language.'"

Martin was also sweet enough to give partial credit to me for his "wild and crazy guy" character, with the fake arrow through his head, which drew from one of my Sheriff Deadeye sketches, where my comic cowboy got a hatful of arrows. And some of Martin's general comments about performing comedy demonstrated just how little things have changed. For instance, I really related to the following insight: "Every entertainer has a night when everything is clicking. These nights are accidental and statistical: like lucky cards in poker, you can count on them occurring over time. What was hard was to be *good*, consistently good, night after night, no matter what the abominable circumstances." So true, though now a distant memory for me.

I recently celebrated my eighty-fourth birthday. It is a mellow age, in fact it is almost rotten. I am often asked how I start my day, living in the smog free part of California. (That means the smog is free. I heard a fellow robbed a bank and ran outside and disappeared in thick air.) I open my eyes in the morning, and if I do not see candles and smell flowers, I get up. Since I'm not up to performing anymore, I focus on my painting, which I'm proud to find so many people enjoy. It makes me feel I'm sharing a gift from God, just as I once brought laughter to so many. I feel truly blessed.

Sadly, for much of my time in this book, I have been apologizing over my habit of slighting people who meant a great deal to my career and/or personal life, such as Buster Keaton and my first two wives, Edna and Georgia. Thankfully, I've never done that to my old Vincennes mentor, Clarence Stout. But lately, I've been wondering why. Maybe it was because his influence came so early. Maybe it was because he doubled as a father figure. Still, to be brutally honest, which is the goal of this memoir, maybe I just didn't see him as a threat to my fame—someone who would take away from my desire to make it look like I created it all.

All this was going through my mind even before I came across a shoebox of correspondence from Clarence that dated back to the early 1930s. The letter which especially moved me was a response to something I'd written him about being an entertainment failure. His thoughtful reply, which again taps into that persistence/resiliency factor, was this: "Don't despair, but if you despair, work on in your despair." Evidently, my correspondence to him had also included the concern that whatever routines I then had were merely "sentimental hokum—100 percent goo." Again, Clarence's reply was right on the money: "Any 'aw' shucks hokum from you will surely stand the test of time. Your innate sincerity will keep any sappiness at bay." Clarence's support helped me continue to focus on the feel good approach to comedy, and that made all the difference.

Speaking of my comedy work, I think if someone sat down and watched every episode of my television series, he would know me for sure. Of course, it would probably have to be a bright someone. Still, my small screen stuff felt so personal, I believe this idealized viewer would know exactly who and what I am. I finally realize, however, that while I used to think of myself as a simple man, I'm anything but that.

Many pages ago I mentioned that Georgia and I had seen the spirit of our departed son dancing on the yard of a Palm Springs home we eventually bought. Later, I also shared that Ella periodically drops in on me. For some readers, I'm sure that simply added to the "this guy is crazy" quotient. Well, catch your breath. Since entering my ninth decade, I've been visited by a host of other spirits from my past. Let me hasten to add, there's nothing scary or threatening about it. This is *not* an updated version of *A Christmas Carol*. But come to think of it, the comfort I have received from some of the contacts has probably contributed to my decision to set the record straight. Like my hero Lincoln, while I've never been much for organized religion, I am a student of the Bible. And I'm a great fan of the passage about casting bread on the water.

Of course, at this point in my life, I should probably follow W. C. Fields' example and be closely studying the Bible for any loopholes to heaven. Or, maybe I'll just hope for that old folktale of a free pass through the Pearly Gates. The story goes that if you die on Christmas, St. Peter ushers you right in, no questions asked, other than some insurance forms. I'm reminded of this by the fact that my two favorite hell raising comics, Chaplin and Fields, both died on Christmas.

My writing mentor, Gene Fowler, was a great friend of Fields', and frequently talked about how the comedian faced the end stoically. W. C. was essentially his own executioner (via drink), yet self-pity was a stranger to him. The comic was even poetic about death, referring to the Grim Reaper as "The Man in the Bright Nightgown," which almost sounds like Fields bought into that previously mentioned Christmas loophole. Personally, I think Fields felt the government wouldn't let him die until they found a safe place to bury his liver. But as the most cynical of Hoosier humorists, Ambrose Bierce, once observed, "Death is not the end... there remains the litigation."

Regardless, if I had my life to live over, I would try to keep a better handle on the truth. Besides the general platitudes about the subject, such as Lincoln's comment, "Let the people know the truth and the country is safe," it also just makes life easier. Like W. C. Fields, I found it increasingly hard to discuss my fabricated past with the passage of time, because I had spun so many whoppers through the years. People who claim they wouldn't change a thing in their life... "because it made them who they are today"... are MAJOR NUT JOBS, the one time a MAJOR outranks a GENERAL. All the screw-ups everyone makes over the years, and they wouldn't correct a thing? Really? No, these folks are living the lie. Since one can't really go back in time and fix things, they're suggesting "I'm ok with everything." Well, to that I say, "Blessed are the cracked, for they let in the light." If you own-up to nothing else in life, admit your mistakes. Yes, from time to time it's healthy to say, "I've been—what's the ugly word?—wrong!" You don't think my man Lincoln wouldn't have rethought that decision to go to the theatre?

Still, I wouldn't miss knowing any of the people—especially the ones whose leaving hurt the most. Will Rogers always said, "I never met a man I didn't like." Well, I think Will was a better fellow than me, though I've *tried* to like every man and woman I've met. Ironically, my biggest regret, after the fibbing and fumbling a second bloom of love with Georgia, was not meeting one particular guy, an alcoholic grocer I made over into a world class clown, my father Joe Skelton. I have no illusions about him. His mother, my beloved Ella, made sure of that. Still, he was my father, and I am forever curious.

Well, I think that about says it all. But how does one close a memoir? Let me take yet another cue from the aforementioned humorist, Irvin Cobb. He simply advised, "Avoid using the term 'The End.' Who knows what the end of anything is? Who knows where a thing begins or when it may end?" In fact, though I know all things must eventually die, I've always rather hoped an exception might be made in my case. We shall see. But if "the Man in the Bright Nightgown" does come for me and it is difficult for me to "exit laughing," let me leave you with Grandma Ella's rural Indiana take on death: "In the city a funeral is just an interruption in traffic; in the country it is a form of popular entertainment."

Select Bibliography

"A well-written life is almost as rare as a well-spent one."

– Thomas Carlyle

THOUGH THIS IS A "NONFICTION FICTION" TEXT, it is so anchored in basic biographical research I feel compelled to recycle the bibliography of my most recent Red Skelton biography — *Red Skelton: The Mask Behind the Mask* (2008). Ironically, given some new developments in my ongoing Skelton research, the following bibliography is actually *longer* than it appeared in the *Mask* text. Besides drawing from the memoirs of several additional Skelton contemporaries, I was able to spend four days with the comedian's granddaughter, Sabrina Alonso, when I brought her to Ball State University as a visiting filmmaker/speaker in November 2007. And finally, interviews with two Vincennes University archivists, who wished to remain anonymous, revealed that their collection of Red Skelton private papers had, until recently, contained some notes from the comedian's third wife which would not pass for love letters. (See the Gehring interview section of the bibliography.)

SPECIAL COLLECTIONS

"Clarence Stout Papers." Lewis Historical Library, Vincennes College, Vincennes, Indiana.

MGM Legal Department Records (1941-43). Margaret Herrick Library, Academy of Motion Picture Arts and Sciences, Beverly Hills, California.

MGM Script Material (Red Skelton). University of Southern California Cinema-Television Library, Lost Angeles, California.

"Red Skelton Clipping Files." Margaret Herrick Library, Academy of Motion Picture Arts and Sciences, Beverly Hills, California.

"Red Skelton Clipping Files." Performing Arts Library, New York Public Library at Lincoln Center, New York, N. Y.

"Red Skelton Clipping Files." Vincennes Public Library, Vincennes, Indiana.

"Red Skelton Collection." Archives and Special Collections, Western Illinois University Library, Macomb, Illinois.

"Red Skelton Collection." Vincennes College, Vincennes, Indiana.

BOOKS

Blair, Walter. *Native American Humor*. 1937. Reprint, Scranton, Pennsylvania: Chandler Publishing, 1960.

Blesh, Rudi. *Keaton*. 1966. Reprint, New York: Collier Books, 1971.

Bran, Christopher. *Father of Frankenstein*. 1995. Reprint, New York: Plume, 1996.

Brown, Joe E. (as told to Ralph Hancock). *LAUGHTER is a Wonderful Thing*. New York: A. S. Barnes and Company, 1956.

Capra, Frank. *The Name Above the Title*. New York: Macmillan, 1971.

Cavinder, Fred D. (ed.) *The Indiana Book of Quotes*. Indianapolis, Indiana Historical Society Press, 2005.

Curtis, James. *James Whale: A New World of Gods and Monsters*. Boston: Faber and Faber, 1998.

Day, Richard. *VINCENNES: A Pictorial History*. St. Louis: G. Bradley Publishing, Inc., 1988.

Dunning, Johnny. *On The Air*. New York: Oxford University Press, 1998.

Edwards, Larry. *BUSTER: A Legend In Laughter*. Brandenton, Florida: McGuinn & McGuire, 1995.

Ephron, Nora. *And Now... Here's Johnny!* 1967. Reprint. New York: Avon Books, 1968.

Evans, Peter. *Peter Sellers: The Mask Behind the Mask*. 1968. Reprint, New York: Signet, 1980.

Fein, Irving A. *Jack Benny: An Intimate Biography*. 1976. Reprint, New York: Pocket Books, 1977.

Fowler, Gene. *Minutes of the Last Meeting*. New York: Viking Press, 1954.

Freedman, Benedict and Nancy. *Lootville*. New York: Henry Hold and Company, 1957.

Gable, Kathleen. *Clark Gable: A Personal Portrait*. Englewood Cliffs, New Jersey: Prentice-Hall, Inc., 1961.

Gehring, Wes D. *Carole Lombard: The Hoosier Tornado*. Indianapolis Historical Society Press, 2003.

Gehring, Wes D. *Charlie Chaplin: A Bio-Bibliography*. Westport, Connecticut: Greenwood Press, 1983.

Gehring, Wes D. *The Charlie Chaplin Murder Mystery*. Shreveport, Louisiana: Ramble House Press, 2006.

Gehring, Wes D. *Film Clowns of the Depression: 12 Memorable Movies*. Jefferson, North Carolina: McFarland & Company, Inc., 2007.

Gehring, Wes D. *Forties Film Funnymen: The Decade's Great Comedians at Work in the Shadow of War*. Jefferson, North Carolina: McFarland & Company, Inc., 2010.

Gehring, Wes D. *Groucho & W. C. Fields: Huckster Comedians*. Jackson: University Press of Mississippi, 1994.

Gehring, Wes D. *Irene Dunne: First Lady of Hollywood*. Lanham, Maryland: Scarecrow Press, 2006.

Gehring, Wes D. *James Dean: Rebel With a Cause*. Indianapolis Indiana Historical Society Press, 2005.

Gehring, Wes D. *Joe E. Brown: The Baseball Buffoon*. Jefferson, North Carolina: McFarland & Company, Inc., 2006.

Gehring, Wes D. *Laurel & Hardy: A Bio-Bibliography*. Westport, Connecticut: Greenwood Press, 1990.

Gehring, Wes D. *Leo McCarey and the Comic Anti-Hero in American Film*. New York: Arno Press, Inc., New York Times Company, 1980.

Gehring, Wes D. *The Marx Brothers: A Bio-Bioliography*. Westport, Connecticut: Greenwood Press, 1987.

Gehring, Wes D. *"Mr. B" Or Comforting Thoughts About the Bison: A Critical Biography of Robert Benchley.* Westport, Connecticut: Greenwood Press, 1992.

Gehring, Wes D. *Parody as Film Genre: "Never Give a Saga an Even Break."* Westport, Connecticut: Greenwood Press, 1999.

Gehring, Wes D. *Personality Comedians As Genre: Selected Players.* Westport, Connecticut: Greenwood Press, 1997.

Gehring, Wes D. *Red Skelton: The Mask Behind the Mask.* Indianapolis: Indiana Historical Society Press, 2008.

Gehring, Wes D. *Seeing Red… The Skelton in Hollywood's Closet: An Analytical Biography.* Davenport: Robin Vincent Publishing, 2001.

Gehring, Wes D. *Steve McQueen: "The Great Escape."* Indianapolis: Indiana Historical Society Press, 2009.

Gehring, Wes D. *W. C. Fields: A Bio-Bibliography.* Westport, Connecticut: Greenwood Press, 1984.

Gehring, Wes D. (For more on the author's other books, simply google his name.)

Gottfried, Martin. *Nobody's Fool: The Lives of Danny Kaye.* New York: Simon & Schuster, 1994.

Hiney, Tom. *Raymond Chandler: A Biography.* New York: Grove Press, 1997.

Hubbard, Kin. *Abe Martin of Brown County, Indiana.* Indianapolis: Levey Bros., 1906.

Hubbard, Kin. *Abe Martin's Almanack [for 1909].* Indianapolis: Abe Martin Publishing Co., 1908.

Hubbard, Kin. *Abe Martin's Barbed Wire.* Indianapolis: Bobbs-Merrill Company, 1928.

Hyatt, Wesley. *A Critical History of Television's "The Red Skelton Show," 1951-1971.* Jefferson, North Carolina: McFarland & Company, Inc., 2004.

Jenkins, Henry. *What Made Pistachio Nuts? Early Sound Comedy and the Vaudeville Aesthetics.* New York: Columbia University Press, 1992.

Keaton, Buster (with Charles Samuels). *My Wonderful World of Slapstick.* Garden City, New York: Doubleday & Company, 1960.

Kelly, Fred C. *The Life and Times of KIN HUBBARD: Creator of Abe Martin.* New York: Farrar, Straus and Young, 1952.

Kendall, Paul Murray. *The Art of Biography*. 1965. Reprint, New York: W. W. Norton & Company, 1985.

Knipfel, Jim. *Quitting the Nairobi Trio*. 2000. Reprint, New York: Berkley Books, 2001.

Knipfel, Jim. *Slackjaw*. 1999. Reprint. New York: Berkley Books, 2000.

Lardner, Ring. *You Know Me Al: A Busher's Letters*. 1914. Reprint, New York: Collier Books, 1991.

Levant, Oscar. *The Memoirs of an Amnesiac*. 1965. Reprint, New York: Bantam, 1966.

Latham, Caroline. *The David Letterman Story*. 1987. Reprint, New York: Berkley Books, 1988.

Lax, Eric. *WOODY ALLEN: A Biography*. New York: Alfred A. Knopf, 1991.

Maltin, Leonard. *The Great Movie Comedians: From Charlie Chaplin to Woody Allen*. New York: Crown, 1978.

Marx, Arthur. *Red Skelton*. New York: E. P. Dutton, 1979.

Marx, Groucho. *Groucho and Me*. 1959. Reprint, New York: Manor Books, 1974.

Meade, Marion. *Buster Keaton: Cut to the Chase*. New York: Harper Collins Publisher, 1995.

Meyers, Jeffrey. *Hemingway: Life Into Art*. New York: Cooper Square Press, 2000.

Miller, Frank. *LEADING MEN: The 50 Most Unforgettable Actors of the Studio Era*. San Francisco: Chronicle Books, 2006.

Minnelli, Vincente (with Hector Arce). *I Remember It Well*. New York: Samuel French, 1974.

Nelson, Ozzie. *Ozzie*. Englewood Cliffs, New Jersey: Prentice-Hall, 1973.

Raphael, Frederic. *Eyes Wide Open: A Memoir of Stanley Kubrick*. New York: Ballantine Books, 1999.

Riley, James Whitcomb. *The Best of James Whitcomb Riley*, Donald C. Manlove, ed. Bloomington: Indiana University Press, 1982.

Rogers, Ginger. *GINGER: My Story*. New York: Harper Collins, 1991.

Rollyson, Carl. *A Higher Form of Cannibalism?: Adventures in the Art and Politics of Biography*. Chicago: Ivan R. Dee, 2005.

Sandburg, Carl. *ABRAHAM LINCOLN: The Prairie Years and the War Years.* 1926, 1939. Reprint. New York: Harcourt, Brace & World, Inc., 1966.

Schickel, Richard. *D. W. Griffith: An American Life.* New York: Simon and Schuster, 1984.

Skelton, Red. *Gertrude and Heathcliff.* 1971. Reprint, New York: Charles Scribner's Sons, 1974.

Skelton, Red (ed.). *A Skelton In Your Closet.* New York: Grosset & Dunlap, 1965.

Smith, David L. *Hoosiers in Hollywood.* Indianapolis: Indiana Historical Society Press, 2006.

Smith, Ronald L. *Johnny Carson.* New York: St. Martin's Press, 1987.

Steinberg, Cobbett. *Reel Facts: The Movie Book of Records.* New York: Vintage Books, 1978.

Strausbaugh, John. *BLACK LIKE YOU: Blackface, Whiteface, Insult & Imitation in American Popular Culture.* New York: Penguin, 2006.

Summers, Harrison B. (ed.). *A Thirty-Year History of Programs Carried on National Radio Networks in the United States, 1926-1956.* New York: Arno Press, 1971.

Thurber, James. *My Life and Hard Times.* 1933. Reprint, New York: Bantam Books, 1947.

Twain, Mark. *A Connecticut Yankee in King Arthur's Court.* 1889. Reprint. Scranton: Chandler Publishing Company, 1963.

Twain, Mark. *The Selected Letters of Mark Twain.* Charles Neider, ed. 1982. Reprint, New York: Cooper Square Press, 1999.

Wallace, Daniel. *Big Fish.* New York: Penguin Books, 1998.

Wertheim, Frank. *Radio Company.* 1979. Reprint. New York: Oxford University Press, 1992.

SHORTER WORKS, INCLUDING SCRIPT MATERIAL, LETTERS, AND INTERVIEWS

Adams, Jennifer. "Why the Skeltons Parted." *Movieland*, March 1943.

Agee, James. "Comedy's Greatest Era." *Life*, September 3, 1949.

"Ailing." *Newsweek*, December 22, 1952.

Allen, Steve. "Jackie Gleason." In *The Funny Men*. New York: Simon and Schuster, 1956.

Allen, Steve. Letter to Red and Georgia Skelton, May 20, 1958, "Our Dear Sweet Beloved Richard" Funeral Scrapbook (1). Red Skelton Collection, Vincennes College, Vincennes, Indiana.

Allen, Steve. "Red Skelton." In *The Funny Men*. New York: Simon and Schuster, 1956.

Als, Hilton. "Shining Hours." *The New Yorker*, May 22, 2006.

Arnold, Maxine. "Clown In Civies." *Photoplay*, February 1948.

Baytos, Betsy. Interview with Red Skelton, February 20, 1996. In the Dance Collection Oral History, New York Public Library at Lincoln Center.

Bergson, Henri. "Laughter." In *Comedy*, Wylie Sypher, ed. Garden City, New York: Doubleday & Company, 1956.

Blum, John M. "Retreat From Responsibility." In *The National Experience: A History of the United States*, John M. Blum, ed. New York: Harcourt Brace, 1968.

Busch, Noel F. "Red Skelton—Television's Clown Prince." *Reader's Digest*, March 1965.

Carroll, Doug. "Red Skelton—Ed Wynn Legend [e-mail to the author]," February 28, 2011.

Cosby, Vivian. "Edna Skelton's Lasting Loyalty." *American Weekly*, November 13, 1949.

Davidson, Bill. "'I'm Nuts And I Know It.'" *Saturday Evening Post*, June 17, 1967.

Davis, Sammy. Telegram to Red and Georgia Skelton, May 1958, "Our Dear Sweet Beloved Richard" Funeral Scrapbook (1). Red Skelton Collection, Vincennes College, Vincennes, Indiana.

"Demure Du Barry." *Newsweek*, June 28, 1943.

Dudley, Janice Thompson, Letter to the author, July 10, 1991.

Eisenhower, Mamie. Letter to Red and Georgia Skelton, May 20, 1958, "Our Dear Sweet Beloved Richard" Funeral Scrapbook (1). Red Skelton Collection, Vincennes College, Vincennes, Indiana.

Engle, William. "Out of Love Into Business." *American Weekly*, July 27, 1947.

"Everyone's a Kid is Basis for Skelton's Philosophy." *McGuire Banner* [military hospital publication], February 1, 1945.

Felton, Verna. "Love That Red-Head." *Radio Mirror*, January 1948.

Flight Command review. *Film Daily*, December 23, 1940.

Franchey, John R. "Exs Can Be Friends." *Screenland*, September 1943.

Friedrichsen, Frank. "The Short Tragic Life of Jimmy Dean." *Movie Star Parade*. December 1955.

The Fuller Brush Man review. *Time*, May 31, 1948.

Gehring, Wes D. "The Gentile Clown [Red Skelton]." *USA Today Magazine*, September 2006.

Gehring, Wes D. Interview with Anita Mykowsky, 2000.

Gehring, Wes D. Interview with Brenda Hopper, February 6, 1994.

Gehring, Wes D. Interview with Cheech Marin, January 31, 2004.

Gehring, Wes D. Interview with Earl Williams, September 24, 1997.

Gehring, Wes D. Interview with Eleanor Norris Keaton, late 1980s.

Gehring, Wes D. Interview with Lothian Toland Skelton, December 9, 1998.

Gehring, Wes D. Interviews with Marvin L. Skelton, December 12, 14, 2006; and February 6, 2007.

Gehring, Wes D. Interview with Pandro S. Berman, June 1975.

Gehring, Wes D. Interview with Paul Cooley, September 21, 2000.

Gehring, Wes D. Interview with Red Skelton, September 18, 1986, as well as various conversations during his 1980s visits to Ball State University (Muncie, Indiana).

Gehring, Wes D. Interview with Sabrina Alonso, March 7, 2007. Also, I spent extended time with her when I brought her to Ball State University as a visiting documentary filmmaker (November 27-30, 2007). This contact also included a side trip to Vincennes University (Vincennes, Indiana) to show her the Skelton archives.

Gehring, Wes D. Interviews with Valentina Skelton Alonso, February 27, March 5, 13, 14, 2007.

Gehring, Wes D. Interviews with two Vincennes University archivists over controversial materials recently removed from the Red Skelton holdings, November 29 & 30, 2007. (They wished to remain anonymous.)

Gehring, Wes D. "The Mentor and the Clown: Clarence Stout and Red Skelton." *Traces of Indiana and Midwestern History*, Fall 2000.

Gehring, Wes D. "The Neglected Career of Kin Hubbard's Abe Martin: Crackerbarrel Figure in Transition." *Indiana Magazine of History*, March 1982.

Gehring, Wes D. "Red Skelton and Clem Kadiddlehopper." *Indiana Magazine of History*, March 1996.

Gehring, Wes D. "Red Skelton: It All Started With the Donuts." *Traces of Indiana and Midwestern History*, Winter 2009.

Gehring, Wes D. "What Would Red Have Said?" *USA Today Magazine*, July 2007.

"Gene Fowler." In *Current Biography 1944*, Anna Rothe, ed. New York: H. W. Wilson Company, 1945.

Glatzer, Hal. "Red Skelton Isn't Clowning Around When It Comes to His Paintings—They Fetch $40,000 Per." *People*, April 28, 1980.

Great Diamond Robbery review. *Time*, February 15, 1954.

Greer, Gloria. "Red Skelton: At Home on the Desert." *Palm Springs Life*, April 1963.

Hall, Donald. "Simple Things: A Poet's Poet." *Home and Garden*, September 2003.

Hamburger, Phillip. *Three Little Words* review. *The New Yorker*, August 26, 1950.

Hift, Fred. *A Southern Yankee* review. *Motion Picture Herald*, August 7, 1948.

Hoover, J. Edgar. Letter to Red and Georgia Skelton, May 12, 1958, "Our Dear Sweet Beloved Richard" Funeral Scrapbook (1). Red Skelton Collection, Vincennes College, Vincennes, Indiana.

"How Red's First Wife Arranged His Second Marriage." *TV Picture Life*, March 1969.

I Dood It review. *Time*, November 29, 1943.

"It Hasn't All Been Laughs." *TV Guide*, February 20, 1960.

Jefferson, Sally. "The Skelton In Hollywood's Closet." *Photoplay*, July 1942.

"Johnny Carson." In *Current Biography 1964*, Charles Moritz, ed. New York: H. W. Wilson Company, 1965.

Keaton, Buster and Edward Sedgwick. *A Southern Yankee* "retakes," April 20, 1948. *Yankee* script material folder number 4, University of Southern California Cinema-Television Library, Los Angeles, California.

Keaton, Buster and Edward Sedgwick. *A Southern Yankee* "retakes," April 27, 1948. *Yankee* script material folder number 4, University of Southern California Cinema-Television Library.

Keaton, Buster, Roy Rowland, and George Wells. *Excuse My Dust* addendum, "NOTES," May 9, 1950. In the *Excuse My Dust* script material, folder number 1, University of Southern California Cinema-Television Library, Los Angeles, California.

Keaton, Eleanor. Letter to the author, late 1980s.

"Laugh Clown." *Newsweek*, July 9, 1951.

Lovece, Frank. "Red Skelton: Old Jokes Never Die." *Newsday*, September 12, 1990.

Loventz, Pare. *Free and Easy* review. *Judge* magazine, May 17, 1930.

Marshall, General George. Letter to Red and Georgia Skelton, May 15, 1958, "Our Dear Sweet Beloved Richard" Funeral Scrapbook (1). Red Skelton Collection, Vincennes College, Vincennes, Indiana.

McCullough, David. "The Unexpected Harry Truman." In *Extraordinary Lives: The Art and Craft of American Biography*, William Zinsser, ed. Boston: Houghton Mifflin Company, 1986.

"Money Can't Buy a Daughter's Happiness." *Modern Screen*, September 1970.

Muni, Paul. Telegram to Red and Georgia Skelton, May 1958, "Our Dear Sweet Beloved Richard" Funeral Scrapbook (1). Red Skelton Collection, Vincennes College, Vincennes, Indiana.

Pachter, Marc. "The Biographer Himself: An Introduction." In *Telling Lives: The Biographer's Art*, Marc Pachter, ed. Philadelphia: University of Pennsylvania Press, 1985.

Panama Hattie review. *Newsweek*, October 5, 1942.

Panama Hattie review. *The New Yorker*, October 3, 1942.

Panama, Norman and Melvin Frank. *The Spy*, August 12, 1947. In *A Southern Yankee* script material, folder number 1, University of Southern California Cinema-Television Library, Los Angeles, California.

Peterson, Marva. "The Two Mrs. Skeltons." *Movieland*, April 1948.

"Radio Notes." *Newsweek*, September 24, 1945.

"Radio Warm-Ups #3." *Radio Life*, August 29, 1948.

"Red Skelton." In *Current Biography 1947*, Anna Rothe, Ed. New York: H. W. Wilson Co., 1948.

"Red Skelton: Master of Ad-Lib." *Hollywood Lean Sheet*, May 1948.

Red Skelton photo showcase with text, *Look* magazine, May 14, 1946.

"Red Skelton." *Time*, July 9, 1951.

"Red Skelton, TV Clown, Dead at 84." Site visited September 30, 1997.

Rhine, Larry. Letter to the author, November 16, 1998.

"Right Up There: Red Skelton's Back On Top And Here Are [the] Reasons Why." *TV Guide*, April 28, 1956.

Roos, Robert De. "Television's Greatest Clown" (two-parts). *TV Guide*, October 14 and 21, 1961.

Ross, Sid. "Red Skelton… His Plane Was In Trouble." *Parade* magazine, September 23, 1951.

Rosten, Leo. "How to See Red—Skelton That Is (Part 2). *Look*, November 6, 1951.

Rottenbery, Josh. "The Piracy Debate." *Entertainment Weekly*, July 14, 2006.

"Rubber Face on TV." *Life*, October 28, 1951.

Ruskin, Harry and Jeanne Bartlett. *Watch the Birdie* treatment, October 18, 1948. In the *Birdie* script material, folder number 1, University of Southern California Cinema-Television Library, Los Angeles, California.

Schlesinger, Arthur M., Jr. "The World in Flames." In *The National Experience: A History of the United States*, John M. Blum, ed. New York: Harcourt Brace, 1968.

Shearer, Lloyd. "Red Skelton: He Never Stops Clowning." *Parade* magazine, May 8, 1955.

Ship Ahoy review. *Showman Trade Review*, April 18, 1942.

Skelton, Edna and Red. Letter to Inez and Clarence Stout, February 27, 1939. "Clarence Stout Papers." Lewis Historical Library, Vincennes College, Vincennes, Indiana.

Skelton, Edna and Red. Letter to Inez and Clarence Stout, March 30, 1938. "Clarence Stout Papers." Lewis Historical Library, Vincennes College, Vincennes, Indiana.

Skelton, Edna and Red. Letter to Inez and Clarence Stout, May 28, 1937. "Clarence Stout Papers." Lewis Historical Library, Vincennes College, Vincennes, Indiana.

Skelton, Edna and Red. Letter to Inez and Clarence Stout, undated [1937]. "Clarence Stout Papers." Lewis Historical Library, Vincennes College, Vincennes, Indiana.

Skelton, Edna and Red. Postcard to Clarence Stout, November 21, 1937. "Clarence Stout Papers." Lewis Historical Library, Vincennes College, Vincennes, Indiana.

Skelton, Edna and Red. Telegram to Inez and Clarence Stout, December 15, 1938. "Clarence Stout Papers." Lewis Historical Library, Vincennes College, Vincennes, Indiana.

Skelton, Edna Stillwell (as told to James Reid). "I Married a Screwball." *Silver Screen*, June 1942.

Skelton, Georgia Davis. "Do Comics Make Good Husbands?" *Screenland*, June 1952.

Skelton, Georgia. Letter to Red Skelton, May 19, 1971, "Letters to Big Red from Little Red" (1971)—bound. Red Skelton Collection, Vincennes College, Vincennes, Indiana.

Skelton, Georgia. Letter to Red Skelton, October 5, 1971, "Letters to Big Red from Little Red" (1971)—bound. Red Skelton Collection, Vincennes College, Vincennes, Indiana.

Skelton, Georgia. Letter to Red Skelton, undated, [1971], "Letters to Big Red from Little Red" (1971)—bound. Red Skelton Collection, Vincennes College, Vincennes, Indiana.

Skelton, Georgia. "My Autobiography," 1934. Biography of Red and Georgia folder, Red Skelton Private Papers box, Red Skelton Collection, Vincennes College, Vincennes, Indiana.

Skelton, Lothian Toland. Card to Red Skelton, undated, Valentina's Personal Items Box, Red Skelton Collection, Vincennes College, Vincennes, Indiana.

Skelton, Red. "Glamour Will Get Me Nowhere." *Movieland*, August 1952.

Skelton, Red. Letter to Georgia Skelton, April 2, 1967, Box 8, "Letters to Georgia & Some to Valentina"—bound. Red Skelton Collection, Vincennes College, Vincennes, Indiana.

Skelton, Red. Letter to Georgia Skelton, August 21, 1968, Box 8, "Letters to Georgia & Some to Valentina"—bound. Red Skelton Collection, Vincennes College, Vincennes, Indiana.

Skelton, Red. Letter to Georgia Skelton, August 2, 1969, Box 8, "Letters to Georgia & Some to Valentina"—bound. Red Skelton Collection, Vincennes College, Vincennes, Indiana.

Skelton, Red. Letter to Georgia Skelton, March 28, 1945. "Red Skelton Collection." Archives and Special Collections, Western Illinois University Library, Macomb, Illinois.

Skelton, Red. Letter to Georgia Skelton, undated [probably 1969], Box 8, "Letters to Georgia & Some to Valentina"—bound. Red Skelton Collection, Vincennes College, Vincennes, Indiana.

Skelton, Red. Letters to Godfrey Cambridge, August 15, 1967, Box 10, "R. R. S. Letters to Friends." Red Skelton Collection, Vincennes College, Vincennes, Indiana.

Skelton, Red. Letter to Hedda Hopper, January 31, 1951. "Hedda Hopper Collection." Margaret Herrick Library, Academy of Motion Picture Arts and Sciences, Beverly Hills, California.

Skelton, Red. Letter to Sabrina Alonso, September 6, 1991, Box for Valentina, "Letters to Valentina and Sabrina" folder. Red Skelton Collection, Vincennes College, Vincennes, Indiana.

Skelton, Red. Letter to Sabrina Alonso, undated [1990s], Box for Valentina, "Letters to Valentina and Sabrina" folder. Red Skelton Collection, Vincennes College, Vincennes, Indiana.

Skelton, Red. Letter to Valentina Skelton, undated [1965], Box 8, "Letters to Valentina & Friends"—bound. Red Skelton Collection, Vincennes College, Vincennes, Indiana.

Skelton, Red. "The Role I Liked Best..." *Saturday Evening Post*, February 28, 1948.

Skelton, Red. Rough draft letter to Georgia Skelton, December 27, 1968. "Little Red and Miscellaneous Writing" folder, Red Skelton Collection, Special Collection Library, Western Illinois University, Macomb, Illinois.

Skelton, Red. Rough draft letter to Georgia Skelton, undated [1960s]. "Little Red and Miscellaneous Writing" folder, Red Skelton Collection, Special Collection Library, Western Illinois University, Macomb, Illinois.

Skelton, Red. Rough draft letter—short fragment—to Georgia Skelton, undated [1960s]. "Little Red and Miscellaneous Writing" folder, Red Skelton Collection, Special Collection Library, Western Illinois University, Macomb, Illinois.

Skelton, Red. Telegram to Clarence Stout, March 15, 1937. "Clarence Stout Papers." Lewis Historical Library, Vincennes College, Vincennes, Indiana.

A Southern Yankee review. *Cue*, November 27, 1948.

Stout, Clarence. Letter to Lou Levy, October 31, 1947. "Clarence Stout Papers." Lewis Historical Library, Vincennes College, Vincennes, Indiana.

Stout, Clarence. Letter to Thomas Gerety, April 18, 1947. "Clarence Stout Papers." Lewis Historical Library, Vincennes College, Vincennes, Indiana.

"Success Story." *Cue*, September 20, 1941.

Tugend, Harry. *A Southern Yankee* script material, filed July 19, 1948. *Yankee* script material, folder number 1, University of Southern California Cinema-Television Library, Los Angeles, California.

"The Unflappable Miss Morrison." *TV Guide*, July 11, 1964.

Vincennes Public Schools Records (RHC #370), Enumeration—District 2 (1923 and 1924). Courtesy of a Red Skelton private collector.

Watch the Birdie review, *Film Daily*, November 28, 1950.

"We Point With Pride to Red Skelton." *Silver Screen*, October 1947.

Whitehead, John. "Red Skelton as the 'Little Brat.'" *Radio Life*, April 12, 1942.

Whitney, Dwight. "'A Clown Is a Warrior Who Fights Gloom'... and Red Skelton Fights Harder Than Anyone." *TV Guide*, August 20, 1966.

Whitney, Dwight. "The Weekly Ordeal of Red Skelton" (Part One). *TV Guide*, April 20, 1963.

Wild, David. "Steve Martin: The 'Rolling Stone' Interview." *Rolling Stone*, September 2, 1990.

Williams, John A. and Dennis A. Williams. *If I Stop I'll Die: The Comedy and Tragedy of Richard Pryor*. 1991. Reprint, New York: Thunder's Mouth Press, 2006.

Wissing, Douglas. "Red Skelton: THE LAST VAUDEVILLIAN." *Traces of Indiana and Midwestern History*, Winter 1998.

Yagoda, Ben. *WILL ROGERS: A Biography*. 1993. Reprint, New York: HarperCollins, 1994.

The Yellow Cab Man review, *Motion Picture Herald*, February 25, 1950.

Young, Jordan R. *The Laugh Crafters: Comedy Writing in Radio and TV's Golden Age*. Beverly Hills, California: Post Times Publishing, 1999.

Zinsser, William. "Introduction." In *Extraordinary Lives: The Art and Craft of American Biography*, Zinsser, ed. Boston: Houghton Mifflin Company, 1986.

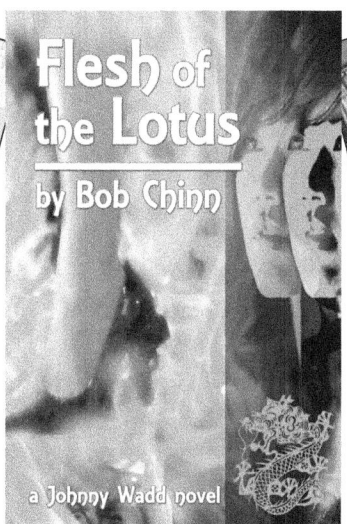